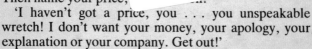

'You climb into my ... death. You cause me ... killed me. You ruin my ... five pounds' compensa...

'Hah!' Matthew gr... ...ore? Then name your price, ...

'I haven't got a price, you . . . you unspeakable wretch! I don't want your money, your apology, your explanation or your company. Get out!'

'You sanctimonious little prude, I'm going!' he shouted back at her. 'Let me know when you're pre-pared to listen. In the meantime, you can think what you like. Next time someone climbs through your window at night, turn on the light. That should frighten him off!'

There was a silence that fairly prickled with emotion, charging the air like an electrical experiment.

Verity sat bolt upright and drew a deep breath. 'Mr Burton,' she said icily, 'you are not a gentleman.'

Matthew stepped swiftly forward, stooped, seized her face in his cupped hands, and before she could guess what he was about, or begin to protest, kissed her firmly on the mouth.

'Oh dear, Miss Lyndon, I fear that *you* are not a lady!' he said softly.

Ann Hulme was born in Portsmouth and educated at the Royal Holloway College—part of the University of London—where she took a degree in French. She has travelled extensively, and it was the fascination of the various countries in which she made her home—France, Germany, Czechoslovakia, Yugoslavia and Zambia—which made her begin to write. She now lives in Bicester, Oxfordshire, with her husband and two sons.

Ann Hulme has written eight other Masquerade Historical Romances. Recent titles include *The Garden of the Azure Dragon*, *The Hungarian Adventuress* and *A Woman of the Regiment*.

INTERLAKEN INTRIGUE
Ann Hulme

MILLS & BOON LIMITED
15–16 BROOK'S MEWS
LONDON W1A 1DR

*First published in Great Britain 1986
by Mills & Boon Limited*

© Ann Hulme 1986

*Australian copyright 1986
Philippine copyright 1986
This edition 1986*

ISBN 0 263 75592 4

*Set in 10 on 11 pt Linotron Times
04–1286–75,700*

*Photoset by Rowland Phototypesetting Limited
Bury St Edmunds, Suffolk
Made and printed in Great Britain by
Cox & Wyman Limited, Reading*

CHAPTER ONE

VERITY CLIMBED down from the omnibus at the corner of Regent Street and was immediately assailed by a swirling blast of cold air, bearing on it dust and grit which stung her eyes and caused her to clutch at her hat. She grasped her long skirts in her hand and scuttled round the corner out of the draught, wondering why, in England, the onset of summer was usually signalled by a marked deterioration in the weather, rainclouds, gusting winds and occasionally even a late frost, nipping at the new buds which had unwarily emerged from their cocoon of leaves. She retreated into a doorway to wipe a speck of grit from her eye. It was already occupied by a news-stand, decorated with two hand-printed bills that flapped in the wind, threatening to break loose and bowl away towards Oxford Circus.

One read: HMS DREADNOUGHT UNDERGOING SEA TRIALS. BRITAIN TO BE INVINCIBLE AT SEA.

The other read: FRENSHAM EMERALDS STOLEN IN AUDACIOUS ROBBERY.

The newsboy, with whom she shared her refuge, grinned at her sympathetically.

'Bloomin' cold, ain't it, miss?' he said cheerfully. He had a pinched urchin's face, and a cloth cap pulled well down over large ears. 'Flamin' June, this is,' he added conversationally. Then, in deafening tones, he bellowed, 'Read all abaht it! Jool robbery in famous London 'ostess's town 'ouse. Fortune in emeralds stolen by cat burglar!'

'Do you happen to know the St Lambert's hotel?' she asked.

'Right down the street there, can't miss it,' he told her. He cast an old, wise eye over her, obviously judging her not to be quite the class of person who usually put up at such expensive hotels. 'Lookin' for a job?'

'Don't be cheeky!' she rebuked him.

'Garn!' he said amiably.

Verity did 'go on', she hoped with dignity. All the same, it was unnerving to think that even this street urchin could assess her so accurately. Her plain tailored costume was good. It had cost all of five pounds new, but was, alas, far from new now. She had retrimmed her hat herself and had a gloomy feeling the wind had added its own touch of fancy. But she walked on briskly through the early evening crowds until she came to a spotless portico of white stone and a discreet notice of polished brass announcing the hotel she sought.

A uniformed commissionaire stood on the pavement, casting a lacklustre eye up and down the street. He ignored Verity completely. Obviously he was another who thought her unlikely to be a guest. As she stood there irresolutely, the doors at the top of the well-scrubbed steps swung open, and a man came out, hurrying down. He turned up his coat-collar against the wind as he did, so that she could not see his face. He ran lightly past her, nodded to the commissionaire, and set off up the street at a fast pace.

Verity, unconcerned, did not even glance at him. On such a small omission turned an extraordinary sequence of events, which finally took on the frightening trappings of a nightmare.

Emboldened by the commissionaire's temporary distraction, she marched past him, head held high, up the steps, through the still swinging doors and into a lobby dominated by a smell of recent wax polish and two huge aspidistras on stands. A dragon in black bombazine bore down on her and eyed her through steel-rimmed spectacles.

'I've called to see Contessa Giulini,' Verity said loudly, before the redoubtable receptionist could give voice. 'She's expecting me. I'm Miss Lyndon.'

'Ah, yes,' said Bombazine in a voice like chipped glass. 'Albert!'

A pageboy of about fourteen years of age, who bore a startling resemblance to the newsboy at the corner, appeared from a cubby-hole and said importantly, 'Follow me, madam, if you please.'

He led her upstairs and along a corridor, stopping before a door and announcing succinctly, ''Ere it is.'

Verity hunted in her purse for a sixpence she could ill afford, and asked quickly, and in a low voice, 'Tell me, the Contessa, the Italian lady who is staying here, is she—is she an elderly lady?'

'No,' said Albert, pocketing the sixpence with alacrity. 'She's a young 'un. And she ain't no Italian, neither. She's English, she is. Speaks just like you and me.' His snub nose wrinkled as he decided how much more information made up sixpennyworth. 'Been a gent here twice, asking about her. Not wanting to see her, just asking questions, on the sly. He was a real rum 'un. Looked like a prizefighter, but was a gent anyway. He give me a shilling.'

When Verity declined to take up this hint, Albert stalked off. She took a quick look in a pocket mirror to see if any dust smeared her face, and tapped on the door.

'Come in!' called an unmistakably English voice. Albert was reliable, at least. Verity pushed open the door and entered.

It was a hotel sitting-room of the more costly kind, with much reproduction rococo furniture and heavy lace curtains draping the tall windows which gave out on the street. A woman rose from a chair to greet her. She was,

Verity supposed, about thirty-five or six and unquestionably very beautiful. So much so, that Verity caught her breath. The Contessa was not tall, but slender and graceful, with abundant ash-blonde hair piled up in a chignon and obviously all her own—no need of a false 'transformation' here. Her gown had that simple elegance which speaks of a Paris fashion house and a great deal of money, and the hand she held out glittered as the light struck flashes of white fire from a cluster of diamonds.

'Miss Lyndon? Do come in. How very prompt you are. Please sit down.'

All this was delivered in a cool, welcoming, yet businesslike voice. Verity became aware of a very sharp stare and of a hard line to the rouged lips. The Contessa had no old-fashioned objection to make-up. There was also, she decided immediately, a personality of steel beneath that feminine exterior. She sat down warily and waited.

'My dear Miss Lyndon,' the Contessa began without preamble. 'I won't beat about the bush. I have your name from my good friend, Mrs Cavendish, to whose children you were, I believe, governess?'

'Yes,' Verity said. 'Until they were sent away for their education.'

'I have no children,' Contessa Giulini continued briskly. 'So I am not offering you a similar post. What I do need is a companion. Mrs Cavendish thought you had not yet taken up any new employment, and that you might do very well. I want someone intelligent, presentable and of a good family.' The sharp eyes flickered rapidly over Verity, assessing the tailored costume. 'I see you are presentable; I take it you are intelligent; and Mrs Cavendish assures me you are of good family. I travel a great deal, especially on the continent. It is extremely disagreeable to do so with only a maid. Sitting and eating alone in hotel dining-rooms is very boring, so that is why I need a companion. All your travelling expenses, hotel bills,' the Contessa shrugged, 'that sort of thing will be met by me, naturally. In addition, I propose a salary of one hundred and twenty pounds a year. Do you think we might come to terms on that basis?'

She raised her fine, arched eyebrows interrogatively. Verity gulped. She had been out of a job since her position at the Cavendishes had terminated three months before, and her modest savings were beginning to run low. To be offered the position of a companion to someone who travelled extensively on the continent seemed too good to be true.

'Might I ask,' she answered unsteadily, 'what duties I should have to perform?'

'Why, just to be a companion,' the Contessa said vaguely. She stood up and went to stand by the window, looking out. 'You know . . . Accompany me when I have no other social engagement . . . Take care of small matters. There is my jewellery, of course.' Glancing towards Verity and seeing her puzzled, she went on in explanation, 'I have a great deal of jewellery, from my marriage. I am a widow, incidentally. I insist that every night it is locked in the hotel safe, wherever I may be staying. Sometimes you would be required to see that done. Perhaps you could also undertake some little secretarial work for me. Address cards, that sort of thing.'

'I am not a typewriter,' Verity said hastily.

'It doesn't matter. They're noisy machines, and any-thing I wanted you to do would need to be done in longhand. As you were a governess, I presume you can write legibly, and spell?'

'Yes, I can do that,' Verity assured her.

Jessica Giulini smiled at her charmingly and released

the lace curtain. 'How nice. My handwriting is totally illegible! Even my best friends can't read it, and I never could spell. Well, Miss Lyndon, I'm sure you would suit very well. There is just one last thing. Can you be ready to leave England at once?'

'I . . . At once?' Verity was caught unawares.

'Yes.' A slight note of impatience touched the Contessa's voice. 'I want to take the boat-train tomorrow night. I have to be in Paris on Friday, and hope to be in Switzerland by the end of the following week. There I shall stay for a month or so. Can you leave so soon?'

Verity thought feverishly. 'Yes, I suppose so.'

'Good. Then, Miss Lyndon—Verity, isn't it? I shall call you Verity, and you shall call me Contessa, since mine is an Italian title. Then, Verity, I suggest you go home and pack your trunk. Tomorrow, about midday, put yourself and it into a cab, come over here, and then your things may be collected and taken to be put on the boat-train with mine.' Jessica Giulini smiled her charming smile again and left the window, holding out her beringed hand. 'Until tomorrow, Verity.'

Verity found herself outside the door in the corridor again, almost before she had time to take a decent farewell of her new employer. 'Well!' she exclaimed to herself. She straightened the jacket of her tailormade and set off down the staircase.

As she neared the foot of it, Bombazine's voice drifted from some private nook behind the reception desk. 'I shall be glad to see the back of her. She's complained about everything; not a thing pleases her. A thoroughly spoiled piece of goods, if you ask me. Too much money and no husband to keep a check on her.'

'Does she get any men visitors?' enquired a different voice.

'One called this morning,' said Bombazine disapprovingly. 'They had some kind of a quarrel. The chambermaid heard them arguing, and a little afterwards he came storming down the stairs and out. Also there's been another gentleman asking after her. It's not the sort of thing we expect at the St Lambert's. She's been playing fast and loose, if you ask me. Keeping too many admirers dangling on a string, and now it's all getting into a tangle and she's going to cut and run. Good riddance, say I!'

Verity could not listen any longer without risk of being caught. She descended the last few stairs and Bombazine, alerted by some instinct, appeared from behind a curtain and bade her a gracious farewell.

As soon as Verity arrived indoors, she knew Jack was there ahead of her, even before she saw or heard him. A blue haze of cigarette smoke hung in the air with its sour tobacco smell which made the membranes of her nose itch. She stifled a sneeze, shut the door, and called out sharply, 'What are you doing here at this time of day?'

Her brother didn't answer. Verity unpinned her hat, and briefly surveyed the damage the wind had wrought to the trimmings before putting it on the table. She opened the door of the tiny living-room and stood, looking despairingly at the havoc even a few minutes' occupation by Jack could create. Newspapers littered the floor. Unwashed glasses and cups stood in a row. Jack never washed up a cup, but always took another, clean, one. Every ashtray was filled to overflowing with cigarette stubs. Jack lay sprawled on the sofa, his feet sticking out over the end, ostensibly asleep.

Verity automatically picked up and folded the nearest sheet of newspaper. It was the one the newsboy had been selling, with its *Dreadnought* headlines, set above a paragraph boasting of Britain's naval superiority. She walked across the room and gazed down at her brother's handsome young form, with its ruffled hair and look of a fallen angel. He was in his shirtsleeves, his shirt-collar, together with the studs, thrown down on the floor by the sofa. His waistcoat was unbuttoned, and their father's gold half-hunter watch and chain, which should have decorated the front of the waistcoat, was conspicuous by its absence.

Going out again, into the cramped kitchen, Verity put the kettle on the hob. While it was coming to the boil, she went to her bedroom to change out of the tailored costume into a blouse and old skirt. By the time she returned to make the tea, Jack had given up his pretence of sleeping and had appeared in the kitchen, where he hovered uselessly, eyeing the steam from the kettle with detached interest.

'You can make the tea, you know,' Verity said to him crossly, wrapping a knitted holder round the kettle handle and lifting it off the hob. 'I asked you, what are you doing here at this time of day?' She stopped in the act of pouring the boiling water into the chipped earthenware teapot. 'You haven't been dismissed from Benson's, have you? You've only been there five months!'

He flushed dully, and thrust his hands into his pockets. 'You might as well know,' he said sullenly. 'I haven't been at Benson's for the past two weeks. I'm sorry,' his voice grew louder and his flushed cheeks redder, at the expression on her face, 'I would have told you, but I knew how you'd take it. You make it damn difficult for a fellow, Ver'.'

'Why did they dismiss you?' she asked coolly.

He shrugged. 'I don't know. The old boy was always carping. I was late a couple of times. Not my confounded fault . . .' A peevish, self-justifying note entered his voice.

'Where's Father's watch and chain?' She put the tea-things on a tray, trying to sound composed.

'I popped them, what do you think? So that you wouldn't ask me where my wages were.' He made no attempt to carry the tray, but followed her back into their living-room, justifying himself as he went. She listened in silence until he ran out of excuses and threw himself down, defiant still, on the sofa where he'd been when she came in. 'Where have you been, Ver'?'

'Out looking for a job!' she said tartly.

He brightened. 'Any luck?'

'Yes. I've been offered the post of companion to an Italian Contessa. That is to say, she's an Englishwoman, widow of an Italian Count.'

He expelled his breath in a whistle of surprise. 'I say, Verity, that's fine! Better than governessing to those spoiled Cavendish brats. What will she pay?'

'All found, and one hundred and twenty a year.' She saw his forehead wrinkle with the effort of calculating, and a pain entered her heart, as it always did at his ruthless self-interest.

'Look, Ver'. I'll be strapped for money until I get another job. Benson won't give me a reference, and it will be difficult. You'll have to send me the rent for this place, until I get fixed up.'

Verity sipped at her tea. It had happened so often before, but this time it was going to be different. It was possible for it to be different, because she would be going abroad. Before, whenever she'd tried to make a stand against Jack's fecklessness, he'd got round her in the end by a combination of wheedling, moral blackmail and his sheer inability to fend for himself. But no longer. This time she was going to be firm, and she would be out of reach of his blandishments and entreaties. She set down her cup carefully, but it rattled in the saucer, even so, betraying her inner tension.

'Listen to me, Jack. You're twenty-eight, and I just can't support you. You've hardly contributed anything to the upkeep of this place, even when you were at Benson's. We've been living on *my* savings.'

'A fellow's got expenses, Ver',' he interrupted passionately. 'Damn it, I've got to keep up at least the appearances of a gentleman!'

'Why? You haven't a gentleman's income. It's not enough to whine that you were born a gentleman and society owes you some sort of a gracious living. It doesn't, and I don't. I've never said, "I'm a lady, and can't soil my hands." For the past ten years I've worked as a nursery governess, and I haven't enjoyed it particularly. As a matter of fact, the Cavendishes were the nicest of the families I worked for, and it's thanks to Mrs Cavendish that Contessa Giulini offered me this new post.'

'You're the practical sort, Verity,' he said, almost wistfully. 'I'm not.'

'Rubbish! You're just lazy and a first-rate sponger. Don't glower at me, Jack. It's the truth! You've sponged off me here, and last summer you sponged off those Scottish friends of yours.'

'That's not so!' he defended himself with vigour. 'They invited me up there on a climbing holiday. I was a house guest, along with half a dozen other fellows.'

'All of whom were in a position to offer some kind of hospitality in return. You weren't.'

'That's unkind, Verity,' he said, in the reproachful voice which he knew made her feel guilty.

She hardened her heart against it. 'It's a fact. So I'm not going to be sending you either the rent or any other money. If I did, you'd never go out and get another job. I'll give you ten pounds before I leave, and—mark you!—it's ten pounds I can ill afford. After that, you're on your own.'

He bit his lip and stared at her appraisingly. 'Where does she live, this Contessa of yours?'

'I gather, mostly in hotels. She travels a lot. I'm going to the continent with her tomorrow night.'

'*What?*' Jack leapt up, upsetting the teacups, sugar, and the nearest overflowing ashtray. 'Hang it all, Verity, you can't just go off abroad and leave me here with *ten* pounds!'

'I could easily leave you here with nothing, Jack, so don't tempt me!'

He fell back on the sofa. The news that she was leaving England had obviously shaken him badly. Several times before she had 'cut up rough', to use his own phrase, but he'd always known he'd talk her round in the end. Dash it, he depended on her. She couldn't just go and leave him. It wasn't fair . . .

'What's she like, the Contessa, I mean?' He tried to sound nonchalant.

'About thirty-five, very attractive, wealthy. Used to getting her own way, I shouldn't be surprised.'

A speculative look entered his handsome face. 'She sounds interesting.'

'She'd eat you for breakfast,' Verity said rudely.

A spiteful look flickered in his eyes, which were so like hers, grey and widely spaced. As brother and sister they did closely resemble each other, and there were only fourteen months between them. But in character they'd had always been as unlike as chalk and cheese.

He said, 'Just because *you* have never caught a husband, it doesn't mean I can't catch the eyes of a good-looking woman, even a wealthy widow. That's your trouble, Verity. You've always wanted to be independent and pay your way. Any other woman wouldn't have wasted her best years; she'd have played helpless, and found a husband somehow. Hang it, when you were with the Cavendishes or the other families, you must have met dozens of fellows with independent incomes! Couldn't you have got your hooks into one of them?'

'Governesses aren't supposed to flirt with the young gentlemen of the family. They either get unwished motherhood, or instant dismissal, and generally both!'

He grinned. 'How about that, Ver'? Did you ever, you know, with anyone? There must have been opportunities.'

'I suppose there were, but I'm not that stupid.'

'No, you're too damn clever and self-righteous for words!' he said sourly. 'If you'd tried, been a bit more encouraging, you'd have got yourself a wealthy husband by now, and we'd both have our money worries behind us.'

'You'd let me do that, wouldn't you, Jack?' she said softly. 'Just to get money to support you.'

He got up and kicked a sheet of newspaper out of his path. 'Dash it, you talk as if I wanted to send you out on the streets! All I meant was, be nice to a few chaps, get them to buy you a few presents, that sort of thing. One of them would have come across with a ring eventually. You're not bad-looking.'

Verity rose. 'I'm going to start packing. You can sweep up all that sugar you spilled, wash up *all* the cups, including that horrible collection over there, pick up all these papers, and generally tidy up. I'll cook some supper later.'

'If it's lamb stew again, I'll throw up,' he said moodily. 'You know I hate lamb, it's fatty.'

'It's cheap.' She glanced at him, and seeing him so downcast, weakened. 'Oh, go out and buy some sausages.'

'Give me the money?' He held out his hand, a beseeching look in his eyes. 'Come on, Ver'. I haven't a brass ha'penny!'

She hunted in her bag and gave him a florin.

'Thanks,' he said wryly. 'We'll have a feast.'

'It's enough for the sausages. We have potatoes and bread. You can bring in two pennyworth of tea. The grocer at the corner will weigh it out and do it up for you in a twist of paper.'

'Oh, all right.' He pushed the florin into his pocket, where it jingled against other coins. So he wasn't as short of money as he claimed! She let the deception pass. She was used to his lies and tricks.

'I say, Ver',' he said, as he pulled on his coat. 'That ten pounds you say you'll give me, you couldn't make it twenty, could you?'

Jack insisted on coming to the station to see her off, but she knew, as soon as he appeared, that his real intention was to make the acquaintance of the wealthy woman who had engaged the services of his sister. He'd put on a clean shirt and collar, actually pressed his suit. He'd persuaded her, after all, to make the ten pounds up to ten guineas, and run down to the pawnbroker to redeem the gold half-hunter with some of the money. It decorated his waistcoat now, resplendently. He was a handsome young man, with what elderly ladies call 'breeding'. His confident look, of a man about town of modest but independent means, would have led no one to guess that the remaining guineas jingling in his pocket were all he had. Jack lived from day to day, sure that someone would 'pick up the bill' and look after his needs. Generally, somebody did.

Jessica stood on the concourse in a pale grey travelling suit and silver fox fur, with a large veiled hat. She was directing porters to dispose of her mountain of luggage. Through the veil, her sharp eyes rapidly assessed Jack, who bowed elegantly.

'Who's this?' she demanded abruptly of Verity.

'My brother.' Verity gave Jack a warning look that she knew was in vain.

'I'm very honoured to meet you, Contessa,' Jack said with just the right mixture of admiration and deference. The admiration, at least, was real. Jessica's beauty was not obscured by the veil: her clothes were straight from a Paris fashion plate, and even her luggage had an expensive look. But she was clasping a large bag, not very fashionable and at odds with her elegant ensemble.

Verity thought, 'The jewel-box . . .'

Jack, unaware of the probable contents of the bag, made the mistake of offering to carry it. He was dismissed with a curt, 'No, I'll do it myself!' and retreated a step or two.

Clearly, either because of the valuable contents of her bag or for some other reason, Contessa Giulini did not wish to stand about on the platform. To be true, it was draughty and crowded. Porters were pushing luggage through the throng and the engine coughed smoke and soot at them. But, once or twice, Verity saw her glance over her shoulder, or look about her, as if she searched for someone, a face in that hurrying crowd. But no one came to bid her farewell, and she did not seem disappointed. She gave final directions to the porters, tipped them, and allowed Jack to hand her up into the compartment, where she drew the blind.

'Damn good-looking woman,' said Jack disconsolately, knowing he'd been treated like an amateur footman. He gave Verity a peck on the cheek. 'Take care, old girl, and send me a postcard.' He strode off briskly, the guineas burning a hole in his pocket. He'd go to a music-hall tonight, he thought, take one of the chorus girls out to supper. He whistled and hailed a cab, even his jealousy of his sister's good fortune forgotten for the time being.

*   *   *

The journey as far as Paris was uneventful and comfortable. Verity, who had made the trip only once before, and that third class, noticed ruefully all the differences first-class travel and plenty of money made. Officials were polite, no one pushed or shoved or expected you to carry anything. Cabin crew found you a seat out of the breeze, unasked, and stewards appeared from nowhere asking if madam wished tea. The sea was calm, and Verity frankly enjoyed the crossing.

It was during the three days spent in Paris that she first began to experience the problems that being the companion of Contessa Giulini threatened to make daily affairs. Jessica's avowed purpose in stopping over in Paris at all was to make a visit to the fashion house of Worth, who was her couturier. She ordered Verity to accompany her, and they descended on its elegant portals, where they were greeted, Verity fancied, with a certain coolness.

She soon found why. The Contessa set about complaining bitterly and at length about everything, but chiefly about the prices, threatening to take her custom to Paquin. Verity began to suspect that there was a strong streak of miserliness in her new employer. It manifested itself in petty and selfish ways. For example, Verity was told to look presentable and to dress quietly but suitably—suitably, that was, for someone in the company of such a wealthy woman, who stayed at expensive hotels. But just how Jessica thought that Verity would do this on a hundred and twenty a year was unclear. If silk stockings cost Contessa Giuilini two shillings a pair, they also cost Verity that sum. It was immediately apparent that the salary she had been offered and accepted was a low one for the appearances she would be expected to keep, and Verity was sorry she had not taken a leaf from Jack's book and bargained for a higher one. Had she done so, she might well have gained it,

since it was obvious that Jessica, anxious and ready to
leave, had been in desperate need of a companion and
would have surrendered, even if with bad grace. Now,
however, they were on the way to Switzerland in a
reserved first-class compartment, and there was nothing
Verity could do about it.

But she had learned that the threat to change couturiers was a real one. The Contessa, it seemed, changed
couturiers, hairdressers, maids and companions with
tempestuous regularity. This information Verity had
from the lady's present maid, Maddox. Maddox was a
stern-looking woman with iron-grey hair, dourly competent and not generally given to gossip. But during
their last hours in Paris, both of them having suffered
Jessica's criticisms, Maddox had unbent to the extent of
telling Verity that she had worked for the Contessa for
only six months, and that if 'things go on like this', she
would be relinquishing her post as soon as they returned
to England.

Yet to be travelling was such an adventure in itself that
Verity did not feel she could complain—not so soon,
anyway. After all, scarcely a week ago she had been
without a job and with no prospect of finding one, living
in damp, windy England. As they progressed across
Europe, the weather had improved dramatically and
they had reached the Swiss frontier in unseasonable
heat. It was much warmer than it should be for the time
of year, Jessica grumbled. She reclined in the corner of
the railway carriage and fanned herself slowly with an
oriental fan. Verity pushed down the window and
looked out on to the platform.

The Customs officials had finished their business with
the train passengers, but there had been a slight delay on
account of a pair of cyclists who wanted to take their
machines into Switzerland. To do this, they were required to pay a sizeable deposit and get lead seals affixed

to their bicycles to show it had been done. It took a few minutes, as did the explanation of the numerous regulations covering bicycles in the Swiss cantons, but at last they were loaded back into the guard's van, and the guard himself raised his flag.

At that precise moment, a pony and trap clattered noisily up to the station entrance. Verity could just see it across the platform and through the station gate. A late traveller was hurriedly decanting himself and his baggage from it. He ran on to the platform, shouting to the guard to hold the train. The guard shouted back that they were a minute late already, and resolutely blew his whistle.

The newcomer began to race across the platform to the moving train. He was a very tall man, topping six feet, and strongly built, but he sprinted with the co-ordination and ease of a trained athlete. As Verity held her breath, he reached the train and managed, despite its gathering speed, to wrench open a door. He hurled his bag inside and leapt after it. The door slammed.

'Whew!' thought Verity, expelling her pent-up breath. 'That was close!'

'Do bring your head inside, Verity,' Jessica said from her corner. 'You'll be struck in the face by a cinder from the engine.'

She withdrew her head and pulled up the sash. 'Someone just jumped on the train at the last moment. I thought he wouldn't make it!'

The fan stopped its gentle motion. 'Oh? What sort of person?'

'A tall man, in a Norfolk jacket. He ran very fast. I should think he was a sportsman of some kind.'

'Which compartment is he in?' Jessica asked.

Verity looked at her in surprise. 'I don't know exactly. Two or three down from this one, I should think.'

There was a pause, before Jessica said calmly,

'I'm going to take a nap. Do draw the blinds on the corridor side. I hate to be gawped at by people passing by.'

CHAPTER TWO

THE EUROPE through which Jessica and Verity travelled
in 1906 had enjoyed unprecedented security and peace
for almost forty years. Before then it had seen several
wars, but all of them, savage and cruel though each had
been, had at the same time been localised affairs, brief,
bloody and decisive. Since 1815 there had been nothing
like the spread of the Napoleonic campaigns that had
dragged on, year after year, in one form or another,
making the whole of Europe into one vast, armed camp.
By the time the twentieth century dawned, Europe, to
all outward appearances, was safe, prosperous, elegant
and pleasure-loving. Not, of course, for all. But for
those who had even a little money, life was good. And
for the rich . . .

For the rich, life was generous in the pleasures it
offered, and they travelled as never before in order to
sample as many of these delights as possible. Not only
did they visit the recognised tourist stopping-places
of the old Grand Tour. The new peace and security
meant they could venture into wild regions, hitherto
inaccessible.

But most liked comfort, and could pay for it. A swift
and efficient rail network covered the continent and
bore them to the luxurious playgrounds upon which they
descended in droves, accompanied by husbands, wives,
lovers, mistresses, children, maids and valets, nurses
and footmen. It was sometimes necessary to hire a
private train to transport the menagerie of hangers-on.
The ladies went to Paris for their gowns: the gentlemen
went there for the can-can. They fished in Scandinavia

and shot game in Bohemia. They went to Baden-Baden
for the races, to Deauville and Trouville to take healthy
sea air, to Monte Carlo for the gaming, to Marienbad for
the spa waters and to revive their jaded constitutions.
Above all, they went to Switzerland . . .

It was the playground of all Europe, and of the very
rich. That Switzerland, like England, also harboured a
number of social malcontents in exile, who doggedly
plotted to upset the whole degenerate applecart, was
something of which the pleasure-seekers were blissfully
unaware. Other turbulent currents, too, ran beneath the
glittering surface, undermining the whole edifice. But
few, as yet, took them seriously.

Small wonder that Verity was filled with curiosity and
excitement at the prospect of seeing the fabled fairyland.
Here German barons, Austrian counts, Russian princes
and English aristocrats of all kinds rubbed shoulders
in the fashionable cafés and hotels, and undertook a
variety of healthy outdoor activities in the beautiful
Alpine surroundings; shielded, of course, from any real
discomfort or effort by an army of guides, coachmen,
chairbearers, cooks and others. What was more, she,
Verity Lyndon, was going to be a part of it. In Jessica's
elegant shadow, she would see it all, at first hand.

Jessica had decided upon Interlaken. Not unexpectedly, she took some dislike to the suite of rooms
offered her at the first hotel and removed herself, Verity
and Maddox to a large, rambling wood and brick establishment on the outermost fringes of the town. There she
engaged a suite of rooms giving on to a long balcony and
affording a breathtaking view of the mountains.

There was only one drawback. It was on the second
floor. Regretfully, the first-floor suite was taken already,
the manager explained, 'by an English milord'.

'Oh?' Jessica raised her eyebrows. 'What is his name?'

'A Sir Miles Frensham, Frau *Gräfin*, who holidays

here with his wife, Lady Frensham. Such a fine gentle-man, very gracious.'

An expression of genuine pleasure crossed Jessica's face. 'What a surprise! But I know the Frenshams. I was at a dinner party in their London house barely two weeks ago.' She turned to Verity. 'And, just imagine, the following night they were burgled and poor Emma Frensham lost her emeralds.'

A memory picture flickered into sharp relief in Verity's brain: a flapping bill with a crudely printed headline: Frensham. She had been so much occupied with her coming interview at the St Lambert's that she had not realised the import of the words.

'Oh my goodness! Lady Frensham!' she exclaimed.

Jessica stared at her. 'What do *you* know of the Frenshams?'

'Only that Lady Frensham called several times on Mrs Cavendish, so that I have met her. I've never met Sir Miles. I only know he holds some important position at the Admiralty.'

Jessica turned this information over in her mind and eventually dismissed it as having no importance. 'It will be nice to see the Frenshams,' she announced at last. 'I had no idea they were coming to Interlaken. What a strange coincidence.'

It might be a coincidence, but Contessa Giulini wasted no time before building on it, and renewed her acquaint-ance with the Frenshams that very evening. They were an elderly couple, Sir Miles very dignified, but with a twinkle in his eyes, his wife a plain, unaffected woman, a few years his junior, who remembered Verity and spoke kindly to her.

'How nice to see you, Miss Lyndon. I know Elinor Cavendish was very sorry to part from you, but children will grow up so quickly! If you haven't been in Switzerland before, I'm sure you'll find it most interesting. We come every year. I always insist Miles takes a holiday. If I didn't, goodness knows, he'd never leave his desk at the Admiralty.'

'Well, well, my dear,' Sir Miles said amiably. 'Someone has to keep an eye on what the Admiral of the Atlantic is doing!'

'Who is the Admiral of the Atlantic?' Verity asked.

'Ah, that is the title the Kaiser has given himself!' Sir Miles chuckled. 'We'll see about that, however, or the *Dreadnought* will!'

'That wretched battleship,' Lady Frensham said firmly, 'is constantly with us. I feel as though she were a member of the family. We never leave her behind. When I said that I'd persuaded Miles to leave his desk at the Admiralty and take a holiday, I should have added that, in a sense, he brings his desk with him, wherever he goes. Our sitting-room here at the hotel is like an office, I swear! Despatch-boxes everywhere, telegrams arriving daily, and couriers coming down from our embassy with papers . . . I'm sure, I have to force Miles even to look out of the window and admire the view! Only yesterday I was watching a superb sunset over the Jungfrau and remarked on it to Miles. I said, "How beautiful the mountain looks, so rose-pink." And there he sat, buried in some report, and only replied, "Mountain? Which mountain?"'

Lady Frensham looked and sounded her exasperation, but Jessica laughed and said, 'How very devoted to your work you are, Sir Miles!'

'I wish he were as devoted to his health!' said his wife fiercely. 'He will not take a rest.'

'Were you at the launching of the *Dreadnought*?' Jessica asked. 'Everyone seems to have gone there. Quite a social occasion. Of course, the King was present.'

'And, of course, it rained,' said Lady Frensham, determined to find no good in the *Dreadnought* or anything connected with her. 'It always does, when it's a royal occasion. A howling gale, pouring rain, and naturally all the ladies in totally unsuitable garden-party dresses. The rain ruined our hats, our gloves and our shoes. I tied *my* hat on with a veil, such as ladies do now when they go motoring. But Miles's top hat blew off and bowled away merrily, and would have been swept clear into the Solent, had not a very charming young naval officer chased after it and seized it in the nick of time.' Lady Frensham looked distinctly pleased at the thought of her husband's mishap.

'I was so sorry,' Verity said, remembering, 'that your emeralds were stolen. I saw the headlines, in a newspaper.'

'Very tiresome,' agreed Lady Frensham. 'Though they were very old-fashioned—my mother's—and I never cared for them. I kept intending to have them re-set, and so, in a way, I have been spared the bother of it.'

How nice, thought Verity, to be able to treat the loss of a valuable set of emeralds as no more than a minor inconvenience.

'My dear Jessica,' said Lady Frensham. 'It happened the very night after you came to dinner at our house, just before the weekend. As luck would have it, that dinner party was the last we gave at home, before getting ready to leave for Switzerland. I was the whole weekend closing the house up for the summer, and getting dust-sheets put over everything. It was all very vexing. The police detectives insisted on taking all the dust-sheets off again, looking for clues. It upset the maids; and, of course, they found nothing. Then they upset all the maids again, asking questions. I ask you, men!' exclaimed Lady Frensham finally. 'If any of them ever had to run a house, they'd learn to organise themselves better!'

'Pretty girl, that,' said Sir Miles to his wife, when Jessica and Verity had departed.

'Jessica?'

'Lord, no. La Giulini is a handsome woman, I suppose, but a damn tartar beneath it! No, Miss Lyndon. Didn't Elinor Cavendish tell you that she came of quite a decent family, but down on her luck?'

'Yes, she did. But, Miles, I know perfectly what's in your mind, and you'd be most ill advised to go matchmaking! At your age, too,' said Lady Frensham rudely.

'I'm fond of the boy. Besides, the fellow needs a wife.'

'No, he doesn't. And he doesn't want one. What's more, he'd be a thoroughly bad husband. Besides, the girl is too sensible, and understands her situation, poor child. I mean, no money at all . . . It just doesn't do. Elinor was a little afraid, when Miss Lyndon first came to her, that she might just, well, set her cap at her eldest boy Toby, who is up at Oxford. It's always a worrying possibility when a governess is attractive. But the girl behaved very well, and put the young man firmly in his place, I gather, when he did try a little foolishness.'

'Toby Cavendish is an addle-pated young idiot! Burton is a different kettle of fish altogether.'

'He looks like a gorilla,' said Lady Frensham dismissively.

'Ah? And do *all* ladies object to that as much as you do, my dear?' asked Sir Miles with deceptive calm.

'I know to what you're alluding, Miles!' she said sharply. 'But I'm not going to repeat vulgar gossip. Some women will do anything for a novelty!'

'Really?' said her husband, retiring behind his newspaper. 'I wish I'd known that when I was younger.'

'Oh, do stick to your Admiralty papers, Miles! They'll give you far less trouble than meddling in Burton's life would.'

To the relief of both Verity and Maddox, Jessica remained in excellent temper after the meeting with the Frenshams, apparently satisfied with something at long last. As she prepared to retire to bed that night, she was in high fettle, even humming a little tune as Maddox brushed out her blonde hair.

She leaned forward and peered at her reflection in the dressing-table mirror with every sign of pleasure. 'Do take my jewel-box downstairs, Verity, and see Inebnit locks it away. Emma Frensham might not miss her emeralds, but I certainly don't want to lose anything of mine.'

Verity picked up the double string of pearls the Contessa had worn that evening and laid them, almost reverently, in the blue velvet groove in the box. They lay gleaming dully up at her in the uncertain light of the new-fangled electric light bulbs sprouting from a five-pronged light fitting that dangled above their heads like an illuminated monster spider. Verity was struck by the opalescent, cold beauty of the pearls, so much like that of their owner. The string must be priceless. The diamond clasp alone, winking as the electric bulbs flickered, was probably worth almost the entire amount of the salary Jessica proposed paying her companion.

Maddox glanced dispassionately and with the faintest tinge of disapproval at the jewel-box, and Verity forced herself resolutely to concentrate on the business in hand. She shut the box, which was of metal and about the size of a large biscuit-tin, and locked the little padlock which secured it. As she reached the door, Jessica called after her.

'They seem to have a very poor library in this hotel,

but when you've seen my jewels safe, bring up a book. I don't want any trish-trash! Bring something interesting.'

'Why don't you go down and look for a book yourself?' demanded a sudden rebellious voice in Verity's brain. She felt shocked at finding herself meditating this revolt, and a little ashamed. Aloud, she said, 'Yes, of course.'

She carried the box carefully downstairs. The hotel foyer was almost deserted, lined with potted palms like so many silent green sentinels. It was an old building —boasting that Lord Byron had once dined there and written in its visitors' book (remarking on the view but not on the dinner). Since those romantic days, the hotel had had the electricity installed. It was erratic, and they had been warned that occasionally it failed entirely. As Verity approached the reception desk, it flickered alarmingly yet again.

Herr Inebnit, the manager, small, rotund and balding, was waiting for her, rubbing his pale soft hands nervously. He led the way into his inner office, apologising for the electricity as he went. 'It was installed only six months ago, Fräulein. We like to have all modern amenities. Our guests expect it. But I must say that we never had such trouble with the old lamps.' He took out his keys with ceremony and with a flourish opened the cumbersome old-fashioned safe by the wall. Verity stooped down and put the box on a shelf beside a leather document-case, which she noticed was initialled 'M.F.' 'The gracious lady need have no fears, Miss Lyndon,' Inebnit said politely, as he relocked his impressive antiquity of a strong-box.

Verity's mouth twitched at this inappropriate description of her employer, as she went back into the silent foyer. It was at that point she remembered she had to ask for the key to the glass-fronted bookcase which held the hotel's library. She turned back quickly, and to her surprise saw a young man leaning against the reception desk and watching her closely.

She was startled, because she was sure he had not been there when she went into the office. For a moment, in the shadowy hall, with its sinister array of silent palms, she was tempted to believe in some Byronic reincarnation, for if ever a young man looked as though he ought to be a poet, this one did. He was of medium height, slightly built and somewhat pale. He had long, loose black hair, and was an undeniably attractive figure, dressed in expensive tailoring. Once she had decided that he *was* real, her immediate thought was to wonder if he was one of the many chest sufferers who came to the Bernese Oberland for their health. But perhaps that was also her imagination. Possibly the ivory skin went with the jet-black hair, a Mediterranean combination of features often found in the south of France, where it is called a *'teint mat'*.

Seeing her eyes rest on him so curiously, he smiled. 'You look lost, mademoiselle. What have you forgotten?' His voice was pleasant and easy.

'The key to the bookcase,' Verity told him, embarrassed.

He shrugged, and leaning over the reception desk, unhooked a small, discoloured brass key from a nail, presenting it to her with a flourish.

'You can't do that,' she protested. 'You can't just help yourself!'

'*Pfui*, if you were the manager, how would you like to be bothered just for a bookcase key?'

'I shouldn't,' Verity confessed.

'Well, then, let us go and choose your book, and then I shall return the key and no one will even have missed it,' he said complacently.

He was difficult to refuse. There was a sort of innocent assumption in his voice that she would agree with him.

Had she not been so tired—it was late and the upset over
the change of hotel exhausting—she might have de-
murred. But she followed him meekly to the bookcase.
There he repossessed himself of the key and unlocked
the glass door, pulling it open with a tug.

'The lock is stiff,' he said disapprovingly. 'They should
oil it. I shall tell the good Inebnit so. What do you like to
read?' He peered critically at the well-thumbed contents
of the bookcase, mostly German Tauchnitz editions in
English of obscure novelists.

'It's not for me. It's for . . . for the lady whose
companion I am.'

'*La bella Contessa?* Beautiful as a diamond, and as
expensive. I suspect also as hard! Tell me, is she truly a
countess? I heard Inebnit call her Contessa, but she
hasn't the look of an Italian to me.'

'She isn't,' Verity said. 'She's English, but her
husband was Italian . . .' She broke off and flushed,
realising she was telling all this to a perfect stranger.

But he seemed unconcerned. 'These books are all
falling to pieces.' He began to riffle through them with a
practised hand.

Verity decided to do a little fishing for information on
her own account. 'I can't place your accent. You speak
very good English. Are you Swiss?'

He pursed his lips and shook his head. 'No, I'm
French. My name's Alain Bernard. They know me well
in this hotel. I come here every year. When I was a child,
I had weak lungs.' He tapped his chest. 'I'm quite fit
now, but my family still sends me to the mountains every
year. It's tedious. Life in these hotels is excruciatingly
boring. The only entertainment is to speculate on your
fellow guests. That's why I was watching you. I've been
watching you since you arrived this morning with your
Contessa. Here'—he pulled a stout leather volume
from the shelf and thrust it into Verity's hands—

'that should keep her happy.'

'Thank you,' Verity said stiffly. She did not like to think she had been spied on and speculated about. No doubt he'd summed up the situation without difficulty. A wealthy lady and her impoverished, browbeaten companion.

Alain had relocked the bookcase. They went back to the reception desk, where he replaced the key deftly. 'Dear Miss Lyndon—oh, I read your name in the hotel register—don't be cross! I know you're as bored as I am. Do you ever escape from the Contessa for an hour of an afternoon?'

'Sometimes she takes a nap after lunch,' Verity admitted.

'The next time she does, ask for me at the desk. We can go for a walk. Are you a strong walker? Never mind. You need only sensible shoes. I wouldn't suggest we attempt to walk up the Harder Kulm, which is Interlaken's own mountain and celebrated for breaking the ankles of unwary tourists. No, we can walk to the top of the Kleine Rugen, that woody hill not far from the hotel. There is a path up it through the trees, and a fine view from the top.'

'Perhaps,' Verity said cautiously. Briskly she added, 'I must go now. She'll wonder where I am.'

She stepped back as she spoke, out of the way of two Russian ladies, chattering volubly in their curious, heavily accented St Petersburg French, who had emerged from the hotel dining-room. One, a dumpy figure in a mauve gown, held clasped to her bosom a small, white, long-haired dog with a pointed face, called in England a Pomeranian, but in Europe usually called a 'Spitz'.

'The plump lady with the dog is Princess Detkine,' Alain whispered. 'She owns an estate in Russia which is the size of an entire Swiss canton, but is slow to settle her bill. Despite all protests, she insists on taking the dog into the dining-room, where it sits on her lap and is fed with titbits from her plate.'

'You are a gossip, Monsieur Bernard!' Verity told him a little sharply.

'Only about some things. In other ways, I'm discretion itself. Good night, Miss Verity. Do try and get away from your walking jewel-case of a Contessa, so that we can make our excursion.'

He bowed courteously, and went to take one of the newspapers hanging on rods at the back of the foyer, walking quickly and moving lightly on his feet, almost like a dancer.

It had been a thoroughly exhausting day. Alone at last in her own room, Verity pushed open the french windows on to her share of the balcony to let in some cooling air, and stared out into the night. It was very dark, but to her right she could see the lights of Interlaken flickering like fallen stars. The wooded hill, the Rugen, of which Alain Bernard had spoken, lay ahead of her at the foot of its mightier neighbour of the same name. Between it and the hotel lay a large field of pasture. From this arose the monotonous tinkle of the bells of the cows and goats turned out to graze on it. Otherwise it was painfully quiet. The Swiss were early to bed, and the hotel guests, perhaps exhausted by healthy exercise taken during the day and the large dinner consumed after it, had also taken themselves to their rooms.

Turning back into the room, she unpinned her hair as she went. It fell round her face in long chestnut-brown curls. She would have liked to wear it more attractively dressed than scraped back and pinned into a simple knot, but one thing she had realised very early in her career was that companions and governesses were not expected to look attractive. Those who did were soon dismissed before they caused any trouble. So Verity had learned to pin back her hair and wear plain dresses. The only item of jewellery she possessed was a gold locket of her mother's, and even that she wore only occasionally at dinner. Well, it was a fashion which suited her lean purse. She was satisfied she had achieved insignificance, and would have been surprised if anyone had pointed out that natural good looks are hard to disguise, even in dowdy dresses. Verity's oval face, with its wide-set blue-grey eyes and generous mouth, caught the eye of onlookers without the slightest effort on her part. Often, watchers wondered what made such a young woman look so grave, until they saw the smile which lit up her features and which someone had once likened to the sun coming out from behind a cloud.

Verity pulled her nightgown over her head and thrust her arms into its long sleeves. Then she sat down on the edge of the bed. She wondered how long she would be able to put up with Jessica Giulini's whims and temper. Certainly, at the moment, life offered little by way of alternative. Many a young woman in her situation would have envied her a position of companion, offering opportunities of travel and of living in fashionable hotels, otherwise hopelessly beyond her purse. She was twenty-seven years old, and Jack her only living relation. She had been modestly educated, since there had been no money left for an expensive girls' school after fees had been paid for Jack at a minor public school. As a result, she could not offer her services as governess to any but the least demanding family. Governess was, in any case, an overcrowded profession filled with young women like herself, of respectable birth but no fortune, who were forced to fend for themselves. But Verity had early learned tenacity, and did not give up anything easily once she had set her mind to it. She was not ready to give up Jessica just yet.

She scrambled into bed, rolling back the heavy feather quilt with which it was decked, despite the warm night. The cool air from the balcony played pleasantly over her lightly-clad body. She extinguished the light, and settled down to relax her tired muscles and fall immediately into an exhausted slumber.

She awoke because she had become chilled in the low night temperature without the quilt. At least, she supposed that to be the reason. She did not know what time it was, only that it must be in the early hours, and she fancied that somewhere a clock chimed twice. It was pitch dark, but a cool breeze was blowing over her most distinctly from the balcony, and she could hear the rustling of the trees outside. A wind had sprung up, perhaps heralding a break in the hot weather and a coming storm. The balcony windows, which she had left ajar, now stood wide open and the curtains moved slightly to and fro.

Verity slipped out of bed and padded across on bare feet to close the windows. As she reached them, the long dark shape she had taken to be a fold of the curtain moved in a way no curtain moved, and very faintly her ear caught the unmistakable sound of another person breathing. A shiver of pure horror ran up her spine, mixed with incredulity. Someone was standing there, in the shadow cast by the curtain, inside her room. She drew in her breath with an audible gasp, and though frozen with panic, managed to whisper through dry lips, 'Who . . .'

She was allowed to say no more. The shadowy figure leapt out of his hiding-place with the rapidity of a springing animal. A hand, supple and smooth like polished leather and as strong as steel, was clasped over her mouth. The rough texture of a man's jacket brushed against her cheek and neck as she twisted, trying to free herself, and he flung his other arm round her, holding her tightly against him. She could feel his fingers, through the thin cotton of the nightgown, pressing into her flesh, and she kicked out wildly with her bare feet, trying in vain to escape that powerful grip.

'Keep still, you silly little fool,' hissed a voice in her ear, in English. 'I'm not going to hurt you, for pity's sake! Stop struggling, and I'll let you go.'

Verity became still, holding herself tensely in his arms, her heart beating painfully in her breast.

'That's better,' he muttered, it seemed to her with some relief in his voice. 'Are you alone in here? Nod, or shake your head.'

With difficulty, since he held her head tight against his chest, Verity nodded.

'Then listen to me,' he ordered her, speaking quickly into her ear in a low tone. She could feel the light warm touch of his breath on her neck. 'Promise that you won't start shrieking your head off once I take my hand from your mouth, and I'll release you. Agreed?'

Again she managed to nod. Anything, if only he would free her from this terrifying grip that held her powerless and almost unable to breathe! In response, he released his hand cautiously, ready to clamp it back over her lips if she attempted to break her word. When she remained silent, he took his arms away from her completely, expelling his breath as he did so.

Verity stumbled back, away from him. She was silent not from obedience to his command, but from a nervous paralysis that temporarily gripped her throat. At last, forcing the words out and rubbing her sore arms where his strong fingers had pressed tightly on the flesh, she demanded, 'Who are you?'

It was a foolish question, little likely to be answered, but the mere fact that she had been able to speak, gave her courage, and helped her to pull herself together and regain some of her shattered presence of mind.

As expected, he ignored her question. He stepped away from the shadows of the curtain, and now that her eyes had become adjusted to the gloom, she could see his tall form standing in the middle of the room, dimly lit by the moonlight filtering through the windows.

'Close the window,' he ordered, and she jumped at the sound of his voice.

He was standing between her and the door, and, more than anything, she was determined to reach the door. Once through it and into the corridor, it would be easy to raise the alarm. When she had pushed the windows to, as bid, she took a cautious step forward, sidling carefully round him.

'Stand still!' He threw out a hand and caught tightly at her elbow. Verity froze again, and the hand relaxed its pressure and fell away. Somehow she had the impression he was listening, fearing perhaps that someone had overheard them.

'I don't know how you got in here,' Verity said as evenly as she was able. 'But you can get out again, this minute!' Sarcastically she added, 'I haven't any valuables, no jewellery and little money.'

'You talk too much,' the intruder said unkindly. 'If you had any sense, you'd keep quiet and not annoy me! Just hold your tongue, will you? And stay where you are.'

Now she was sure he was listening. He had not turned his head towards her as he spoke, possibly lest even in the dim light she might be able to discern his features, but more likely because his attention was elsewhere. Now or never! He might not be distracted again. She made a sudden desperate lunge past him, diving for the door.

She had reached it, and her fingers, clammy with perspiration, touched the handle before she was seized roughly by the shoulders, dragged away, the handle sliding through her hand, and hurled down on the bed. She gave a cry of fear, sprawling back against the pillows. The man leapt towards her, throwing himself across her to hold her down, and clamping his hand firmly over her mouth again.

'Confound you!' His voice came hoarsely, right against her ear, as his face was pushed close to hers. 'I told you to keep quiet and keep still.'

Verity made inarticulate cries against the pressure of that iron hand, and pushed at his chest, wriggling desperately to get away from him. Managing to free her hand, she reached up to his head and grasped a handful of his close-cropped hair, pulling it as hard as she could.

'Ouch!' he exclaimed. He sounded more surprised than angry, but there was no gentleness in the hand which seized her wrist and thrust her arm away. 'Listen to me, my would-be tigress, that was a very stupid thing to do!'

Verity held her breath and waited.

He sat back on the edge of the bed and unexpectedly took his hand from her mouth. 'I'm a great deal stronger than you are,' he said, 'and in any struggle you're going to come off worse. Do you understand?'

'Yes,' Verity croaked from the pillows.

'Hmm,' he muttered. 'Are you frightened?'

It seemed such an odd question that she speculated briefly as to whether it would amuse him to think he terrified her, which he did. But since to lie would be obvious and serve no purpose, she said vehemently, 'Of *course* I'm frightened! What do you expect me to be? But I'm angry, too. How dare you? For the last time, will you get out!'

'All in good time. What's your name?'

'This is ridiculous!' Verity exploded.

'Your *name* . . .' repeated a cool voice in the darkness, which so impressed her that she told him.

She saw him nod, his head silhouetted against the windows. 'Verity, be a good girl, and no harm will come to you. I want you to keep absolutely quiet.'

'And let you do as you want? You must be mad!' she gasped.

'Good heavens, girl,' he said, almost wearily. 'I'm not after your body. You unmarried women are all the same. You think the world is one conspiracy to assault your virtue. Verity, you can go to the grave in your maidenly innocence for all I care. As it happens, I prefer nice, feminine women to hysterical prudes. In any case, I haven't the time just now.'

'I'm not a hysterical prude!' she cried furiously, outraged. She sat up suddenly, and with such force that she bumped into his chest and cracked her forehead on his chin.

'You're a menace. The moment I let go of you you go berserk, and if I hold you still, you think . . . Ssh!' He broke off and put his fingertips lightly against her lips to silence the retort trembling on the end of her tongue.

More nervous now that he spoke to her almost reasonably than when he had seized her roughly, Verity obeyed. His hand on her shoulder felt hot through her nightgown, and the fingertips against her lips seemed held there in an almost intimate caress. His breath skimmed gently across her temple, and she drew back a little, her loose hair falling over the hand on her shoulder, which tightened its grip warningly.

'I said, don't move.' But there was less urgency in his order now, making it almost a request. He took his hand from her shoulder and pushed the heavy damp locks of hair back from her face. 'Just pretend you dreamed all this, Verity,' he whispered. 'And give me five minutes to get away before you raise the alarm. Come on, you're the sort of girl who keeps a promise.'

Unwillingly, she muttered, 'All right, if you'll only *go*!'

'Good girl.' He caught her chin lightly and, leaning forward, stooped to kiss her forehead. 'Perhaps we'll meet by daylight sometime.'

'I trust not!' she said coldly, pushing away his hand from her face.

A chuckle was the only response. He stood up and opened the door to the dimly-lit corridor, and she had only a glimpse of a tall, solid silhouette before he was gone.

Verity leapt up, ran to the door, pushed hard on it to ensure it was shut and turned the key firmly in the lock. Then she went to the windows and pushed up the bolt, locking those, too. Finally she switched on the bedside lamp and sat down to take stock of it all.

It had all taken place so quickly, that she could scarcely credit it had happened at all. Her alarm clock ticked reassuringly, telling her it was ten past two, so that if she had indeed heard a clock chime the hour, the whole episode had lasted ten brief minutes. And he had been here, for there was the imprint on the bed where he had sat, and a scuffed mark on the carpet where they had struggled. Her visitor could only have been a hotel sneak-thief. He had certainly chosen the wrong room! He'd have found nothing of value among her simple possessions. But how had he entered? Verity glanced thoughtfully at the now bolted window. Through that? Only if he'd climbed up the outside of the building!

She frowned. That would be a remarkable feat, for they were on the second floor, and it was quite dark outside. He'd been a big, strong fellow; and a cat-burglar, so she imagined, would be someone lithe and small. Perhaps he had, after all, entered by the door, and stepped into the shadows of the curtain when she stirred and woke.

She climbed back into bed, pummelled the pillows into a backrest and clasped her arms about her hunched knees. The solution ought to seem so logical and obvious, yet she felt as though what she had witnessed had been a tiny part of an explanation much more complex. Most strange of all, there was a sort of familiarity about her alarming nocturnal visitor, which was a total nonsense, for of one thing only could she be sure. He had been an Englishman.

CHAPTER THREE

THE HOTEL might have progressed as far as electric light, albeit uncertainly, but it had yet to achieve running water in every room. Verity was woken in the morning by a knock on the door and slid out of bed to unlock it, yawning. It had been a disturbed and almost sleepless night. A sturdy Swiss country girl in a dirndl, bearing a jug of hot water, marched in with a cheerful *'Gruotsi!'* She set the jug on the marble-topped wash-stand and flung back the curtains before hurrying out to see to the next room.

Verity went to the windows of the balcony, and involuntarily caught her breath. Before her lay a magnificent mountain vista dominated by the snow-clad slopes of the great Jungfrau. It towered in the distance, set with crystal clarity against a periwinkle blue sky, decked in the maiden-white veil of snow which it never lost, although the surrounding mountains were free of their winter overcoats of ice and snow, and which had gained it the name of the 'Virgin'.

In the town it was possible to buy saucy postcards, in which the mountain was given female features and expressed surprise at being assaulted by a determined swarm of mountaineers. It was the sort of thing that would amuse Jack, and mindful of his parting request, she had sent him one. For it was indeed a real person, the Jungfrau. The mountain had a personality, and a living existence, all of its own and quite unique. It seemed to beckon to the young woman who stood on the balcony in the early sunlight, gazing at it. Verity gained a slight understanding of the lure which led men to climb the fearsome precipices scattered through the Alpine region.

At least the threatened storm had not materialised, and it was going to be another fine day. In the sunshine, the events of the night before seemed even more improbable and unreal, as if she must have dreamed them. She grasped the carved wooden balustrade and leaned over perilously, trying to see the exterior walls of the building. There was certainly a great deal of ornamental frieze-work full of heart-shaped holes, and it looked solid enough. Nevertheless, she couldn't imagine a man scaling it by night. It would require an iron nerve, a complete disregard for heights and the climbing ability of a rock lizard. Perhaps she *had* dreamed it all.

Verity went back, washed and dressed, and went through the intervening sitting-room to the door into Jessica Giulini's room, her hand raised to knock. But, at that moment, a piercing shriek split the air, causing her to freeze with surprise, her hand arrested in mid-gesture. The cry came from further along the corridor on the side not taken up by the Giulini suite. Someone, a woman, was shouting at the top of her voice, and a dog was barking hysterically. She opened the door on to the corridor and ran out to see what had caused such an extraordinary commotion, and so early in the day.

She almost collided with Inebnit, hurrying along, alarm printed on his round face. Princess Detkine, a portly and, but for the real anguish on her features, ludicrous figure in an apricot satin négligée cut to resemble a small tent, her hair confined by a lace boudoir cap decorated with yellow rosebuds, stood in the middle of the corridor, shrieking in broken, distraught German, interspersed with Russian and French. Her harassed maid hovered ineffectually in the background, and the

Spitz raced madly up and down the corridor, yelping shrilly.

A click beside her made her turn her head. Jessica stepped out into the corridor, cool and elegant as ever in a crisp lawn blouse and beige walking-skirt, her hair swept up and coiled on the top of her head.

'What on earth's going on?' she demanded. 'Why is that wretched woman howling? And can't anyone do something about that ghastly dog?'

'Volée!' screamed Princess Detkine, bearing down upon Inebnit in a flurry of apricot satin and rosebuds. 'Volée—on m'a volée! I have been robbed! Stolen, you understand? Stolen while I slept! Even Ninochka heard nothing. Hush, my precious . . .' She scooped up the Spitz, a frenzied ball of long white hair, and Verity realised that it was the dog, and not the maid, who bore the name Ninochka.

'Madame . . .' faltered Inebnit, white with apprehension. 'What has been stolen?'

'My rings!' The Princess thrust the struggling Spitz into the arms of the maid, so that she could seize the unfortunate Inebnit by his lapels. She shook the poor man as if he had been a doll. 'While I sleep! I put them on the bedside table. They are gone! Two emerald rings and one sapphire with diamonds.' For Verity and Jessica's benefit, perhaps, she had chosen to speak in heavily accented English.

'Are you sure, madame?' the manager stammered.

'Of course I am sure, you idiot! Fetch the police, search everywhere! What kind of an establishment do you keep here, where defenceless women can be robbed as they sleep?' The Princess pushed Inebnit away, and he staggered back.

'Barinya . . .' murmured the maid, clasping the writhing Spitz to her flat bosom. She whispered something into the Princess's ear.

The Princess turned majestically to Jessica. 'My dear Contessa Giulini, you have not suffered such a loss also, perhaps?'

Jessica shrugged her slim shoulders. 'I take no risks. My companion, Miss Lyndon, or myself, sees all my jewels are safely locked away at night in the manager's safe.' She turned to Inebnit and raised an arched eyebrow. 'I take it that has not been forced, Herr Inebnit?'

'Indeed, not, Contessa!' Inebnit looked shocked. 'My dear lady,' he went on, attempting to placate Princess Detkine, who still stood, irate and smouldering like a half-extinguished volcano in the middle of the corridor. 'I shall send for the police immediately. A search will be made. Please, I beg of you . . .'

'I am going to faint,' said Princess Detkine portentously. She began to sway from side to side, like a large tree about to be toppled.

Inebnit blenched and the maid put down the Spitz hurriedly. Two other guests, who had appeared in their dressing-gowns to see what caused so much uproar, stepped back hastily, out of the way.

'*Not* in the corridor!' Verity said loudly and firmly. Everyone turned to look at her in astonishment, including Princess Detkine, who momentarily ceased swaying to and fro. Verity walked across to her, ignoring the Spitz snapping at her skirts. She took the Princess by one plump, apricot-satin-clad arm. 'Come along! Come and sit down in your room.' To the maid, she ordered, 'Shut away that dog before someone falls over it. Then bring your mistress some strong tea.' She turned back to the Princess. 'Now then, Madame la Princesse, I'm sure you want to be ready and dressed to receive the police whom Herr Inebnit will have here shortly.'

'Yes, yes,' Princess Detkine agreed tearfully, the moist drops trickling down her plump cheeks. 'My dear young lady, you are right . . .'

She subsided like a pricked balloon, and leaning her considerable weight on Verity's arm, allowed herself to be escorted into her own room. The maid, interpreting Verity's instructions literally, shut the Spitz in the wardrobe, where it barked furiously in muffled frustration and scrabbled at the door with its sharp claws. Princess Detkine sank in folds of satin on to a chair, and Verity left her to the ministrations of the maid, who seemed competent enough, if not overly bright.

Jessica Giulini gave a musical chuckle of delight and tapped Verity indulgently on the cheek. 'My dear Verity, that was very well done! I thought the awful woman was going to collapse at our feet, and we should all have to drag her back into her room. You know, like a dead stag.'

'She really is very upset,' Verity said thoughtfully. 'Little wonder. Contessa, last night . . .'

'Do come along,' Jessica interrupted, linking her arm through that of her companion in a rare show of friendship. 'Let's go and have our breakfast on the balcony before that lovely view. It's the only moment of peace we shall get today. Mark my words, the place will be crawling with officious little Swiss gendarmes. We shall all have to comfort the Princess, and every lady in the hotel will be in a frenzy of excitement. That woman does speak the most extraordinary French. When she was shrieking *volée*—robbed—*I* first thought that she was screaming *violée* . . . Now *that* would have been amusing! Can you imagine anyone having the courage to ravish her?'

'I wouldn't call any of it amusing,' Verity exclaimed, as they seated themselves at a table ready laid for breakfast on the balcony.

'Pah! The woman won't feel the loss of a couple of paltry rings. She's as rich as Croesus, and thoroughly mean. It serves her right. She should do as I do, and make sure her jewels are locked up at night. If people will be foolish, what can they expect? Do pour out the coffee, Verity dear.'

So saying, Jessica shook out a snowy white napkin and helped herself serenely to a mouth-watering croissant.

Jessica was certainly right in her predictions. The day was thoroughly taken up with the robbery. Excitement was doubled when it was discovered that the Princess was not the only one to have suffered a loss. An elderly gentleman on the top floor had lost his gold watch and chain in similar circumstances, taken from his bedside table.

Princess Detkine had no intention of allowing this relatively trivial and humble loss to vie with her own. She had set up court in her sitting-room, splendidly encased in a rigid whalebone corset and a purple plush gown, with the Spitz on her knees and the sal volatile at her elbow. A silver samovar bubbled on the table, as she received visits of sympathy and repeated her story over and over again for each newcomer.

'We are all to take tea with her,' Jessica said. 'Didn't I tell you? We are all to sit around and listen to her woes and offer her comfort. I believe the ridiculous woman thinks she's Catherine the Great. And she's been fortifying herself with more than *tea*—Maddox saw the bottle being taken up to the room. I just hope she doesn't let that horrid dog loose. It jumps on my lap, ugh!' Jessica shivered. 'You needn't come, Verity. You've nobly done your duty, and it will be a fearful crush in there. Go and amuse yourself. Go for a walk, or something.'

Princess Detkine's misfortune had obviously put Jessica Giulini in high good humour. The mood was unlikely to last very long. Verity realised that she should seize the opportunity offered, since it was unlikely to be repeated soon. She had had no time to herself, as Jessica clearly expected her 'companion' to dance a constant attendance. So, if Jessica had given her a free afternoon, Verity did not mean to waste it. After lunch, she laced up her strong walking-shoes and went downstairs.

Behind the reception desk, Inebnit was mopping his bald head. 'Ah, Fräulein? I hope you have a pleasant time.'

'Thank you.' Verity hesitated. 'Is Monsieur Bernard in the hotel, do you know?'

'I saw him not five minutes ago, Fraülein. I will send someone to call him for you.'

Alain arrived, grinning broadly and pushing his long dark hair out of his eyes with a nervous gesture. 'What a day! You see, Miss Lyndon? You make things happen. I knew, when I first set eyes on you, that from now on, nothing could be boring any more.'

'I didn't commit this robbery!' she objected.

He waved the point away. 'No matter, you make things happen. You are, what is it? A catalyst.' He eyed her shrewdly. 'You're going for a walk. Show me your shoes.'

Verity raised her skirt high enough to reveal a pair of strong Oxfords.

He nodded approvingly. 'Good! You'd be surprised at the stupid footwear some women choose to walk in. They twist their ankles and blister their toes, and wonder why.' He thrust back the rebellious lock of hair again with his long, tapering fingers.

With a sudden flash of intuition, Verity exclaimed, 'You're an artist, or a musician!'

He smiled. 'Something of an artist. Not a good one. I take my sketch folder out with me most days. I was going to take it this afternoon. Let me get it, and I'll come with you.'

Together they walked across the pasture to the trees which began at the foot of the hill called the Rugen.

Alain, his folder of sketch-paper under his arm, and a disreputable broad-brimmed straw hat on his head, said, 'It's hot, but under the trees it will be cool. Watch out for midges.'

A beaten path, narrow and in places crossed by surface tree-roots, led in zig-zags up the steep slope, It was quiet and peaceful, especially after the commotion at the hotel. A female blackbird ran among the fallen leaves, searching for insects to feed her brood. She put her head on one side and eyed them as they passed her by.

'Such a relief!' said Verity in heartfelt tones. 'But I'm surprised *you* want to leave the hotel, now there's so much excitement going on there.'

'This morning it was interesting. Now it's old news.'

'How quickly you're bored,' she chided him.

He shrugged, dismissing the charge. 'Oh, these things happen in hotels from time to time. What do you expect? Switzerland is full of wealthy visitors, English lords, Russians, even Americans with wallets stuffed with dollars . . . The Russian nobility are especially vulnerable to being robbed, because they are all used to the grand gesture.' Alain waved his free arm expansively. 'The Princess left priceless rings lying about like glass baubles. Even though they're lost, I don't suppose she truly worries about it. But she has an opportunity to be the centre of attention for twenty-four hours, our fat, plain Princess, so she means to take it. Who can blame her?'

He stopped, and pointed through the trees. Below them lay the fields and villages which fringed Interlaken, like a child's set of wooden models, tiny cattle, doll's houses.

'How high up we are 'already!' she exclaimed in surprise.

'I told you it was an easy hill to walk,' Alain said. 'This

is only the small hill, the little Rugen. There is a greater
Rugen, that mountain over there. It takes much longer,
but everything takes time . . .'

Something in his voice caught her ear. Glancing at
him, she saw his pale cheekbones were touched with two
patches of scarlet.

'I should like to sit down for a moment, all the same,'
she said carefully. 'I'm just a little breathless.'

'Are you?' He raised his eyebrows. 'Just a little
further on, and we'll come to a seat.'

When they reached the bench, he seated her at one
end of it, and stood back and stared at her critically.
Then he darted forward and redraped her skirt.

'What on earth are you doing?' she asked, laughing.

'Arranging my model. Keep still.' He untied the
ribbon round his sketch-folder, put his hat on the
ground, and searched in his pocket for a crayon.

'I smoke when I work . . . That doesn't trouble you?'
He lit his cigarette, stuck it rakishly in the corner of his
mouth, propped his sketch-board on his knees and,
frowning ferociously, began to work.

'Am I allowed to talk?' she asked.

'Mmm—yes . . . if you must. But don't move.'

'Will you give me the portrait when you've finished
it?'

'Only if it's good enough.' He sketched on quietly for
a few moments, the smoke from his cigarette curling into
the air. Then he paused, took the cigarette from his
mouth, but without looking up from the sketch-board,
said, 'Verité. In French, it means "truth". Do you
always tell the truth, Verity Lyndon?'

'Nearly always,' she said cautiously.

'Ah, a wise reply. Because you told a lie just now.'
When she would have protested, he shook the crayon at
her admonishingly. 'Yes, you did. You said you wanted
to sit down because you were out of breath. If you had

been out of breath, *I* should have seen it, and *I* should have suggested we sit down. You thought *I* should sit down.'

'All right,' Verity admitted. 'I did.'

'I told you, I'm quite fit now!' There was undisguised annoyance in his voice, and he threw the cigarette away in an angry gesture.

'You were red in the face.'

'Passion,' he said promptly. 'You're a very attractive woman, and I'm a Frenchman.'

'What nonsense!' Verity exclaimed, laughing at him.

'Not so. You are attractive, and you have it in you to be beautiful, if you wished. Why do you put up your hair like that? You should wear it loose, as the American girls do.'

'It wouldn't be suitable,' she answered quietly.

He said, 'Ah . . .', but made no further comment, and she knew he'd understood. Abruptly, he pushed the crayon into his pocket, and turned the sketch to face her.

She drew in her breath with a gasp. 'You *are* an artist, Alain! It's very good, but it flatters me.'

'A good artist doesn't flatter his sitter. He draws what he sees. And I *did* draw what I saw.' He put the sketch back in his folder and tied it together with the ribbon. 'I'll work on it at little, back at the hotel, and then you can have it—if you wish and if I'm satisfied.' He picked up his hat and shook the dust and leaves from it. 'Are you ready to go on to the top?'

They climbed on, up to the summit. Alain had taken off his linen jacket and slung it over his shoulder, hooked on one finger. In his shirtsleeves he was a slender but lithe figure, perhaps as fit as he claimed, because he was still breathing easily when he stretched his hand to help her over the last few feet. She was surprised, too, at the strength of the slim fingers that gripped her.

'I told you,' he said, 'I'm quite fit now. I walk all the

time. A man doesn't have to be built like a Colossus to be healthy.'

At the top, the sunlight filtered down through the tall trees, and a cool breeze wafted over them, as they sat down, side by side, on a patch of dry leaf-mould.

'Down there,' Alain said, pointing to the valley, 'the men of Unspunnen used to meet and vie to see how strong they were by hurling great boulders. Not a sport for me! There's a ruined castle there, too. It was not always so peaceful.'

'Alain!' Verity said impulsively. 'There's something I'd like to talk to you about. I know I hardly know you, but I don't know anyone else here. It's on my mind. I ought to talk to the Contessa, I suppose, especially as she's in such a good mood today, for once. But she probably wouldn't listen. I did begin to try and tell her, but she wanted her breakfast.'

'You realise,' Alain told her gravely, 'that you're making no sense?'

'That's because it's so embarrassing. Alain, you said you could be discreet. Can you really? It's something very serious. At least, I think it is.'

He folded his jacket as a pillow and stretched out on the ground, putting his hands under his head. Looking up at her through half-closed eyes, he mumbled lazily, 'Well, then?'

Although he looked more as though he were going to fall asleep than listen, Verity began anyway, picking her words slowly. 'Last night, as it was so warm, I left the balcony windows open . . .'

'And a man climbed through them,' he said promptly.

'Yes! How did you know?' Verity twisted round to stare at him in astonishment.

There was a silence. Alain opened his eyes wide, and said incredulously, 'I was joking! Verity, you're not serious? You're making fun of me.'

'No, I'm serious. Never more so in my entire life. I swear it.'

Alain sat up in a sudden burst of energy, muttering to himself in French. He ran his hands through his long black hair so that it stuck out wildly. 'It's impossible, you're on the second floor!' he objected. 'Did you see him climb in?'

'No, but I think he did. He was inside my room, by the balcony windows.' As briefly as possible, she told him the essentials of what had occurred, leaving out the details of their undignified and alarming struggle. 'He just left, suddenly. Should I tell the police, do you think?'

'No!' Alain said emphatically. He gave her a quick glance. 'Think, Verity. They will ask you why you didn't raise the alarm at once. Why you didn't call for help. Why you didn't tell the Contessa this morning, or the policemen who came to see Princess Detkine.'

'Yes, I realise that.' She bit her lip. 'I went outside this morning and studied the wall. There's a lot of ornamental carving, and I suppose it just could be done. The handholds would be very far spaced, but he was tall.'

Alain shook his head. 'I think you're mistaken, my dear. Your visitor came by the door. You should keep it locked. There,' he grinned at her briefly, 'I give you this advice, even though it may work against me!' He grew sober again. 'If this man was Princess Detkine's thief, you are a danger to him. Would you know him again?' His eyes searched her face anxiously.

'I don't know. I didn't see his face. I might recognise his voice.' Verity sighed, and automatically stretched out her hand to pick off the fragments of dried leaf that clung to the back of his shirt. She did not find it difficult to talk to him like this. She felt quite at ease with him, almost as if she were sitting here with Jack.

'You know,' Alain said softly, 'I don't wish to alarm you, but he might have had motives other than robbery . . .'

She flushed. 'I suppose so, but I don't think so. He said not—and he let me go.'

'You struggled. You showed you would fight. He couldn't risk waking others. Perhaps you were just fortunate,' her companion said soberly. 'If you think you see this man again, Verity, tell me.'

At the hotel, Jessica Giulini's good temper had evaporated after an afternoon spent drinking tea with Princess Detkine. As Verity came into the suite of rooms, she could hear the Contessa berating Maddox loudly. Jessica whirled round as Verity entered, and snapped, 'Where have you been?'

'Walking. You told me I could go . . .'

'Not for the entire afternoon and half the evening!' Jessica sounded vehement. 'Oh, go and get changed, it's nearly time for dinner. If Princess Detkine brings that horrid little dog into the dining-room again, I'll scream. It ran round our feet all afternoon, and leapt on my lap just as I picked up a dish of scalding hot tea. It's a wonder there wasn't an accident! My skirt is covered in white hairs. I just hope I haven't caught a flea from it.'

Verity went to dress for dinner as bid, but that unquenchable spirit of rebellion was simmering away inside her again. She was tired of Jessica's whims and fancies and more than usually resentful. Perhaps the afternoon spent in Alain's company had something to do with it. She brushed out her thick hair vigorously, releasing some of her pent-up wrath. When she had finished, instead of pinning it up, she caught it at the nape of her neck in a cascade of curls secured by a black silk bow. She took out her mother's locket and fastened it round her throat, so that it lay in the scooped neck of the simple dark blue dinner dress.

'My!' Jessica Giulini said, raising her finely arched eyebrows. 'You have made an effort this evening, Verity. May I ask why?'

'I felt like a change,' Verity replied defensively.

'Well, it's time! You were beginning to look very dowdy, and I was intending to speak to you about it.' Jessica's eye fell on the gold locket. 'That's a pretty trinket. Don't leave it lying about, will you, as old Detkine did her rings?'

They were a little late going down to dinner, and the room was already crowded. The chatter of voices and clink of glass and china filled the air. Alain was dining alone in a far corner, and discussing the menu with the waiter with French thoroughness. Verity pushed a piece of fish from one side of the plate to the other with her fork.

If Alain had not told her of his childhood lung trouble, she would have had no reason to suppose him other than as fit as a fiddle. Yet she could not forget that hectic flush that had momentarily stained his pale cheeks. She liked him tremendously, but found him in many ways an enigma. The family which sent him on these yearly convalescent trips must be wealthy, yet Alain himself seemed curiously alone and friendless. Perhaps he simply preferred it that way. Yet it seemed odd that if the family was so concerned, no watchful friend or companion travelled with him, as she did with Jessica Giulini.

A shadow fell across her plate, breaking into her conjectures. Someone had just entered the room, and stopped at their table. He stood at her shoulder, looking across the plates towards the Contessa.

'Good evening, Jessica,' said a man's voice drily. 'I thought, after what happened at Montreux, you had crossed Switzerland off your list.'

Jessica's fork fell from her hand, clattering on her plate as she looked up, startled. 'Matthew!' she whispered.

Verity had never seen her so disconcerted, and turned her head quickly to see who could possibly have had such a devastating effect on her self-possessed employer.

The newcomer, one sunburned hand resting carelessly on the back of Verity's chair in a familiar manner, appeared to her eyes a total stranger. She judged his age at somewhere between thirty-four and thirty-eight, tall and strongly built, with powerful shoulders pulling on the seams of the dinner-jacket which sat incongruously on his muscular frame. The skin stretched across the broad cheekbones was darkened to a brown, shiny tint that reminded her of the Irish tinkers who used to call by the kitchen door in her childhood. His hair was thick and coarse, greying a little already, its tendency to curl curbed by a ruthless haircut which had cropped it to lie close to the well-shaped skull. A practical man's haircut, and one which stirred a chord in her memory. Deep creases carved by weather lined his cheeks and ran round the sides of a wide, firm mouth. The jaw was square and obstinate, and the eyebrows very straight, dark and thick, overhanging like mountain ledges, deep-set, intelligent blue eyes. His nose had a battered appearance, as if it had at some time smashed into some solid object, being broken and pushed out of its original shape. He made Verity think of those gritty portraits hewn out of solid rock, staring uncompromisingly from the mountainsides of which they are so solidly a part.

'Looked like a prizefighter, but was a gent . . .' So Albert had described the stranger who had enquired after the Contessa secretively in London. A tremor ran up Verity's spine, as if some great bird of ill omen had alighted at her side.

The man smiled at Jessica, and Verity saw that one of his otherwise even, white teeth was chipped. Whatever he did, she thought, puzzled, he led an extraordinary life—out of doors, hard, violent—even dangerous. Who, or what, on earth was he? Yet it was Jessica's expression which was the more startling, for the Contessa looked frightened. The fear did not stay long on her face, but Verity saw it, and it aroused in her breast a loyalty to her employer she would not have imagined existed. Whoever the stranger was, Jessica was afraid of him, and he knew it.

But the Contessa had rallied, smiling now as if nothing had ever been amiss. She held out her beringed, slender hand to the newcomer in welcome.

'Matthew, my dear! How nice to see you. Have you come to scale precipices and break your neck clambering over ravines and glaciers, as you always seem set on doing?'

He bowed over her hand, moving gracefully, for all his size and weight. 'Dear Jessica! Perhaps you would like me to break my neck, but I haven't done so yet, and God willing, won't do it this year.'

Jessica withdrew her hand and turned to Verity. 'Verity, dear, may I present an old—friend?' There was a perceptible hesitation before she chose the last word. 'Matthew Burton, the celebrated alpinist. He climbs mountains. Don't you, Matt? This is Verity Lyndon, my travelling companion.'

'Miss Lyndon,' Burton said politely, his eyes resting briefly on her with no show of any interest. They were blue as the alpine sky, yet somehow chill, like the waters of a mountain lake. 'I am delighted.'

The lacklustre way in which he spoke these last words, so obviously observing a mechanical formality, contrived to make them sound like an insult. Verity felt herself colour, her throat and face burning.

'I'll see you later, Jessica, in the lounge?' He raised his bushy eyebrows questioningly. 'Who knows? We might even crack a bottle of champagne to celebrate our unexpected reunion.' Now there was no hiding the sarcasm in the voice.

'How lovely,' Jessica answered in a bright, brittle voice, but if she were really pleased at the prospect, her eyes did not show it.

Matthew Burton passed by them to the far side of the room, pausing on the way to greet the Frenshams at their table.

'Is he an old friend?' Verity asked curiously, watching the burly figure whose hand Sir Miles was shaking enthusiastically.

'What?' Jessica looked up sharply. 'Oh, yes, indeed. I've known Matt for years, since I was a girl. He's quite eccentric, you know. I think that's the polite word for it. Anyone who spends nearly all his time clinging to sheer rock-faces like a mountain goat has to be a little mad.' She twisted the stem of her wine glass in her fingers, nervously. 'I haven't seen him for over a year.'

'At Montreux?' asked Verity, as innocently as she could.

'Oh, yes, Montreux. So stupid. I think Matt thought . . .' Jessica pushed her glass away. 'I was engaged to him once,' she said in that same bright, brittle tone. 'Oh, long, long ago when I was very young, only nineteen, and, of course, it didn't last. He was mountain-mad, even then. *Not* good husband material! I broke off our engagement, returned his ring, all the usual sort of thing. He took it quite badly at the time. But then he went off, climbing in the Dolomites, perhaps to celebrate his freedom!' Jessica gave a little laugh. 'I think that's what Matt really wants, to be free of all encumbrances—free of a wife, certainly. He'd lead any woman a wretched life. Such a surprise to see him here.' She picked up her fork and recommenced her dinner as calmly as if nothing had happened.

Verity looked across the crowded room to where Matthew Burton was conferring with the wine waiter. So, he was no stranger to Jessica. But neither was his voice, at least, completely unknown to herself. He was a mountaineer, was he? A skilled climber? Here, in Switzerland, she should have thought of such a person immediately, realised that such a person would find little difficulty in scaling a knobbly wooden façade to reach a balcony.

'I suppose Matthew wants to talk old times,' Jessica said idly. 'I won't need you this evening, Verity. Go and have some fun. Go into Interlaken. All the cafés are open, and some of them have music.'

Verity took her departure with some relief. She had not been looking forward to an evening spent in the company of Jessica and Matthew Burton, especially since she was practically sure that he had been her nocturnal intruder.

Back in her room, she went out on to the balcony. The sun was setting, and in its rosy rays a transformation was wrought on the Jungfrau. The mountain's veil of white became pink, so that it now resembled some huge sugar confection, iced in cerise and mauve, and touched with gold. Its magical spell seemed to be woven more strongly than ever, reaching out and touching the watching girl with gentle, caressing fingers.

'Free,' the mountain seemed to whisper. 'Free to be whatever you want, as I am, the mystical virgin mountain, ever changing, ever the same.'

She sighed and closed the window, drawing the curtains before she turned away. Gradually the room grew dark. But she sat in a chair, quite still, turning over and over in her mind what had happened, and trying to work out what it could all possibly mean. From that, she arrived somehow at speculating on her future, reflecting wryly that just now it did not hold out any great promise but that it had gained a note of uncertainty. She had recognised Matt Burton. But had Matt Burton recognised her? Almost certainly. Then what would he do about it?

She could just run away, something she'd never done in her life. She could go back to London and take lessons to be a lady typewriter. But London meant returning to Jack, admitting she had failed to keep her post, and facing another indefinite spell of miserably genteel poverty, searching for another job.

Jack would be delighted to see her, of course, his bread and butter. But for the first time in their lives she had resolutely turned her back on him and she must not seem to waver, or it would all have been for nothing. She ought to have done it years ago, to have obliged Jack to stand on his own feet or leave him to sink in a quicksand of idleness and misplaced pretensions. He was, after all, the elder by fourteen months, and the man of the family. Most people would say that he should have been looking after her all these years. If she'd thrust him out of the door at twenty, to make his own way, he might have been saved. But she had hesitated, misled by her own love for him into an indulgent weakness, and it was probably too late. Jack couldn't change now.

Verity felt a pang of anxiety. Suppose he starved? Suppose, for want of money, he turned to crime?

Crime! That brought her back, full circle, to Matthew Burton. He had climbed through her window. There had been two robberies in the hotel that same night. Yet, today, he had arrived boldly at the front entrance and taken a room like any self-respecting guest. A man everybody seemed to know, a famous mountaineer. It was impossible to make sense of any of it.

There was a faint noise from the next room, the sitting-room between her bedroom and that of Jessica. People were moving about in there, and there was a click as the balcony windows were opened. A sudden shiver ran through Verity as she heard the murmur of a man's voice. Jessica had not returned alone, and that low masculine tone was already horribly familiar.

'She could be eavesdropping.' His voice suddenly came clearly from outside. He had stepped out on the balcony. 'Her windows, too, open on to this balcony.'

He could only refer to her, and Verity flushed angrily. Yet, if she remained, she would be doing just that. She hoped he would go back into the sitting-room, but instead, Jessica came out and joined him.

'Don't fret so, Matt,' her voice came impatiently. 'You can see that her windows are shut, the curtain's drawn and it's quite dark in her room. I told her to go into town. She's probably sitting in some café, devouring a mountain of ice-cream. Or else she's gone to bed. Verity is a distressingly virtuous soul, always early to bed and early to rise, and never puts a foot wrong. She's frightfully sweet, and rather a dull little mouse. I'm sure men terrify her, so behave yourself!'

'I don't go about seducing meek little governesses or companions. She probably can't afford to be anything but good. Not like you, Jessica! Tell me, what brings you to Interlaken?'

'I really quite like the place. I suppose I am free to travel about as I wish without your permission, Matt? I confess, I didn't expect you to be here. You're not following me about, are you?' A coquettish note entered her voice, but it was false. The question was in deadly earnest.

Harshly, Matthew said, 'You told me in Montreux that I was wasting my time. You took great pains to tell me why, in detail, if you recall.'

'Oh, I was feeling out of sorts that day,' Jessica replied quickly. 'Don't sulk, Matt. It doesn't become a grown man. Of course I'm pleased to see you. You're one of my oldest friends. I like you, even though you are a grouch, and prefer mountains to people. Do you still like me, just a little?'

'I always liked you, Jessica,' he said hoarsely. 'And you know it, damn you for it!'

'Oh, poor Matt . . .' Jessica gave her light, musical chuckle, and Verity knew the Contessa felt surer of herself. She had been afraid of the man, but now she had found his weakness. Verity heard the rustle of Jessica's skirts, and could imagine the scene as clearly as if she herself stood out there on the balcony with them. The man, angry, angry at his own weakness, and the woman, sensing her power, moving to brush against him, and slipping her arms round his neck.

'I do believe,' Jessica whispered throatily, 'you're still just a little bit in love with me.'

'If I ever loved you, Jessica, I paid for it.' His voice muttered the words almost indistinctly. 'It was a higher price than any man should have to pay for bitter experience. I don't believe that, even now, you have the slightest notion of what you did to me all those years ago. I sometimes think you destroyed something in me that no other woman has ever put back. But it taught me one thing—don't repeat a mistake. Perhaps I ought to hate you.'

'No, don't say that!' Jessica's voice changed, and Verity detected the former note of panic in it, as the fear returned. 'Don't, Matt, don't hate me, please! I never meant to hurt you. I was very young, and very foolish. Can't you understand that? Can't you forgive?' Her voice trembled, almost pleading. 'Say you don't hate me.'

'No, I don't hate you.' Verity was astonished at the

change in his voice. It held a note of defeat, quite unexpected and seemingly out of character. 'But not because I haven't tried!'

'Then don't try. Let me mean something to you, Matt, as I used to.'

There was a scrape of a foot, and a silence. Verity, fearing to move lest she be heard and discovered, closed her eyes tightly, as if she could shut out the picture from her imagination, and pressed her hands over her ears until the blood rang in them.

On the balcony, the man and the woman drew slowly apart and stood looking at one another in the gathering dusk. Then Jessica turned and went in through the glass balcony doors. Matthew hesitated, before following her and closing the windows after him, and Verity could no longer hear them.

Jessica switched on the light and walked, hips swaying, across the room to the further door which led into her bedroom. Matt remained where he was in the middle of the sitting-room, and watched through the open door as Jessica switched on a bedside lamp, so that its yellow glow fell across the pillows. She glanced over her shoulder at him.

'Aren't you coming in?' She smiled at him invitingly. 'You weren't always so shy, Matt.'

Matthew Burton came into the room and stood staring down at her moodily. The dull lamplight emphasised his battered and distinctive features. He looked as solid and immovable as one of the mountains now lying hidden in the darkness.

Jessica turned her back on him and put a hand to the neck fastening of her dress in a simple, provocative gesture. 'Unhook me? I don't know where Maddox is.'

'You can send for her,' he said brusquely. But he stretched out his hands to unhook the dress.

Jessica gave a little sigh as his fingers touched her bare

skin. She wriggled out of the unfastened bodice and let the whole gown fall about her feet. Stepping out of it, she turned towards him in her chemise, petticoat and stays, and moved close to him, running her hand over his chest. 'Now unlace me, Matt . . .'

He shook his head. 'I'll call your maid.'

'No.' Her hand moved up to his neck, in which the tendons seemed strained like cords, and circled it, forcing his unwilling head down to meet her upturned face. 'Don't be old-fashioned, Matt! It's no fun being a widow. Not that poor Gianni was much good in bed. Don't believe all they say of Italian men, Matt.'

'You disappoint me. I thought all those tomatoes in the cooking were supposed to act as an aphrodisiac? But your husband, as I recall, was a trifle elderly.'

'It was a bore of a marriage. He liked to sit and watch the maid undress me. Mostly, that was the total achievement for the night.'

Something like amusement gleamed briefly in the frosty blue eyes looking down at her, mellowing them. 'What a pity! Still, better an old man's darling than a young man's slave, as the proverb has it.' He detached her hand from his neck and moved away from her. 'And you *were* his darling, Jessica, even if he wasn't an ardent young lover. Look at the jewellery he bought you.'

'You heard about that?' For a second, her face held suspicion. 'Who told you?'

'Renzo did.'

Her hands clenched into tight little fists, the knuckles gleaming white. 'I didn't know you'd met Renzo.'

'You forget, there's an international brotherhood of climbers. Renzo is one of the finest of the Italian alpinists.'

'Renzo is a thoroughgoing brute, a snake in the grass! He'd ruin me if he could! You didn't believe all he told you, Matt?' Anxiety touched her voice.

'Oh, we talked about mountains mostly, not you.' His voice dismissed her, relegating her to her proper place, second to mountaineering. He glanced at her. 'Do you carry the jewellery around with you?'

'Yes, of course I do, but I don't leave it lying about. Renzo would stop at nothing to get his hands on it. I keep it locked in the hotel safe.' Suddenly she darted towards him, her face twisted so that its beauty was distorted. 'Renzo didn't ask you to try and get it back from me, did he? Tell me the truth, Matt, or I swear I'll . . .'

'Do what?' He chuckled. 'Poison me, probably! No, Renzo didn't ask me to get it back. He's confident he can get it back for himself.'

'Never!' She spat the word at him viciously.

'You haven't changed, Jessica,' he said softly. 'Treacherous, vindictive and spiteful. Avaricious, too. What do you pay that poor, drab lady companion of yours?'

'Verity? A hundred and twenty, and all her expenses. It's more than adequate. What does *she* need money for?' Jessica's voice and manner changed. 'Come to bed with me, Matt. I'm tired of being a virtuous widow. I'm a young woman, and I have needs like any other. You can't imagine how tedious it all is.'

'Are you telling me you've been faithful to your husband's memory?' He shook his grizzled head. 'I don't believe it, Jessie my girl.'

'*Don't* call me Jessie! You know how I hate it. Of course I haven't lived like a nun! But no one has counted . . .' She put her hands on his shoulders and breathed, 'I promise you, it will be worth it.'

She had won. His fingers touched the swell of her bosom above the constricting corset, as he caught her towards him in a sudden, urgent demand. Within himself he was angry, angry at her; but, more than anything, angry at himself.

She knew it from the roughness of his love-making, but that was something she had always enjoyed, and added to her pleasure was the sense of power over him. He hated her, but still she knew how to bewitch him. She would always be able to do it—until someone stronger came along. That would never be, because all he really loved was the mountains.

Maddox, arriving a little later to undress her mistress, opened the bedroom door a crack, caught a glimpse of the bed, and closed the door quickly. 'Trollop!' she muttered to herself.

CHAPTER FOUR

JESSICA STRETCHED like a lazy cat in her deckchair on the sunny balcony, and said, 'Matt insists, don't you, Matt? You and I, Verity dear, have to go up to Grindelwald tomorrow and view the glacier ravine. Well, Verity doesn't mind walking, Matt, but *I* never walk. You'll have to hire a pony for me at Grindelwald.'

'It's hardly far, Jessica,' he said patiently. 'Three-quarters of an hour, and you're as fit as a fiddle. It would do you no harm at all.'

'Easy enough for you and Verity, I dare say, but not for me!'

Verity, sitting in a corner, asked uneasily, her eyes fixed on Matthew Burton's bulky frame, 'Do you really want me along?'

He swung round to face her. 'Yes, come!' he ordered abruptly. Perhaps his tone sounded rude even to his own ears, for he added, 'My being in Interlaken is something of a diversion. I came to Switzerland to meet my climbing partner, Karl Hable. He's been making his way to Grindelwald from Vienna. In fact he's already there. We mean to make an attempt on the western slope of the Eiger.'

Verity exclaimed, 'I thought the Eiger was a very dangerous and difficult mountain.'

'All mountains are dangerous and uncertain, just like women.' He grinned at her sardonically, so that she noticed again the chipped tooth. 'Two years ago, on that same mountain, an avalanche missed us by a few feet. A lump of rock from it struck my face, breaking a tooth and my nose, and nearly sweeping me clean away. Had I been climbing alone, I dare say I'd have perished. But I was climbing with Karl, and he held me.' Matthew paused, adding soberly, 'When a climber falls, high on the face, there's not much left of him by the time he reaches the bottom. And if he doesn't fall to the bottom, well, up there where the ice never melts are the bodies of men dead for half a century and preserved, entombed in the ice.'

He saw her shiver, and shrugged. 'So, two years ago we were forced to turn back, but this year we are determined to reach the summit. Karl and I plan to follow, approximately, the route taken by Charles Barrington. He was the first to reach the top in 1858, and when he got back, no one would believe it! But others have done it since, and I don't see why Karl and I shouldn't.' He stared out of the window at the distant panorama of the mountains.

Suddenly he transferred his gaze to Verity and demanded challengingly, 'Aren't you going to ask me why I do it, Miss Lyndon? People generally do.'

She wriggled uncomfortably before the unexpected scrutiny, but replied composedly, 'No.'

'Ah, you don't *care* why I do it!' was the dry observation.

She shook her head. 'That isn't it. I think I understand, a little anyway, why you do it. I stood watching the sunrise on the Jungfrau yesterday, and it was almost as if the mountain called to me . . .'

She broke off as Jessica burst into a peal of laughter. 'Goodness, Verity, what nonsense! I didn't think you so romantic. I thought you quite hard-headed and practical!'

But Matthew didn't laugh. Very quietly he said, 'Yes, you do understand . . .' He glanced out of the window to where the Jungfrau rose in all its magnificence before their eyes. 'The Jungfrau, for all its name means the "virgin", is less a problem to assault than some other mountains'. His eyes swept briefly over Verity. 'The Eiger's name means "Ogre". Once upon a time, and not so very long ago at that, the Swiss peasants believed giants and evil spirits lived up there among its secret places. It's not the highest mountain, but in spirit it is a monster, and a fearsome opponent.' He smiled now. 'But so am I!'

Jessica got her way over the pony, as Verity suspected she would. Perhaps it wasn't only laziness that motivated her. Jessica on horseback, in a salmon-pink riding-habit and a hat with a veil, was an eye-catching figure. The boy hired along with the pony to lead it was gazing up at her in open-mouthed awe. Matthew, too, was staring at the Contessa moodily, and Verity, trim and neat in her tailored costume, wondered what his real feelings for Jessica were. For all the quarrels and the partings, something had brought him back, taking him out of his way to Interlaken. But not necessarily Jessica, she thought. There were rich visitors by the score in Interlaken, profitable prey for a thief.

They took the train up to Grindelwald, and hired a pony for Jessica at the station. It was a magnificent, clear day when they set off, but a little cooler, for which Verity was thankful. Around them lay the mountains, rising sheer from the alpine meadows like a ring of watching giants. Matthew obligingly named the peaks and saddles of rock for them.

'I've telegraphed Karl to meet us at the ravine. He's probably up there already, downing a beer.'

He was right. After they had walked, fairly briskly, for a little over half an hour, Verity was surprised to hear the sound of rushing water, though she could see nothing. Suddenly, on their left, a great cleft in the rock wall opened up, and coursing down it came a white foaming torrent of mountain water, pouring from the great glaciers to join the river in the valley. Near the mouth of the stream was a small *Bierstube*, surrounded by trees, under which some tables and chairs had been set. At their approach a shout went up, and a young man scrambled from his seat under a tree and came hastening to meet them.

He had a great deal of untidy fair hair crowned by an ancient felt hat, and was dressed, like Matthew, in a collarless shirt, a tweed jacket, corduroy knickerbockers and woollen stockings, and wore strong alpine boots. His skin had that same look of fine leather, weathered by icy temperatures, wind, storm and snow. He pumped all their hands enthusiastically.

'This is Karl—Karl Hable, my climbing partner,' Matt introduced the young Austrian. 'You wouldn't believe it, but he's a lawyer by profession, a real dull, sober fellow, until he gets out into the mountains!'

The word 'mountain' seemed to trigger off some immediate response in their new acquaintance. He grasped Matthew by the sleeve and burst out enthusiastically, 'Matt, I was yesterday on the lower slopes with a Swiss guide. I am sure all the signs are good for the ascent, although the Swiss was not happy. The weather has been too warm, and there has been much stonefall on the mountain. He would go no higher, but prophesied rockfall and turned back.' Karl looked his frustration. 'But we can do it! Tomorrow you and I shall make a practice climb, and the day after we make the ascent.'

He looked eagerly at Matt. 'The weather breaks. It will be cloudy and misty by the end of the week, also cold. Up there will be much ice and poor visibility.'

'Take it easy, Karl,' Matthew said placatingly, patting him on the shoulder. 'I came to Switzerland to climb the Eiger, and climb it I shall. But today, you see, I have the honour of escorting these two charming ladies to view the ravine.'

'Oh, the ravine,' the Austrian said in ill-concealed disgust. 'Yes, it is very fine, very beautiful. They have built wooden platforms and put ladders so that you can walk along the face of the gorge.' His contempt for anyone who traversed the wall of a gorge by means of fixed ladders and bolted platforms was obvious. 'I shall stay here,' he said firmly. 'I shall stay here and drink my beer. You, Matt, will take the ladies to view the gorge, and then come back and join me.'

'I, too,' broke in Jessica unexpectedly, 'have already seen all I want of this famous gorge. I shall sit here under the trees with Herr Hable, and wait for you and Verity to come back. Herr Hable . . .' She put her hand on the young mountaineer's arm. 'You shall tell me all your exploits. Do you think they have any iced tea in that little restaurant?'

'I'm sure, *gnädige* Frau . . .' Hable said, looking a little startled, and blushing beneath his tan.

'Come along, Miss Lyndon!' Matthew said, taking Verity's elbow in a firm grip. 'Follow me.'

He propelled her along with him, giving her no opportunity to refuse his invitation, until they reached the foot of the wooden ramp which clung precariously to the wall of the gorge. Here he released her and, to her surprise, chuckled to himself.

'Something is amusing?' she asked him, a little coldly. She hoped she did not sound as nervous as she felt. Here, out of sight of the others, and surrounded by the wild scenery, she felt horribly vulnerable.

'I was just imagining the scene back there.' He jerked his head towards the place they had just left. 'Jessica busy seducing Karl under the trees.'

'You don't mind?' Verity's curiosity overcame her other preoccupations.

He shrugged, and said calmly, 'Oh, Karl can look after himself.'

'That's not what I meant. Don't you mind Jessica —flirting—with another man?'

He turned his sharp blue eyes on her and asked gently, 'Why should I mind, eh?'

She felt her face flush, and her tongue stumbled in her confusion. 'Oh, I thought . . . It doesn't matter.' Wanting to get away from him and from that penetrating glance, she scrambled unurged up the first ladder and set off hastily along the wooden catwalk.

Below them, the torrent foamed and roared, dashing over the great boulders. On either side rose the sheer walls of the gorge, excluding the warmth and the sunlight, so that it was cold and dank. Verity shivered. She looked up to the sky and saw that a fir tree had fallen at the top of one wall of the gorge and hung, lodged in a crevice, looking as puny as a matchstick.

'You're not frightened?' Matthew cupped his hands round his mouth and shouted above the roar of the torrent as they edged their way along.

'Not *this* time!' she called back promptly, and saw from his expression that he understood her. Immediately she wished she had been more prudent, and hadn't said it. She had, in a slang phrase of her brother's, 'tipped her hand'. Suddenly she began to feel really frightened of the man behind her, and to walk quickly, almost carelessly, on the narrow catwalk.

All at once, however, they found their way barred by a pole wedged across the platform, with a red rag fluttering from it. A notice in German announced that work was in progress and visitors could not go beyond that point. To underline the message, the word 'Danger' had been printed in English. Beyond the notice, the catwalk was a line of uncertain, loose planks on steel brackets driven into the rock. The workmen who should have been there were nowhere to be seen. Possibly they were back at the *Bierstube* with Karl and Jessica, making a leisurely lunch.

Matthew, close behind her, called into her ear, 'The glacier has been retreating for the past thirty-one years. Every year the torrent gets a little longer and they build the catwalk out a little more. Take care, it's slippery, and the planks are loose.'

Verity nodded, staring down fascinated at the wild waters beneath their feet. When Matt touched her shoulder, she jumped and looked round quickly. He was pointing to a shallow recess carved into the rock. They edged into its shelter and wedged themselves against the rock wall. Verity looked up at him, and something in his face made her heart leap painfully in alarm.

'Well, Verity, we're as private here as we can be. You have something you want to say to me, I fancy?'

The wall behind her ran with water, but she braced herself to meet the challenge of the question. 'Why did you climb into my room?' There was no point in being less than direct.

'To be honest, it was a mistake. I thought it was Jessica's room, and my motives were less than pure,' he returned coolly.

'Rubbish! If you had wanted to pay romantic midnight visits to Jessica's room, you'd have tapped at her door or arranged for her to let you in.'

'You don't think much of Jessica's virtue, I'll say that!' Matt exclaimed.

'It's what you did last night—you acted openly. You didn't care who knew, nor did she.'

'So you *were* eavesdropping!' he returned swiftly. 'I hope you satisfied your prurient little curiosity and, who knows, even learned something!'

Verity flushed, but stuck doggedly to her theme. 'The

same night as you entered my room, Princess Detkine was robbed, and someone else.'

'Ah, so that's it,' Matt said softly. 'You think I'm a thief.'

'Well, are you?' she countered.

He smiled at her. She could see the chipped tooth. But there was no laughter in his eyes. She could not help thinking how much he seemed to belong out here, amid this wild scenery and in his casual, well-worn clothing. She was the interloper. It was as if she had stumbled upon and disturbed some large and powerful wild animal of uncertain temper, here, right in the midst of his own territory, some battle-scarred wildcat, lord of his mountain realm.

'This is why he brought Jessica and me out here today!' she thought uneasily. 'So that he could challenge me on his own ground. Nothing here helps me; everything aids him.'

'Work it out for yourself,' he said now, in answer to her question. 'After all, mountaineering is an expensive hobby. I'm not a particularly wealthy man, even if the Swiss are all convinced I am. They think any Englishman who comes to climb their mountains must be a lord with bottomless pockets. I'm a man with a modest income, expensive tastes, reasonably enterprising character and a head for heights. But if all that adds up to what you think it does, why haven't you told someone, for example, the police?' When she didn't reply, he added insolently, 'Oh, you little governesses and ladies' companions are all the same! You lead such dreary lives. You didn't really mind an unknown man clambering over your balcony. That's why you didn't raise any alarm at the time. After I left you, there was nothing to stop you running out into the corridor and shrieking "Help! A rough man came into my room and took dreadful liberties with my person!"' Matthew mimicked a shrill female voice. 'But did you? Not you! I'll bet my last shilling that, after I left, you sat patiently on your bed, waiting hopefully to see if I'd come back and finish what I'd started.'

'You think yourself very clever,' she retorted angrily, forced to shout the words because of the roaring spray. 'But perhaps you'll have more difficulty explaining yourself to the Swiss police. When we get back to Interlaken I intend to do what I should have done at once: report the whole thing!'

He shook his head. 'No, Verity, you're not going to tell anyone anything. I came here to climb the Eiger, and I'm not going to be held up because you've roused a hornet's nest of enquiries.'

'You can't stop me!' she shouted unwisely, knowing, as she did that she held his future reputation in her hands.

'I most certainly *will* . . .' He stepped forward and grasped her shoulder.

Verity gasped, and in a moment of blind panic, not knowing what he intended to do, twisted free and darted out on to the narrow catwalk. She had forgotten how close to the end of the solidly supported stretch of it they stood. She stumbled against the pole barrier, and it clattered down, tumbling off the edge of the catwalk into the torrent. Beneath her feet, for a single horrifying moment, she felt the rocking of the unsecured planks beyond it, and then there was nothing, only emptiness. She had a split-second vision of Matt's face, twisted in an indescribable expression as he lunged towards her. His hand reached out to her, to push her or to save her—she did not know. It was too late for either.

Verity fell, plunging with a terrified shriek down the face of the ravine towards the roaring icy waters. There was a sickening thud, and she landed, face down and spreadeagled, on a wide flat boulder that rose up out of the torrent like a small plateau.

At first she was completely winded, and half knocked unconscious. Then the ice-cold spray from the melted glacier struck her face and ran over her outstretched arm, shocking her into awareness. She stirred, and raised her head.

'Verity!' Matt's voice came from above, howling her name down the rocky cliff wall. 'Don't try and move. Stay there, I'm coming down . . . Wait!'

Probably her strongly boned corset and her long skirts had helped to save her and protect her from real injury. That, and her incredible good fortune in landing on this piece of flat rock. Had she landed on any of the surrounding boulders she would have broken limbs and ribs, if not cracked her head open. If she had fallen into the raging torrent, she would have been swept away. As it was, the discomfort of the cold rock and icy water caused her to draw in her breath painfully and roll over on her side, realising that by some miracle she had managed to escape injury.

She could hear Matt shouting distantly to his partner to bring a rope, and then a shower of small stones clattered into the water. Turning her head, she saw that he was clambering slowly down the rock-face beneath the platform towards her. By the time he had reached her, she had sat up.

'I'm all right,' she gasped.

'Wait,' he ordered. 'Move this arm, slowly. Now this. Turn your head . . . Does it hurt your back? Try and move your ankles, but carefully.'

'Nothing's broken, I tell you!' she protested.

A coil of stout hemp rope landed beside them with a heavy smack. Verity looked up, and saw Karl on the catwalk securing the other end of the line he had thrown down. Matt stood and waved both arms in a signal that the Austrian evidently understood.

'Listen, Verity,' Matt ordered. 'I'm going to make a harness, and Karl will pull you up. If you think you're swinging into the rock-face, push yourself away with your feet, but steadily, not wildly. Hold up, now, we'll soon have you out of this.'

There was a rough comfort in his voice which was reassuring, because delayed reaction was setting in, as Verity only now began to realise just what had happened. The cold water had permeated her clothing and spread over her skin, making her shudder. She needed all his encouragement, for going up was in its way almost as terrifying as plunging down. So much depended on that length of rope. If it broke, it would send her hurtling down again, and she could not hope to be so lucky a second time.

At last, after what seemed an eternity, Karl was hauling her up on to the catwalk. It was not until then that Verity realised Jessica had come to join them and see the rescue. She eyed the bedraggled figure of her companion unsympathetically.

'I suppose,' she said tartly, 'I shall have to *walk* back to Grindelwald. You will want to ride the pony.'

Karl Hable looked up quickly. 'Perhaps,' he said, 'the *gnädige* Frau would clear the catwalk, so that we can bring the Fräulein through?'

There was something in his voice that silenced even Jessica.

'You have been very fortunate, Fräulein Lyndon,' the doctor said, preparing to take his leave. 'No broken bones, only bruises. You have had a remarkable escape. But you must rest until tomorrow, and even then, no excursions or long walks.' He opened the door. 'If your head begins to ache, call me back at once.'

He took himself off, and Verity leaned back on the

pillows with a sigh. She had been put to bed by Maddox under the vague direction of Jessica, who still seemed to think Verity had somehow contrived to leap from the catwalk on purpose.

'Such a stupid thing to do!' she said severely.

Verity did not mind. It was preferable to having Jessica enquire as to how, exactly, the accident had happened. It was Matthew who had insisted on the doctor. Now she was alone, sore in every limb, and recovering from a very bad fright. A tap on the door roused her, and she called, 'Come in!'

'I came to see how you were.' Matthew's bulky frame filled the doorway. He entered awkwardly, and stared critically at the girl propped up in the bed, her long chestnut hair loose and curling on her shoulders. She looked very pale, and there was a nasty graze on her cheek, but her grey eyes, fixed on him, were cool and composed. There was a look in them which made him think, 'She must have been a tartar of a governess!' Then he thought, 'Well, she has a right to be angry.'

'I'm all right,' Verity said coldly. 'No thanks to you!'

She saw a dark flush spread over his battered features. He hunched his massive shoulders, but said nothing. Instead, he thrust his hands into his pockets and walked to the window, glowering morosely at the Jungfrau, rose pink in the setting sun.

'I'm sorry,' he said, his back turned to her. 'It was my fault. I frightened you. So near to the unsafe area of the catwalk, it was inexcusable.' His voice sounded strained.

'Yes, it was,' Verity agreed. 'But I don't believe you're sorry. Any accusation I may bring against you now will be put down to my having had a severe bump on the head. They'll think my wits are wandering!'

She was unprepared for the explosive response this called forth. Matthew whirled round, his face red and contorted. 'Damn it, you don't *understand*! I'm a *climber*! A mountaineer! I climb with a partner. Two men on a rope depend on one another. They're a team. Each one trusts the other not to do anything foolish. But I did do something foolish out there on that catwalk, and you *fell*! A foolish mistake on a mountain, and a fall, that's the end! That's why what I did was so inexcusable. Of all men, I should have known better!'

He was so bitterly furious, and so obviously was his anger directed at himself, that she could say nothing, although she still felt that he had not expressed his regret quite as she might have liked. He was distressed at what had happened, but at his own failure, not at her bruises. However, at least it settled one doubt in her mind. He had not intended her to fall. The hand he had flung out in vain had been intended to save her, not to send her hurtling on to the rocks. Verity felt a surge of relief. To be obliged to consider that she might be dealing with an international jewel thief was bad enough, without having to consider the possibility that she dealt with a potential murderer! She told him of the doctor's judgment and advice.

Matthew muttered, 'Good, good . . .', and turned away again.

The slopes of the Jungfrau were turning from rose to crimson. Verity, who could see a glimpse of it through the window over his shoulder, said, almost in awe, 'It's so beautiful in the sunset.'

Almost as quietly, Matthew answered, 'The sun is setting over us all, Verity.'

He must have sensed the surprise on her face, because he turned round and came back to the bedside, pulling up a chair and sitting down, uninvited.

'Jessica is down below, in the gardens, walking with Lady Frensham. There are rich and idle people from the four corners of the western world in this hotel.

They think themselves and their world utterly secure. But the sun is setting on old Europe. The century is turned, and we are entering a new age. In ancient times, every new event was marked by a blood sacrifice. We, too, are preparing to baptise the new age with blood.'

Uneasily, she asked, 'How do you mean?' Her fingers plucked nervously at the quilt, for she had never seen him look like this.

'I passed through Germany on my way here. I wanted to look up some climbing acquaintances. It's like a great military camp. The Kaiser and his generals play war games, and everyone joins in, down to the smallest child. Young men in uniform are everywhere, strutting about with pretty girls hanging on their sleeves and their every word. Karl says it is the same in Vienna. Can you imagine? Dear old carefree Vienna, where no one used to do anything but talk of wine, women and song! Now they talk of the army, and "settling the pan-Slav question once and for all". The old Emperor is entering his dotage. His heir, Franz Ferdinand, has gone out of his way to endear himself to the new brand of hotheads in the officer corps. Europe is like a stable full of restless horses when a thunderstorm approaches.'

'But that's only young fellows boasting and posturing,' Verity objected. 'For the benefit of the pretty girls, as you described.'

He shook his grizzled head. 'No, you're wrong. It's not idle. Would to God that it were! But there's a horrible eagerness about it all. And it's about to get worse.' He saw her questioning expression, and leaned towards her. 'Verity, you've read in your newspapers about the *Dreadnought*?'

'The new battleship,' she said.

'She's more than that. She's a revolution afloat. Overnight, the *Dreadnought* has made every ship of war in the world obsolete. Imagine it. Those prized navies of Germany, Austria, America and Japan—just so many floating museum pieces. All eyes are on the *Dreadnought*, to see how she fares during her sea trials. If they are successful, it will be a mad scramble to modernise the fleet of every maritime nation. Germany, especially, cannot rest until she has her own equivalent fleet of dreadnoughts. And when we have all these wonderful new toys, I fear we shall want to use them.'

'No!' Verity shook her head disbelievingly. 'They couldn't be so foolish, Matt.'

'Couldn't they? There are dangerous new ideas seething in Europe, like water in a cauldron coming to the boil. Ruthless men of ambition and blind young fanatics plot behind every bolted door. It's a powder-keg. All it needs is a spark, one spark, to set it off, and Europe will be ablaze from end to end.' He smiled slightly. 'And you know, Verity, it's in a man's nature to want to prove himself, to test himself against the odds, whether it's in battle, or whether he's a cat-a-mountain like me, driven by a desire to conquer alpine summits and be lord of the high mountains.'

Verity did not reply, but lay back on the pillows thoughtfully, gazing at the lengthening shadows which crept across the mountains. They suddenly seemed sinister. 'What you say,' she said at last, 'makes me think of Jack, my brother. Perhaps what he's always lacked was a chance to prove himself. If Jack could have achieved something, it would have made a real man of him, after all. He's twenty-eight,' she added in explanation, 'and has never truly grown up. I left him alone in England —perhaps I shouldn't have done.'

Matthew caught his breath and leaned forward urgently. 'You're Jack Lyndon's sister? Dear God, what a fool I am! I should have guessed it. It isn't just the name, there's a likeness. I know your brother. We were climbing together, last summer, when staying with mutual friends in Scotland.'

Verity's heart sank. It was a last, unwished, complication. She could imagine the stories Jack had told this man and other guests, the impression he'd given of being an amateur sportsman of independent means, indulging his favourite pastime.

Matt, too, seemed to be trying to reconcile what he knew of Verity with what he'd been told by Jack. He screwed up his blue eyes and stared at her as if she presented a particularly awkward piece of rock. 'I don't understand,' he said at last, in a puzzled voice. 'If you're Jack's sister, what on earth are you doing dancing attendance on Jessica? Surely you don't need to do that?'

'Of course I do,' she told him calmly. 'I have no money. I have to live, to eat. I haven't the aptitude or inclination to be a thief.'

He ignored the last thrust and burst out, 'But, confound it, surely Jack . . .' He broke off, evidently thinking better of what he had been about to say. 'Hmm . . .' He rubbed a hand vigorously over his chin. 'Look, Verity, I owe you an explanation. I should have made it before now, but . . .'

'No!' she interrupted, so sharply that he looked at her, startled. 'No, Matthew Burton, you do not owe any explanation to Jack's sister that you did not owe already to Contessa Giulini's companion! You were not anxious to explain yourself when you believed that was all I was. Don't bother to do so now! I don't want to hear it. I don't even know whether I could believe it. All I know is that I can't trust you.'

Matthew paled. 'I asked for that,' he said huskily.

But she hadn't finished. It all came bubbling up, a mixture of fierce resentment, anger, damaged pride and something else to which she could not put a name. 'Nor do I want any of your apologies, sincere or otherwise! That fall ruined my tailored costume, the only one I possess. It got wet through, and the skirt is torn. Perhaps you don't think that matters, but it matters to *me*! That costume cost me five whole pounds! And it will have to be replaced out of an entire annual salary of one hundred and twenty.'

He looked considerably taken aback, and exclaimed, 'Then I can at least do something about that! Let me reimburse the expense. After all, it was my fault, and I can certainly pay . . .'

'How? By committing another jewel theft? Or are you planning to rob a bank? What on earth makes you think I'd ever accept any money from you? Even if I could believe it wasn't ill-gotten!'

Matthew rose to his feet, his giant frame towering over her. 'I'd better go,' he said abruptly. 'I shouldn't wish to be found sitting here with you in the dark! If you'll check your valuables after I've gone, you should find everything in its place. I haven't pilfered anything. And, of course, the last thing I would want to do is to besmirch your reputation!'

'How dare you take that tone with me?' Verity cried, almost bouncing out of bed in her fury, and, realising just in time that she was only in her nightgown, scrambling back. 'You climb into my room and frighten me half to death. You cause me to fall on to rocks which could have killed me. You ruin my clothes. And now you offer me five pounds' compensation!'

'Hah!' he growled at her. 'You want more? Then name your price, Miss Lyndon!'

'I haven't got a price, you . . . you unspeakable wretch! I don't want your money, your apology, your explanation or your company. Get out!'

'You sanctimonious little prude, I'm going!' he shouted back at her. 'Let me know when you're prepared to listen. In the meantime, you can think what you like. Next time someone climbs through your window at night, turn on the light. That should frighten him off!'

There was a silence that fairly prickled with emotion, charging the air like an electrical experiment.

Verity sat bolt upright, and drew a deep breath. 'Mr Burton,' she said icily. 'You are not a gentleman.'

Matthew stepped swiftly forward, stooped, seized her face in his cupped hands, and before she could guess what he was about or begin to protest, kissed her firmly on her mouth.

Verity struggled and pushed at him in vain. She tried to wriggle away, and when that failed, pummelled his broad shoulders wih her clenched fists. Then something very peculiar and rather frightening happened, which she could neither explain nor deny. The will to struggle seemed to evaporate, and she found her hands gripping his shoulders tightly. She began to panic, because this was a totally new experience, and she did not know what to do about it. Yet, beneath the panic and the fear, some insistent voice inside her seemed to whisper, 'Yes' . . . Although her mind wanted to pull away from him, her rebellious body, acting under some impulse of its own, reached out towards him, every nerve alive and quivering, signalling a message which he, too, must read.

Matthew released her suddenly and pushed her back on the pillow. She gave a little gasp and stared at him wildly. She did not quite understand the expression on his face, but sensed that he, too, fought some kind of inner battle. Then he regained his composure, and said softly, 'Oh dear, Miss Lyndon, I fear that *you* are not a lady!'

'Get out of here!' she stammered.

He stood up and went to the door, where he suddenly turned and said, 'It's up to you, Verity, you know. I won't stop there a second time. If you don't want to play the game to the end, don't do again what you did then . . .'

CHAPTER FIVE

'IT's UP to you . . .' She knew what he meant, and turned hot and cold every time she thought of it. Respectable lady companions screamed for help when strange men climbed into their rooms in the middle of the night, and they did not melt into the arms of their assailants when unexpectedly seized and kissed. He thought she wanted him to make love to her. The worst of it was that, just for a brief moment, that was exactly what she had wanted.

She sought out the company of Alain Bernard and poured into his ears an incoherent tale, chiefly concentrated on her suspicions that the famous alpinist was in reality, a jewel thief.

'You are sure,' he said, 'that Burton was the intruder in your room?'

He brushed away a fly which had had the temerity to alight on the end of his nose, and leaned back against the rickety fence. They sat on the edge of a broad, grassy field. Alain settled himself comfortably, tilting his straw hat over his face so that Verity could only see his mouth and chin. He waved his long, slender hand again, to disperse the flies.

'I don't think it, Alain, I *know* it!' she said fiercely. 'The man as good as confessed it to me . . . He knew I'd recognised him, and he just didn't care. He said mountaineering was an expensive hobby, and he needed the money!'

Verity looked and sounded her frustration and annoyance. It was the following day and, mindful of the doctor's strictures, she had ventured only as far as the near-by pasture, supported on Alain's arm.

Alain had been very angry about her accident, but seemed to blame it on Jessica. 'That spoiled woman! Burton is her *bel ami*, not yours. Why should you be her deputy? Let her go wandering in the mountains with him, if she wishes.'

This argument made Verity feel worse, cast down in spirit and oddly morose. The unpalatable fact was that Matthew was a very attractive man. Something in that fiercely unconventional spirit and obstinate individuality appealed to her, possibly because what he was, she could not be. The image of those sunburned, pugilistic features haunted her memory, as did his kiss. She had never felt this way about any man, and she was unsure what to do about it. Worst of all, this man whom in other circumstances she might have come to admire was, as far as she knew, a daring and totally unscrupulous thief. Not that Matthew seemed to find her accusations more troublesome than she found the flies which buzzed about her head in this meadow. He did not even have sufficient regard for her to consider her a threat, real enough to be taken seriously.

Alain, beside her, gave a sort of growl of exasperation, and said discouragingly, 'Anything he confessed to you, Verity, he confessed in the course of a private conversation. If you told anyone in authority, he'd simply deny it again. You know, police officers get hysterical women coming to them all the time with lurid tales and fantastic accusations. Don't glare at me so! You know I don't mean you. But you have to see it as a police inspector would see it. It's Burton's word against yours. His will be taken. They know him in this country. He's a famous man in alpine circles, and you want to accuse him of clambering in and out of hotel bedrooms, stealing jewellery. Matthew Burton, the celebrated mountaineer, a jewel thief? Pah! Who'd believe it?'

'No one, I suppose. I don't like believing it myself. Sometimes I don't know whether I do. But what was he doing in my room?'

Alain raised his straw hat long enough to give her a look which spoke volumes. Verity flushed a brilliant puce, but replied doggedly,

'I don't believe it! He said he intended to climb into Jessica's room. But he'd have to be in love with Jessica to do that, and—and I don't believe he is.' (I won't believe it! declared an unwished voice in her brain.)

'Hah!' said Alain darkly. 'But does Jessica nurse a secret passion for him? That's the question.'

'I don't think Jessica cares for anyone but herself. But she is attracted to him, I'm sure. But it's odd, when she first saw him, in the dining-room, she looked so frightened, really scared. But afterwards I found out that the previous time they'd met, they'd had a blazing row and she had been thoroughly nasty to him. And if Jessica wants to be unpleasant, you know,' Verity added with feeling, 'she can be. I'm not surprised she had an uneasy conscience. She may have feared he was going to make a public scene.'

Alain didn't comment on this, as at that point a curious nanny-goat approached them to stare suspiciously at the intruders in her field. He clapped his hands. The goat looked mildly surprised, and wandered off. Alain picked a long blade of grass and chewed the end of it thoughtfully.

'Alain, what am I going to do?' she demanded.

'I think, Verity Lyndon, you should go back to England,' he said promptly. 'Why should you be obliged to trail around Europe in the company of that rock-hearted woman?'

'I can't. It's my living. I can't give up this post unless I've another to go to, which I don't. I'd have to pay the expenses of returning to England, and live there till I found another post. I can't do it, Alain. Anyway,' Verity paused, then went on stubbornly, 'anyway, crazy though you may think it, I couldn't let Jessica down in that way. I undertook to accompany her on her Swiss tour. I have to see it through. I can't just leave her in the lurch. Certainly not while Burton is still around, and Jessica is afraid of him.'

'You're too sensitive!' Alain exploded angrily. 'That woman would leave you in the lurch without the smallest scruple!'

'Yes, I know she would. But that doesn't mean I can do the same by her. There's a right and wrong. Because other people behave badly, it doesn't give me or you the right to do so.'

Alain took off his straw hat and rolled over on to his side towards her. He stretched out his hand and tickled her cheek with the blade of grass. 'You're very nice, Verity. I have the solution! Marry me, and we'll travel Europe together. What do you say? I need someone like you to keep me out of mischief. A good woman, the support of every man of honour. Madame de Staël said of Napoleon that he would have been a better man had he been better loved, and blamed everything on Josephine. Think what a fine respectable pillar of the community I'd be if you took me in hand! Not a lost cause, as I am now.'

'I shouldn't be so bold, or so foolish, as to imagine I could take any man "in hand". What would your family say if you suddenly arrived home, accompanied by an English bride with no dowry, and of what they would probably consider an advanced age? I'm twenty-seven.'

'I am twenty-nine. Your Contessa won't see five and thirty again, and as for Matthew Burton, he must be thirty-eight or nine. He'll have to give up climbing over balconies soon, let alone mountains. His elderly muscles won't stand it—they'll give out under the strain. He'll fall, like a stone . . . pssh!' Alain made a swooping movement with his hand.

'Stop it, Alain!' Verity cried out sharply. 'I fell yesterday, not far, but far enough to know how horrible it is. Don't talk that way, not even of Matt Burton!'

'I'm sorry,' he said contritely. 'Well, to answer your question, my family would be delighted to know that I'd settled down at last.'

'And would you?' she asked him, fixing him with a level look. 'Settle down?'

He twitched his shoulders and pulled a face. 'No. Not in one place, anyway. I said, travel the world with me.'

'I don't think,' she told him, smiling, 'that this marriage would last six weeks! Thank you for your offer, Monsieur Bernard, but I'm afraid I must decline it.'

'I really do care about you, Verity,' he said suddenly, in such an altered voice that she was startled. 'I've never asked any woman to marry me before.' He rolled over on his back and replaced his straw hat over his face so that she could not see his expression. 'And if you should mean to change your mind, don't take too long about it, will you?'

Verity looked down at his recumbent figure thoughtfully, her brows creasing in concern. There was that strange note in his voice again, just as she had heard it during their walk on the Rugen, and it was not imagination which identified it as something very like despair.

But after that he seemed cheerful enough, and drew a cartoon sketch of the goats to make her laugh—or to make himself laugh, she was not sure which. As they walked back to the hotel, there was no outward sign that he was in anything but excellent spirits. When they entered, Princess Detkine was just leaving, accompanied by the other Russian lady and the Spitz, which rushed up to Verity and Alain barking madly. At their feet, it recognised them, and began to leap up frantically in joyous welcome.

'It's a very friendly little dog,' Verity observed, 'even if it does look like an animated dish-mop.' She patted the little dog's head, but some idea had suddenly lodged in her own head, and the annoying thing was that she couldn't identify it. Something very significant had just happened, but for the life of her she couldn't say what it was.

'Look at that woman,' whispered Alain disrespectfully of the Princess, sweeping in stately fashion down the hotel steps. 'Just like a battleship.'

Verity wished he had chosen some other simile.

Verity did not see Matthew Burton all day. He had gone, Jessica said, back to Grindelwald to discuss their joint climbing plans with Karl Hable. Jessica seemed to have been much taken with the young Austrian mountaineer.

'Such a sweet boy, and so useful to be acquainted with a continental lawyer. One never knows.' She snapped a stalk of celery thoughtfully in her fingers, as she and Verity sat at dinner that night.

Verity scowled at the dish of *crudités*, and wondered what it was that worried incessantly at the back of her mind, like a terrier with a bone. There was something she should have noticed, but hadn't. She sighed, and wondered what Matthew was doing in Grindelwald. At least he was safely out of the way there, discussing climbing techniques and rock-faces and changes of weather and all the things climbers cared about. Perhaps, even though he seemed little worried by her threat to accuse him publicly, he had taken heed of it, and decided not to risk any further clandestine robberies.

'Do you like Matt?'

The question, so unexpected and yet echoing the

thoughts in her own head, jolted Verity out of her reverie. She stared at Jessica, startled.

'I can hardly say,' she faltered. 'I've only met him briefly.'

'You must be grateful to him,' her employer pointed out, 'for rescuing you when you so foolishly fell off that platform. Really, Verity, I still can't understand why you did it. If you will insist on visiting mountain gorges, you might at least be careful and watch your feet. But what I mean is, being grateful to Matt isn't going to make you fall in love with him, is it? Because it would be very tiresome.'

'I am not in love with Matthew Burton!' she almost snarled.

Astonished, Jessica dropped the piece of celery and raised her finely arched eyebrows. 'Well, at least you sound sure. I'm so glad. You'd be wasting your time sighing over him, anyway. He only cares about wretched mountains. Besides, he needs the money a wealthy wife would bring.'

Verity looked up sharply. 'Are you sure?'

'Oh, positive. He's been waiting for an uncle to die for years, but the old fellow hangs on. When he finally goes, Matt will inherit a baronetcy and a country estate. But he has very little fortune of his own, and spends it all on mountaineering. The uncle was remarkably hale and hearty at the last report. Matt needs a rich wife, if ever a man did.'

Verity's heart sank. He had told her the truth. He needed money. Needed it enough to turn to crime? She fought against the idea, yet everything seemed to point that way. Another thought struck her. A rich wife . . .

'He could perhaps marry you, Contessa?' Verity suggested with a slightly barbed touch to her voice. It was a suggestion which, if taken seriously, seemed to make her heart shrivel up and die within her. That masterful and

unconventional man tied to this spoiled woman and
dependent on her for his pocket-money? Perhaps he
would, after all, rather climb through windows and steal.

Jessica's look was again thoughtful. 'I do like Matt,
but he can be very difficult. Besides . . .' She paused.
'There might be a problem, elsewhere.'

There was somebody else in her life? Was that what
she meant? If it was, Verity had not time to speculate.
It's a strange quirk of the brain's storehouse, that a piece
of required information sometimes refuses to be
dredged up, no matter how hard a person tries to
remember. Only abandon the effort, and then, without
warning, the answer pops up at a quite inappropriate
moment, in the middle of the night, or the middle of
another conversation. This is what happened now.

'Got it!' exclaimed Verity, inelegantly slipping into a
piece of Jack's slang. 'I know what's been worrying me
all day, Contessa! It's the Spitz, it didn't bark!'

But just then the hotel's electricity chose to make
one of its dramatic failures, and plunged them all into
darkness.

'Oh, really!' came Jessica's exasperated voice in the
gloom.

There was a scurrying about with candles, and eventually each table was provided with a guttering light.

'And are we,' demanded Contessa Giulini of the
waiter, 'to peer at our dinner with the aid of one candle?'

'The electricity will return immediately, Frau *Gräfin*,'
the man promised. 'It is a fuse. The fusebox is only under
the main staircase, and Herr Inebnit has gone there to
mend it.'

Eventually the electric light was restored, but not the
Contessa's temper. She grumbled for the rest of the
meal, but Verity, silent and mulling over her discovery,
hardly heard her.

*   *   *

Some distance away, another person was complaining of inattention in his listener.

'May I remind you,' Karl Hable said patiently, 'that I am a respected lawyer and people pay for my time? Yet here I am, trying to discuss a serious matter with you, an assault on the west slope of the Eiger, and I believe you are asleep.'

'I'm sorry, Karli,' Matt apologised. 'It's warm in here, and my thoughts were drifting.'

The two were seated at a corner table of a crowded *Bierstube*. It was hardly the sort of place into which fashionable visitors normally ventured, and was filled with local people, artisans and farmers. But the two mountaineers, with their weatherbeaten, rugged features and their old clothes, blended well into this clientèle, and sat, unnoticed, in their corner.

'Listen, Karl,' Matt said suddenly. 'Do you think I'd make a passable jewel thief? I have several talents compatible with the gentle art of breaking and entering. Mountaineering is a damn expensive business, and I could do with the money.'

'As a lawyer,' Karl told him severely, 'I advise you against saying any such thing, even in jest. There is always some idiot who will believe you are serious. You have a peculiar sense of humour, Matt, and not everyone appreciates it as I do.'

'She's not an idiot. She's a remarkably good-looking young woman with an otherwise intelligent and able brain. But, like a lot of women, having once got a notion—however preposterous—into her head, it would take the devil and a stick of dynamite or two to shift it out again.'

'Hah!' His companion pounced on his words. 'We are talking of Miss Lyndon, are we not? Why does the very attractive Verity think you are a thief?'

'Because I climbed through her bedroom window in

the middle of the night.'

Karl scratched his mop of fair hair. 'Am I supposed to ask why, like an innocent? Or just to let my imagination run riot?'

'Your imagination will get you into trouble! I had not set out to seduce her. I merely mistook the room. I thought it was Jessica's.'

'That was a bad mistake!' Karl said sharply. 'You can't afford to make mistakes. Nor can you afford to get involved with a woman—any woman—just now!'

'I know it. I nearly killed Verity, Karl, out there at the gorge. She was frightened stiff of me, and I knew it, and foolishly tried to use her fear to make her keep her silence. That's why she fell.' He looked up at Karl, a sudden agony in his blue eyes. 'Remember that, Karl, when we're up there on the mountain.'

Karl took a drink of his beer. 'You are the best climber I ever had as a partner. But you are losing sight of *both* the reasons which brought you to Switzerland.' He leaned forward urgently. 'These are dangerous people. I know it better than you. You are engaged in playing two dangerous games here. Up there on the mountain, you would not take unnecessary risks. You cannot afford to take them down here, either. If you get into criminal trouble, as a lawyer I can help you. But if *they* find you out, you will not need a lawyer—you'll need an undertaker!'

Matthew stood up and collected his hat from a wooden peg above his head. 'The last train goes in ten minutes, so I'll have to run. I can't afford to be away from Interlaken for a whole night. Not in my business.' He patted Karl's shoulder in farewell, and pushed his way across the smoky room to the door. Karl watched him with troubled eyes.

*   *   *

Jessica's peevish mood continued until bedtime. 'Oh, give it to me!' she snapped when Verity would have taken the jewel-case. 'I'll take it down myself. I need another library book, anyway, and it's no use sending you. You'll bring another book of sermons, as you did last time!'

'Oh, Alain . . .' thought Verity crossly, not because of the young artist's misplaced sense of fun, but because he had involved her in it.

Jessica marched briskly downstairs with the jewel-case in her hands. It was late, and the night desk clerk was just coming on duty. He was an elderly man who kept himself fortified in the early hours with coffee, which he brewed up on a little spirit stove behind the desk. He was setting out his coffee-making apparatus for use later, and looked up as Jessica bore down on him. *'Guten Abend, Frau Gräfin!'*

Inebnit, the manager, overhearing, shot into the lobby, bobbing and bowing. 'Ah, Contessa, the jewel-box. Wait, I open the safe for you.' He took out his bunch of keys and unlocked the ancient iron safe.

'I suppose it's reliable?' Jessica demanded crossly.

'Such a safe as this they do not make any more, Contessa! In my father's time it stood here.' The heavy door swung open.

Jessica stooped and peered in. 'Where am I supposed to put my box? There is a great leather case in here already. Can't that be taken out?'

'Those are Sir Miles Frensham's private papers!' the manager said, shocked.

'They are a great nuisance,' muttered Jessica, thrusting in her box. 'Has Mr Burton returned yet?'

'Not yet, Contessa. He went to Grindelwald, and we do not expect him. He is a famous *Bergsteiger*, Mr Burton, and it is a great honour to have him here. He has climbed on all our Swiss mountains and now plans to

ascend the Eiger.' Inebnit shook his head. 'Two years
ago he had a bad accident on the Eiger. It is a treacherous mountain. A man should not tempt his luck twice.'

'Oh, Mr Burton has the devil's own luck,' Jessica said
carelessly. 'May I have the key to the bookcase in the
lobby?'

'Of course, Contessa. The desk clerk will give it to
you. When you have made your choice, perhaps you
would return it to him.'

Verity was sleeping badly. Her shoulder ached from the
fall the previous day, and the discomfort increased until it
awoke her in the early hours and left her lying sleepless.
Nor was it the only thing that troubled her. Matthew
troubled her. She hated to think that such a man had
fallen into crime. Apart from anything else, sooner or
later he must surely be caught. She twisted uncomfortably on the pillows. If she could only persuade him,
somehow . . . There must be a way, but he wouldn't
listen to her. Besides, a woman deludes herself badly if
she imagines she can reform a man. Men only change
their ways reluctantly, and to suit themselves. She had
seen it among her young charges in the schoolroom, and
observed that as they grew older, the wilful, obstinate
little boys grew into charming and utterly selfish young
gentlemen, who first bamboozled mama and sisters into
getting their own way, and eventually became engaged
to soft-hearted young ladies who fondly believed they
could 'manage' their handsome young fiancés. She'd
seen it in Jack, who had never mended his ways for all
she had reasoned and pleaded with him. Men seemed to
make two demands of a woman: 'Love me' and 'Don't
tell me what to do.'

She got out of bed, pulled on her dressing-gown, and
went to the wash-stand for some water. As she did so,
her ear caught the faint sound of a movement. In the

quiet of the night even a distant sound was audible, and this came from the corridor, further along at the head of the stairs.

Verity put down the glass, and forgetting her aching shoulder, went quickly to the door and let herself out. For a moment or two she stood, undecided, in the corridor, and then walked softly along it to the head of the stairs. Downwards led to the lobby, passing through the first floor. Another flight led to the floor above. Matthew had a room on the floor above. To reach the lobby, he had to come down this staircase. But had he returned from Grindelwald?

Verity pulled her dressing-gown about her and ran up the stairs to the next floor. Matthew had the corner room, she knew from the number on his key. She stopped before it, and hesitated. Then she slowly reached out her hand and turned the handle. The door opened easily. If he'd been still in Grindelwald, the door would have been locked. She pushed it open a little more, and peeped inside.

In the moonlight, the room was untidy, with strange shapes and bundles lying about in dark unidentifiable humps. But a silver shaft cut clear across the bed, illuminating it. Someone had slept in it. The quilt was thrown back and the pillow crumpled—but the sleeper had gone. Matthew Burton had returned from Grindelwald and was wandering about somewhere in the hotel. On what business?

'Oh, dear heaven,' she breathed. 'The safe in Inebnit's office! Jessica's jewels! All along, he's wanted Jessica's jewels!'

She turned and sped down the corridor to the staircase, dashing madly down, heedless of the poor light and her long dressing-gown that threatened to trip her hurrying feet.

It seemed such a long way down to the lobby, as if she

could never get there, never get there in time to stop him. Yet, when she did reach it, all was quiet, and for a brief moment she felt a surge of relief. The longcase clock by the foot of the stairs struck one, its metallic voice making her jump. It was much, much, too quiet.

Verity made her way cautiously to the desk, looking for the clerk who should be on duty. He was slumbering deeply, his head on his pillowed arm, a half-drunk cup of coffee at his elbow. She leaned across and shook his shoulder. He didn't stir. His breath, deep and regular, continued as before. A rising panic in her heart, Verity shook him again, as hard as she could, but to no avail. A terrible thought struck her and she picked up the half-emptied cup and sniffed at it suspiciously. There was a faint odour that struck a chord in her memory. Only a month or two ago, she had been obliged to have a tooth pulled. Laudanum . . .

She flung down the cup with a cry, and dashed behind the desk to fling open the door of Inebnit's office. A lamp stood on a table, illuminating the scene before her eyes. In a corner stood the safe, its heavy door open wide, and before it knelt the unmistakable burly form of Matthew Burton. At the noise from the door, he turned and leapt up, crossing the room in a flash and seizing her arm.

Verity gave a cry, partly of alarm, and partly because he had wrenched her damaged shoulder. 'What have you done?' she gasped. She pulled herself free and stumbled away from him. 'Jessica's jewels! You meant to take them all along! That's why you came here, to Interlaken!'

'Don't be a fool!' he snarled at her in a low, hoarse voice. 'Damn it, Verity, I've played this stupid charade of yours long enough. I'm not a thief!'

'Then what are you doing?' she accused him. 'Where are they?' She ran to the safe and, falling to her knees, thrust her hand eagerly inside. It struck against the metal jewel-box. She pulled it out and examined it. It was still locked. 'Thank goodness,' she gasped. 'They're still here. I'm in time!'

'No,' Matthew replied coldly, and when she looked up, it was to see that his features might have been carved from granite, so harsh did they look in the flickering lamplight. 'No. They are gone—and *I* am too late!'

She stared at him in bewilderment. 'What do you mean?'

'Look!' He dived past her and dragged out Sir Miles Frensham's leather document-case. 'Can't you see what's happened, woman? It's been forced!' Impatiently, he shook the leather case under her nose. 'Rifled! The confidential Admiralty reports on the *Dreadnought* trials are gone! Gone, and probably already on their way to Germany!'

CHAPTER SIX

'WHAT HAVE you done with them?' Verity backed away from him, at the same time looking frantically about the room.

'Oh, for pity's sake!' he exploded. 'If I'd taken them, I'd still have them. Search me, if you can manage to overcome your maidenly modesty. I'll make no objection. Of course I didn't take the blasted things!'

'Then what are you doing here?' she demanded obstinately, choosing to ignore his offer.

'Locking the stable door after the blasted horse has bolted,' he growled. 'What does it look like?'

'I don't know what to think . . .' she muttered in response.

'Frankly, my dear, it doesn't matter a damn, *now*, what you think.' He turned his piercing eyes on her. 'Come to that, what are you doing here, Verity?'

'I heard someone prowling about . . . No, listen to me, Matthew Burton! *I* don't have to answer your questions—you have to answer mine! You are the one I found kneeling in front of an open safe. That poor old man out there is drugged. How do I know you haven't taken the papers and already hidden them somewhere, or passed them to Karl Hable—he's an Austrian!'

'He's a Czech!' Matt corrected her. 'An Austrian citizen, certainly. But the Slavs of the Austro-Hungarian Empire view the rise of Germany with the greatest alarm. It will do them no good. It will encourage and support only the Germans of the Empire, and hinder the Slavs in their struggle for their own national identity. That's why Karl and I are working together on this.'

There was a silence. Verity thought long and hard. Then, frowning, she said slowly, 'You're not a thief. You're a sort of secret agent. I don't mean one of theirs. I mean one of ours.'

'Something like that,' he agreed. 'I *am* in Switzerland to climb the Eiger—it's my cover. But my real concern is to keep an eye on Sir Miles. I hope I make a better job of scaling the western slope than I've done of keeping the *Dreadnought* papers safe. I've thoroughly messed that up! I was up in Grindelwald with Karl and came back late. The night clerk was awake then to let me in. Perhaps he hadn't yet drunk any of his laced coffee. I glanced in here and saw everything in order, and went upstairs to bed. Then I got to mulling over some problems of our climb, and remembered there were some books on past climbing expeditions in the bookcase. I came down and found the old boy snoring his head off, and realised straight away what must have happened. It's not a difficult thing to do. All you need is an accomplice to distract the clerk for a moment, and a nimble-fingered villain dopes the coffee-pot. The poor old fellow never noticed.'

Verity sat down on the nearest chair and heaved a despondent sigh. Matt eyed her dressing-gown-clad figure and untidy tumbling mass of hair and, despite his troubles, smiled slightly. She looked, he thought, as if she ought to be in bed now, and if he had the time, he'd like to take her there himself . . . But he was getting distracted, and he had work to do.

'You haven't got a hairpin, I suppose?' he asked.

'No, I've taken them all out. What on earth do you want one for?' She looked up and peered at him with renewed suspicion from beneath a lock of chestnut fringe.

'Never mind. Old Inebnit might have something suitable on his desk.' Matt was foraging briskly in Inebnit's pen-tray. 'Ah, this will do it, with a bit of luck.'

'What on earth . . .?' Verity exclaimed, bewildered, as he went to the safe and, reclosing the door, began to do something to the lock.

'Fixing the lock; I hope well enough to fool Inebnit in the morning. The last thing I want is a hue and cry. If Inebnit comes in here tomorrow and finds the safe gaping open, the place will be full of gendarmes before you can say "knife". That will frighten off our culprits, and I don't want that. I believe they are still in the hotel, and I want 'em caught.'

'What about the clerk? Won't he make a fuss?'

'He'll wake up with an almighty headache and not the slighest idea why. He won't go telling Inebnit that he's slumbered all night! It would cost him his job. Ah, that's just about done it.' He gave a snort of satisfaction and sat back on his heels to contemplate his handiwork.

'It seems that I must believe you when you say you are not a thief,' said Verity suspiciously. 'But you seem to have some very odd accomplishments.'

'I'm in a very odd line of business, believe me!' Matt stood up and dusted his knees. 'Right, Miss Lyndon. Now we go upstairs, wake Sir Miles and tell him the sorry tale.'

Sir Miles, his sparse grey hair standing on end, and a venerable plaid dressing-gown wrapped about his dignified person, surveyed his two nocturnal visitors in the sitting-room of the Frenshams' suite. If he was surprised to see Miss Lyndon in her night-attire accompanying Matt Burton, he masked it very well.

'We shan't wake my wife,' he said ungallantly. 'She sleeps like a log.' He poured himself and Matt some whisky, and raised his eyebrows in Verity's direction. 'Miss Lyndon?'

She shook her head.

'Give her some brandy,' Matt suggested. 'She doesn't realise it yet, but she's had quite a shock.'

Sir Miles obliged, and Verity took the glass he offered her. 'Fire away, Matt!' said Sir Miles, raising his own glass. 'Let's hear the worst. I don't suppose you've got me out of my bed for any good news.'

For all his sang-froid, he listened to Matt with an increasingly grave expression. 'Confounded nuisance,' he said at last. 'Don't take it to heart, my boy. Not your fault! They were dashed determined. After all, they tried in London, and they were bound to try again.'

'Yes, sir, but I knew that, and should have been ready for them this time.' Matt glowered ferociously.

'My wife is right,' thought Sir Miles, momentarily sidetracked. 'The fellow does put one in mind of a gorilla. And what's that very pretty Miss Lyndon doing with him in her nightgown?'

He turned to Verity, sitting in the corner. 'We're dealing here with a very professional and competent spy-ring, my dear. They burgled my house in London before I came away, in an attempt to find the papers. When they failed to get their hands on what they wanted, they took my wife's emeralds to make the whole thing look like a straightforward theft. I know I can count on you, my dear, to keep quiet about all this. We have to lay our hands on these people—it's imperative. They're too clever and too successful for my liking.'

'And mine!' Matt growled.

'Ah, Matt, my dear chap . . .' Sir Miles took his scowling subordinate by the elbow and led him across the room out of earshot of Verity. 'That girl *is* to be relied upon, I suppose?'

'Absolutely!' Matt said firmly.

'Ah, mmm, yes . . . I hesitate to ask why she's with you, and, um, somewhat lightly clad . . .'

'She heard a noise and investigated. She thought *I'd*

taken the wretched things! Good God, sir,' Matt said, startled. 'She and I weren't . . .'

'No, no, of course not!' Sir Miles interrupted hurriedly. 'I wasn't suggesting it for a moment. Only you do, ah, enjoy a certain reputation—though blessed if I can understand what the women see in you!' He stared appraisingly and with some fascination at his companion's battered features. 'Ever put the gloves on?' he asked.

'Only in my student days. To be honest, boxing and other sports have never interested me much. I was always a mountain man. Why?' Matt raised bushy eyebrows.

'Oh, nothing, just a thought . . . Well, escort the girl back to her room. It's almost two in the morning. We can't do anything tonight, but we'll discuss it all thoroughly tomorrow. Good night, Matt.' Sir Miles patted the other's brawny shoulder. 'Good night to you, Miss Lyndon. Toss the rest of that brandy back, it won't do you any harm! Matt here will see you safely back to your bed.'

'And into it, probably . . .' he thought to himself, as he prepared to return to his sleeping spouse.

'How on earth are you going to catch them?' Verity whispered, as she and Matt made their way along the dusky corridor to her room. The brandy was pleasantly warming, but burned a hole in the pit of her stomach.

'Sir Miles and I will put our heads together tomorrow and come up with something.' They had reached her door, and Matt opened it and hesitated, his hand on the handle. 'Verity, I have to talk to you. This might not seem a very suitable moment, but a better time might not offer itself. It won't take long.'

'All right,' Verity said uneasily, a thought entering her head not unlike that which had entered Sir Miles's. The brandy had made her feel slightly muzzy. She really wished she hadn't drunk it.

'It's quite all right,' he said, a little impatiently. 'I'm long past the age where I make a lunge for a girl. It's a serious matter I want to discuss with you.'

He followed her into the room, ducking his head beneath the door lintel, and sat down on the chair thoughtfully provided by the hotel to go with the desk at which its clientèle would supposedly write their post-cards home. It looked, beneath his burly frame, uncomfortably spindly and insecure. Matt himself looked grimly determined.

'I never did apologise to you properly for frightening you out of your wits the night I climbed through the window.' He nodded at the balcony doors, and then stared at her belligerently.

'Hic!' said Verity inelegantly. 'I'm so sorry, it's the brandy! I never drink. Don't apologise—I accept you were looking for Jessica's room.' She looked at him a little glumly. 'You are—interested—in Jessica, aren't you?'

'If I hadn't had the brandy,' she thought sternly, 'I wouldn't have asked that. Well, I want to know . . .'

'Yes, I am, but not in the way you think!' Matt retorted.

'But you were following her, weren't you? I saw you run and jump on the train at the border. It was you, wasn't it?'

'Look, Jessica is an old friend of mine,' Matt said evenly. 'I like to keep an eye on her.' He rubbed his hand over his chin, which felt rough and stubbly. He needed a shave. He was cursed with a vigorous growth of hair on his jaw which required scraping off twice a day with a murderous cut-throat razor. He'd last shaved in the morning before going up to Grindelwald. At night, in Grindelwald, he'd given the procedure a miss. No one in the *Bierstube* had minded a blue chin. He sometimes wondered if he wouldn't do better to grow a beard and be done with it.

Aloud, he said, 'How do you come to be Jessica's companion, Verity? Or, come to that, anyone's companion?'

'That's easily explained,' she told him frankly. 'My father invested his money unwisely. He was a man who relied on intuition rather than his banker's advice. Intuition let him down. Ultimately, it let us all down—the entire family. He lost his money, and after he died, Mother was ill and what little was left was spent on doctor's bills. After she died, well, there was no money left at all, so I took a post as governess. I've had several such posts. My last employer kindly recommended me to Jessica, and I was very glad to take the job as companion, I can tell you! Though I can't say I've enjoyed it much!' she confessed, the admission slipping out before she could stop it. Bother the brandy!

'I'm not surprised,' said Matt. 'No one could describe Jessica as sweet-natured. She'd lead anyone a merry dance. Good Lord, do you think *I* don't know it?' He paused, and then asked sharply, 'And what was Jack doing all the time you were earning your keep teaching the three "Rs"?'

Mentally he had already answered his own question: 'Precious little!'

But she was loyal. 'Jack has—has lots of good qualities. But he's impulsive and a little of a dreamer, not good about keeping time or remembering things. He finds it hard to stick to a job, and jobs find it hard to stick to him. He's a little like Father, I suppose.'

'A lot like him!' Matt thought drily. 'A chip off the old block, by the sound of it, and a smooth-tongued unscrupulous, young layabout as well. What's the matter with the young devil? Hasn't he been able to look after his sister better than this?'

It was probably well that Jack wasn't near by at that moment, or he might have suffered short shrift at the hand of an irate Matt Burton. He growled to her, 'A good-looking woman ought not to be running round alone,' and then cursed himself for sounding so damned pompous.

She seemed to be nettled by his manner, too. 'I really have no choice, and I *am* quite capable of looking after myself!'

'Oh, are you, indeed?' he said sarcastically. 'Don't tell me no one ever took it into his head to be a little fresh with you.'

'Yes,' she said calmly. 'You did.'

Matt expelled his breath in a long hiss and commented, 'You didn't object too strongly—or, if you did, I didn't notice it.'

'Oh, you know,' her grey eyes were resting on his face with uncomfortable directness, 'a governess is considered legitimate quarry. Why should she object? I've had all manner of propositions from young gentlemen in dark stairwells—and quite a few from elderly ones! Some snatch a kiss, and some are a good deal blunter in their suggestions. They wouldn't dream of talking like that to a young lady, of course, but *I* was only the governess.'

'And you class me with all of those, do you?' Matt asked her quietly.

Verity looked away, suddenly less self-assured. The effect of the brandy had worn off, and she missed its comforting warmth and the feeling of recklessness it had lent her. She felt dejected and alone. No, she didn't class him with all of those, but she couldn't let him see it. To fall in love with this man would be the height of foolishness. It could only lead to a relationship which in itself led nowhere. This was a man who needed a wife with money and advantageous family connections. He would never think of Verity in those terms—wifely terms. Irregular propositions she could well do without. They had plagued her life.

Seeing her silent, and her averted face, Matt, too, grew thoughtful. In some manner, which he found it difficult to define, she made him feel uneasy. She no longer thought him a thief, and he was sure she wouldn't go running about telling everyone what had happened earlier that night. No, the unease was rooted in something else.

She was both defenceless and exposed to great danger, although she did not realise it. He felt a kind of responsibility for her. It was annoying and ridiculous to feel like this about the girl, but he had, after all, almost killed her up at the gorge, and now, like it or not, she had become embroiled in his business, a risky, volatile business. A professional antagonist, such as himself, was known to his enemies and respected by them. They would want, above all, to avoid him. Only if it became absolutely necessary would they take steps to remove him permanently from the scene.

But this girl was a bystander who had been drawn into the affair, seen by *them* as a meddler and an unknown quantity. Unknown quantities present the greatest danger of all to an enterprise, and it would not be impossible that they might take steps to rid themselves of her. Accidents happened easily hereabouts, witness the lamentable affair at the gorge. If Verity, walking alone on a steep mountain path, were to slip . . .

He did not wish to frighten her by telling her this. Quite apart from it, there was something else which he found dissatisfying. Without independent means of support, she was at the mercy of anyone who offered employment, a captive to spoiled brats in the nursery and spoiled women like Jessica. The good-for-nothing

brother hung round her neck like a millstone. This post
of companion to Jessica could not last long. What next?
Something had to be done about her future, some
permanent arrangement, and it was his misfortune to
find the matter lay in his hands. He hadn't asked for the
responsibility, but a decision had to be made, and
quickly.

Matt's sharp blue eyes ran over Verity, and their
expression softened slightly. Undeniably, she was
attractive, spirited . . . There was a time-honoured, if
irregular, way of dealing with such situations. It was not
one he'd ever employed, but other men had. The girl
was sensible, intelligent enough, surely, to see where her
advantage lay.

He got to his feet and came to the armchair in which
she sat. He bent over her and caught a handful of her
chestnut hair in either hand, trapping her and obliging
her to look straight up at him.

'Let *me* look after you,' he offered softly.

Verity's face burned and her heart sank. She'd expected this, but not quite so soon. All the signs had been
there, but he'd made his move more swiftly than any
of her previous would-be 'admirers'. Resentment and
anger, both born of despair, surged in her.

'I told you, I'm not in line to be seduced! And I don't
want to be set up in some modest little flat in Brighton,
either!'

'You seem to know all about it,' he said in his forthright way, considerably taken aback by the ferocity of
her response.

'I am twenty-seven years old,' she told him, 'and don't
care whether you know it or not. I've looked after
myself—and Jack—out there in a very harsh and
unfriendly world for eight years. I do know how
these things are arranged. That doesn't mean I've
ever been a party to such an arrangement. But you,

perhaps, have, Mr Burton?'

He released her and stepped back. 'No,' he said coldly. 'I've always found that affairs with married women offer a better return on time and effort. A complaisant husband, you know, is the best guarantee against problems one could find.'

'I hope, when you marry, no one ever says that of *you*!' Verity snapped.

'Do-as-you-would-be-done-by, eh?' He chuckled a little ruefully. 'But I'm not a marrying man. The world of espionage and counter-espionage is a pretty murky one. I travel about a good deal, at short notice, and often I don't know myself where I'm going or how long I'll be away. Added to which, fellows like me have been known to disappear suddenly without trace. Not forgetting that I indulge in a very risky sport in which casualties are usually fatalities. That hardly puts me in a position to offer myself as a candidate for domestic bliss. Admittedly I was engaged once—to Jessica—but she threw me over and later married Giulini. So my experiences have rather put me off marriage as an institution. And I'm really wedded to mountains, when all's said and done.'

He turned back to her. 'I wasn't trying to insult you. I'd like to think you were—comfortably settled— somewhere. You can't work for Jessica for ever, and you wouldn't want to. I wouldn't set you up just to abandon you. I'd make a proper settlement on you, drawn up by a solicitor, so that even if I came to grief in the line of duty—or fell off a mountain—you'd have security, a roof over your head, everything.'

Everything except a husband, Verity thought bitterly. Plus no reputation, no self-respect, no children and —lost in the twilight limbo world of the mistresses—no past and no future.

She took a deep, determined breath, and said, just a little unsteadily, 'As long as I look after myself, I know I shall always be uncertain where the next post is to be found, I'll never have money, or a permanent roof over my head, and I'll always have Jack on my hands. But, believe me, Matt, that's a life which I'd prefer *any* time to being a kept woman—your mistress or anyone else's.'

'I didn't mean it dishonourably,' he began, aggressively because he was embarrassed by her level gaze.

Verity shook her head. 'No, you didn't. You meant to be kind, and help.' She felt the tears prickling at her eyelids. 'Go away, Matt, please.'

'Very well.' He stood over her and looked down at her dejected form huddled in the chair. She looked so vulnerable, her pride hurt, defiantly fighting back the tears. He was, he thought bitterly, a clumsy oaf who handled everything badly. He'd let the *Dreadnought* papers be spirited away from under his nose tonight, and as if that wasn't enough, he'd upset Verity when he'd intended to help.

'I must be quite remarkably stupid. Stick to the mountains,' he told himself. 'They can strike back when you put a foot wrong. They send you plunging down.' He rather felt as though he'd suffered a particularly nasty fall now. Her words had left a figurative bruise on his self-esteem, and he thought rather less of himself than he would have liked to do. Oh, what the deuce—he'd tried! His well-meant offer had been thrown back in his face, but it was just as well. Even an understanding mistress tied a man, encumbered him with responsibilities he could do without. A mistress was more of a responsibility than a wife in many ways, since, having no legal rights, she depended utterly on his good faith. Yes, it was a good thing the girl had turned down his offer. He'd made it in a rash moment and, had she accepted, he'd have lived to regret it.

'Lock your door,' he said to her. 'Though you don't need to lock it against *me*.' He had intended to walk out

on those words, but at the last minute he weakened, and
stooping, hurriedly kissed her tangled hair, feeling
almost furtive, like a schoolboy. 'Good night, Verity,'
he muttered huskily.

He went out and closed the door behind him. Verity
rubbed away the tears trickling down her cheeks, stumbled to the light-switch, turned it off and scrambled into
bed. Then the tears would not be stopped. The sobs
welled up in despair, and she buried her head in the
pillow in a hopeless attempt to stifle them.

Outside, on the balcony, the figure which had
been watching them both through the window moved
stealthily away.

'I'm indisposed,' said Jessica irritably. 'Damn it!'

Verity knew what she meant. Whatever else might
determine a woman's plans, these had always to take
into account a regular monthly crisis. Ordinary women
carried on regardless, the wealthy saw out the awkward
days reclining on a chaise-longue, or even in bed,
receiving no visits and generally cossetting themselves.

'Can I get you anything?' she offered.

'I've a book,' Jessica said, arranging a pile of cushions
behind her back on the plush sofa in the little sitting-
room. 'Maddox will look after me. Just draw those
curtains a little, and go and enjoy yourself. But if you
mean to go walking in the woods again with young
Bernard, take care. I don't like that young man. He has a
very insolent way of looking at one.'

'I don't think he intends it,' Verity apologised for
Alain. 'But he's an artist, and he tends to look at
everything very carefully, in case he should want to draw
it.'

'You are far too naïve, Verity!' Jessica said firmly. 'If
you'd had the experience of men I've had, you wouldn't
make excuses for anything any of them did. They are all

single-minded, selfish and deceitful!' Her voice cracked on the last word viciously, like a whiplash. She opened her book and buried her nose in it determinedly.

Obviously dismissed, Verity made her way downstairs. Lady Frensham was in the lobby, elegant in a vast hat with ostrich plumes.

'Ah, my dear Miss Lyndon, and how is the Contessa today?'

'Indisposed,' Verity informed her. 'And bad-tempered', she might have added, but didn't.

'Oh dear. I'll call by later and see if she needs cheering up. But that means you are free, Miss Lyndon, and if you have nothing better in mind, perhaps you and I could take a carriage into town? I've a fancy to go shopping, and it's no use asking Miles to come. He's shut up in the sitting-room with Matt Burton, anyway, discussing something or other. I shan't see Miles today, I know the signs of it. If you ever decide to marry, Miss Lyndon, *don't* marry a man who is already wedded to his work.'

'No,' Verity said dully.

They clattered into the centre of Interlaken in a carriage and spent a busy hour in and out of the shops before retiring to the cool restfulness of a pâtisserie and settling cosily over coffee and strawberry flan. Despite the low spirits with which she had begun the day, Verity had quite enjoyed the morning. It had provided a welcome distraction. She was glad to get out of the hotel, and she liked Lady Frensham.

'Fattening!' pronounced Lady Frensham now, removing the whipped cream from the top of her slice of flan and carefully depositing it on the side of the plate. 'I used to be slim like you when I was a girl. Miles could span my waist with his hands, like that.' She illustrated the gesture.

'Oh?' Verity was a little startled, not only because Lady Frensham was certainly on the portly side now, but because it was hard to imagine dignified Sir Miles indulging in such skittish youthful behaviour.

'Tuck in,' ordered Lady Frensham, pointing her cake-fork at Verity's untouched plate. 'You're as slim as a reed and don't have to worry. You look a little peaky this morning, dear.'

The girl was as pale as a ghost. But that was hardly surprising if, as Miles had told her, Miss Lyndon had been running around the hotel all night with Matt Burton. 'I never did trust that man,' thought Lady Frensham wrathfully. 'Not with women! I hope he isn't going to get this poor girl into trouble.'

'I'm quite well,' Verity said, making a start on her strawberry flan in order to hide her face. 'I—I didn't sleep very well.'

'I always sleep very well,' Lady Frensham said. 'It's being married to Miles.'

'Whatever that means!' thought Verity, her head filling with wild conjectures.

'I suppose Matthew wants to get away up to Grindelwald and climb that wretched mountain,' Lady Frensham continued. 'That young Austrian, Hable, is a very charming boy, but I'm sure I don't know why they want to do it. You can't argue with a man, though—and Matthew is such an obstinate fellow, worse than most of them. He has courage, I dare say, or at least he has the sort of courage *men* admire. Most women would call it foolhardiness. He had a truly terrible accident on that very mountain a year or two ago, and was lucky to get away with such little damage to himself. Goodness knows, he was never any beauty, and what with that broken nose and chipped teeth, and a complexion like an old boot, I wonder at what women see in him!' Lady Frensham affected not to notice her young companion's signs of distress. 'He's what they politely term "a lady's man", I believe. Miles says that Matt Burton has been in more girls' beds than some people have had hot dinners.'

'And if *that* doesn't put the girl on her guard against the fellow,' thought Lady Frensham, 'nothing will!'

CHAPTER SEVEN

BACK AT the hotel, the two women parted amicably in the lobby. Lady Frensham bravely entrusted herself to the eccentricities of the newly installed electric lift, which had just been restored to use after two days' inactivity. Most guests avoided it, because it was known to strand travellers, not infrequently, between floors.

Verity went to fetch her key at the desk, where the manager was deep in animated conversation with a tall, dark-haired man whom she did not recognise.

As she came up, Inebnit caught sight of her and exclaimed, 'Ah, here is Miss Lyndon, the Contessa's companion! I am sure, signore, she can be of more help to you than I can.'

He fled into the office before anyone could deny this, and left Verity to face the stranger. The man turned round and bowed.

He was about twenty-eight, handsome in a Latin way, elegant in a white linen suit and carrying a panama hat in his hands. But he had a leathery complexion strangely at odds with his expensive, almost dandified, dress. Verity had learned to recognise only too well that weather-beaten look. This man, too, was a climber, a cat-a-mountain.

In excellent English, but with a strong Italian accent, he said, 'Forgive me, signorina. You are the Contessa's companion, I understand? Allow me to introduce myself. I am Count Giulini.'

The effect on Verity was as of a bombshell. She stared at him, open-mouthed in shock and disbelief.

'You can't be,' she exclaimed at last. 'You're—he's —dead! I mean, she's a widow!'

'I am her stepson!' he said impatiently. 'Renzo Giulini. Jessica was married to my unfortunate father for a time, until death released him.'

Verity coloured, and muttered, 'I'm so sorry, how silly of me . . .' She eyed him cautiously. 'I suppose you want to see Jessica? I'm afraid she's indisposed. Does she know you're here? I expect she'll want to see you.'

Renzo Giulini gave a tight, mirthless smile. 'No, she does not know I'm here, nor do I suppose she wants to see me very much. If she knew I was here, she'd be preparing to be far away! But *I* want very much to see *her*! Perhaps you would be so good as to conduct me to my stepmother, Miss Lyndon?'

There was something very determined and alarming about his manner and attitude, and Verity made an attempt to gain time. 'I'll go upstairs and see if she's able to receive visitors. It won't take long—the electric lift is working again.'

'No.' Renzo shook his head and took her firmly by the elbow. 'You and I will go upstairs together and enquire if my stepmother is receiving visitors. Believe me, I fully intend her to see *me*.'

He marched her to the lift in a grip like a gaoler and hustled her inside.

'Now look here!' Verity began energetically, as the wire cage whirred them upwards with an occasional lurch. 'This is very rude of you. At least give me a chance to warn her. She's—She's not well today.'

'How unfortunate!' Renzo said suavely, his white teeth gleaming against his nut-brown skin. 'Then she will be bored. Jessica is so easily bored. I shall dispel her boredom. "Stay around", as the Americans say, Miss Lyndon. You will see and hear something very interesting.'

He followed close on Verity's heels as she went down the corridor. In vain she tried to slip into the sitting-room ahead of him and close the door in his face. He was too quick for her, and she barely had time to exclaim warningly, 'Contessa, there's a man here!' before Renzo gave the door a determined shove, so that it flew open. He strode in, brushing past Verity as though she had not been there.

Jessica was lying on the sofa where Verity had left her. The book dropped from her hand and clattered to the floor, and she cried, 'Renzo!'

For a moment alarm showed in her eyes, but almost at once it was replaced by undiluted fury. 'Get out!' she spat at him.

'My dear Stepmother!' Renzo bowed elegantly, and kissed Jessica's hand before she could snatch it from him. He drew up a chair and seated himself, uninvited. 'So beautiful, and so pleased to see me, as ever . . . And you are unwell, I am so sorry. But my business will not detain me here long.'

'You can go *now*!' she stormed at him, pushing herself upright on the pillows, her face distorted with rage. 'How dare you force your way in? How did you know I was here?' Jessica turned her vitriolic gaze on Verity, by the door, and hissed, 'You stupid girl—why didn't you keep him downstairs?'

'That's enough, Jessica!' Renzo said with an authority in his voice that momentarily imposed itself on the Contessa. 'It's not the young lady's fault. You know it would take more than a slip of a girl to keep *me* out.'

'Perhaps,' Verity said nervously, 'I should leave you.' This had all the hallmarks of a first-rate family quarrel, and she had no wish to be a party to it.

But both of the others turned in her direction as one, exclaiming in unison, 'No, stay!'

'Stay here, Verity,' Jessica ordered. 'I want a witness.

I want you to listen to everything *he* says, and if he turns violent, run and fetch the manager!'

'I also want a witness,' Renzo Giulini said, more courteously. 'I should not wish my stepmother's account of this conversation to be the only one to be heard. Don't be alarmed, Miss Lyndon, I am not a violent man. But I am a man with a just grievance.'

'Liar!' Jessica hurled at him.

'Where are they?' he demanded, ignoring her insult. 'Where have you hidden them?'

'They are not hidden, and they are *mine*!' Jessica shouted. 'Gianni—your father—gave them to me!'

'Some he gave you. Some were not his to give!' Renzo leaned forward, his jaw thrust out aggressively. 'I want my family's heirlooms returned, Jessica. I want them *now*.'

'You shan't have them, damn you! They are mine. Your father gave me all my jewellery. It was agreed. *You* agreed!'

'It was agreed he should buy you some jewellery,' Renzo nodded. 'But the family jewels were different, on loan only. They belonged to the family, *not* to any one person. Each and every Contessa Giulini has worn them, but none of them has ever considered she owned them. You held them in trust, Jessica, during my father's lifetime, and *I want them back*!'

'No,' Jessica said very quietly, but with a vehemence Verity would hardly have thought a human voice could hold. 'Never, Renzo! You always hated me. You, and your sisters, forced Gianni to draw up those papers. You forced him to cut me out of the family fortune.'

'You agreed,' he said tersely. 'You signed the paper.'

'I had no choice! What could I do? You were Gianni's children, you all united against me, put intolerable pressure on him! But it was agreed that I could keep all the jewellery he bought me.'

'Yes, but not our family heirlooms! He didn't buy you those!' Renzo thundered, his voice echoing in the little room.

Verity was sure the whole corridor must hear, and anyone in the grounds outside. She went hastily to the balcony windows and closed them. The two antagonists, locked in a fierce battle of wills, hardly noticed her. Renzo had claimed he was not a violent man, but he looked at the moment capable of murder. Verity wondered if it would be wise to fetch Inebnit now.

'Sit down!' Renzo ordered unexpectedly. He did not take his eyes off Jessica, but he flung out one arm and pointed at Verity, to show he meant her.

Verity sat down nervously. Renzo seemed to make some effort to calm his temper.

'I suppose, Stepmama, that you still have our jewels?' he asked silkily.

'Of course I still have them! And safely locked away. I take great care of them. Ask Verity.'

Renzo turned to Verity, who whispered, 'Yes, the Contessa always is very careful that her jewel-box is kept under lock and key.'

'I'm sure she is!' he said swiftly. 'She doesn't want the rightful owners to get their hands on it.'

'I hope you are listening carefully, Verity,' Jessica said. 'All this is slanderous. He is saying I am a thief.'

'You are an unscrupulous adventuress!' he said angrily. 'You took advantage of my father, an elderly man . . .'

'But not in his dotage,' Jessica interrupted furiously. 'He knew what he was doing when he married me!'

'That is a matter of opinion,' Renzo stated. 'The opinion of my family was, and is, that you persuaded him into marriage, thinking he was a wealthy man who would keep you in luxury. You like luxury, don't you, Jessica? You like being a rich woman?'

There was a silence in which Jessica only glanced at him scornfully.

'Very well!' Renzo said suddenly and in an unexpectedly brisk and businesslike way. 'I am authorised by the family to come to a financial arrangement with you. Mark you, we are not obliged to do this. The jewellery in question belongs, without a doubt, to the family. We maintain our position on this. But I am prepared to buy it from you. We shall have it valued—independently —and the family will pay you full market price. For us, it is not only a question of money or the value of the jewellery involved. Those pieces represent our family's history. Some are very old. The pearls which make up the double rope were brought from the Far East in the seventeenth century. The snake bracelet is of Renaissance manufacture. One of the rings was the gift of a pope! So, do you agree?'

'No,' Jessica said coldly. 'I don't agree. You think I'm without principle. But you're wrong. I don't care if you offer me twice—three times—the value of the jewels. They are mine, by *right*. Gianni intended me to have them and to keep them. And what he wanted is what I shall do. If you and your bevy of plain sisters thought the family *really* had a claim to them, you'd take me to court. But you don't! You come here, browbeat my companion into bringing you upstairs, in order to persecute me, hound me, bully me—and finally offer me money. No, Renzo, I will not sell you what is legally *mine*!'

'Any Italian court of law would award them to the family!' he said fiercely.

'But we are not in Italy, Renzo dear. What's more, I don't intend to set foot in Italy, much less take the jewels there. You'll never see them again, Renzo. You have my word on it.' Jessica leaned forward, her eyes glittering. 'Call it my revenge, call it what you like. You slandered me to your father. You told him dreadful tales about me, knowing them to be lies! You turned him against me, ruined my marriage, prevented him leaving me any money! Well, now it is *my* turn to have my little triumph. The family has lost those jewels for *ever*! They are mine, and remain mine!'

Renzo stood up. 'You're wrong, Jessica,' he said softly. 'I'll get them back eventually, see if I don't.'

'Verity!' Jessica ordered sharply. 'Take Count Giulini back downstairs. I see he wishes to leave.'

Renzo walked to the door. 'Oh—I'll be in the neighbourhood for a while, Jessica. I believe Matt Burton is here with the intention of doing some climbing. I'd quite like to do a little climbing myself, if I have time.'

'I hope you break your neck,' Jessica said viciously. 'You and Matt Burton both!'

Verity conducted Renzo Giulini back to the ground floor in the whirring lift. Standing so close to him in the confined space, she could see the perspiration glistening on his swarthy skin and the little muscles about his mouth twitching in agitation. But by the time they had reached the lobby, the Italian seemed to be in control of himself.

As they stepped from the lift, he turned to her and said earnestly, 'I should apologise. You were involved in a very unpleasant scene. I hope you weren't frightened?'

'It was awful!' Verity said with feeling.

'Look, I'd like to explain it to you.' Renzo looked about him. 'The *terrasse* is empty. It's shady there. Won't you join me in a cup of coffee, please?'

She would have refused, but for one thing. He'd mentioned Matt. This man was a mountaineer and knew Matt. For that reason, Verity was curious to know Renzo Giulini better. She allowed him to lead her to the *terrasse*, but when he had ordered the coffee, she said quickly, before he could begin, 'Jessica is my employer.

I don't think I really want to know her private affairs, or that I should know them.'

'You should know this much!' he said firmly. He placed his hat on the table. 'Miss Lyndon, as you can see for yourself, Jessica is nearer to my age than she was to my father's. Let me say immediately that my sisters and I had no objection to our father re-marrying. A man needs a companion in his old age. But to marry a much younger woman is something else. We, his children, were doubtful, but—' Renzo shrugged expressively '—we were prepared to accept it. Until we met Jessica, that is. As soon as we set eyes on her, we saw at once what she was: an adventuress, nothing more!' His voice vibrated with scorn.

'Count Giulini!' Verity interrupted. 'How did you reach that conclusion so quickly and without any tangible proof? Perhaps you, and your sisters, just disliked her? A clash of personalities. Jessica can be very autocratic. But it's not a reason to object to your father's wishes.'

He nodded. 'You are right. But you must understand, Miss Lyndon, that it is sometimes much easier to state facts than it is to convey atmosphere. You didn't know my father. He was a man who greatly loved beauty and all beautiful things. He was a collector of sculpture and paintings. Jessica is still a beautiful woman, but at that time, ten years ago, she was ravishing. My father was enchanted by that beauty. He wished to add it to his collection. Can you understand that?'

Verity nodded. There was something inherently horrible about the whole idea of a beautiful woman being bought like a sculpture, but Renzo didn't see it so. Or, if he did, he didn't find it important.

'She knew it,' he said with deep feeling. 'She played on it. I see you disapprove of the whole thing, but if you could have *seen* how she behaved. She . . . What is the

English expression? She twisted him round her little finger, and so callously, so coldly, with such calculation. He was so much older than she was, and in frail health. We saw he must die before her. She counted on it, believe me. We consulted together and persuaded my father that the family fortune must be kept intact. My sisters were unmarried. They feared to see themselves deprived of their dowries. We drew up papers, legal documents. Jessica renounced any claim to inherit from our family fortune after my father's death. We agreed, willingly, that she should keep all gifts my father made her during his lifetime. He was a *very* generous man. She had only to express a fancy to have a thing, and he would have moved heaven and earth to obtain it for her. But she wasn't satisfied. She persuaded him to let her wear our family jewels. He liked to see her wearing them, because she was such a beauty and he felt her beauty and that of the jewels—they complemented one another. But when he died, Miss Lyndon, she packed together everything portable she could lay her hands on, and fled from Italy before we could prevent her. I don't believe she shed one tear for him,' the Count said with deep bitterness. 'She took them all—not only his gifts to her, but his personal rings, his watch, and our family heir- looms. Miss Lyndon, I have to get them back!'

'I understand,' Verity said uneasily.

He leaned forward urgently. 'Then will you help me?'

'No, of course not! Jessica is my employer. Whatever the rights and wrongs of the matter, I couldn't do anything so underhand. Count Giulini, I do understand how you feel, but my advice to you is to take the matter to court.'

'You have a faith in the law which is very touching, signorina,' he said drily. 'Very well. I appreciate your loyalty. But will you at least confirm that she still has the pieces in her possession? It is our greatest fear, you see, that she might dispose of them, either to prevent us recovering them or just out of pure spite.'

'I cannot let you see them,' Verity assured him. 'She has the key, anyway. I sometimes put the jewel-box away, but she always keeps the key.'

'But you've seen the jewellery?' he asked eagerly. 'Tell me, is there a double rope of pearls, with a diamond clasp? And a gold bracelet, made like a snake, with ruby eyes?'

'Y—Yes,' she agreed. 'There are pieces like that. You can see her wearing them in public, so I'm not betraying any secrets to you.'

'And a very heavy gold ring with a curious seal?'

'I'm not sure about that one. There are two or three rings she doesn't wear because they are too big—a man's rings. One is a signet ring of some sort, but I don't know if it's the one you mean.'

'The papal ring—it has the *Agnus Dei* upon it. Will you check that for me? When you next have a chance, just look in the box and tell me, I beg you,' Renzo leaned towards her earnestly.

'I don't know, I'll see,' she said hurriedly. 'I want to think about it.'

'I shall be staying nearby. I shall call at the hotel again. I wish, in any case, to see a friend, Matthew Burton. He's a fine English alpinist who's staying here.'

'Yes, I know,' Verity said.

Jessica was lying with a cologne-soaked handkerchief over her brow.

'Just leave me, Verity. I don't know how the wretch found me—unless . . .' She sat bolt upright and snatched the handkerchief away. 'No, Matt wouldn't tell . . . Or would he?' She lay down again, looking thoughtful.

Verity was also looking very thoughtful as she made

her way back to her own bedroom. But when she walked
in, she gave a cry of surprise. Looking at her, as she
opened the door, was the face of a young woman, her
own face. The eyes regarded her questioningly, the lips
were parted as if to speak. Tendrils of curling hair had
escaped the pins and caressed her cheekbones. The
woman in the picture leaned back in a graceful, relaxed
way on a bench, the partly drawn trunk of a pine behind
her.

She went to the table and picked up the portrait. As
she did, there was a movement behind her, and turning,
she saw Alain leaning against the door-frame.

'Do you like it?' He raised his dark eyebrows.

'Do I *like* it? But, Alain, it's a wonderful piece of
work! Only, you know, I was never so pretty. I know you
said you don't flatter your sitter, but, well, let's say
you've glossed over my bad points.'

He strolled into the room, his hands in his pockets,
and stared critically at the portrait, pursing his lips, and
then at her, before returning to the portrait.

'You don't have "bad" points: no one does—not to an
artist. You have interesting features and dull ones, but
not bad ones.'

'It's a comforting thought,' Verity said. 'Thank you,
Alain, I shall always treasure it. You are a fine artist.
How did you manage to smuggle it in here to surprise
me?'

'Bribed the chambermaid to open the door for me,
while you were out this morning with the English
milady. I've been hiding since then in the corridor,
waiting for you to go into the room and discover it.'

'Oh,' Verity said, putting down the portrait. 'Then
you heard all the commotion?'

'I did. La Giulini forgetting to be gracious, and
screaming like a fishwife, and the Italian fellow roaring
like something out of Grand Opera. Very entertaining! I

came and put my ear to the door. I didn't want to miss any of it.'

'You are quite shameless,' she told him severely.

'Am I not?' He grinned at her, and took his slim, tapering hand from his pocket to push his black hair out of his eyes. He went over to the window and looked out at the soaring Jungfrau, dominating the horizon.

'You've sketched or painted the mountain, I suppose?' Verity asked.

'Many times. Every time I've come here.' Alain was silent for a moment, then he said, 'I don't think I shall spend another summer here.'

'Why not? Don't you like it?'

'I like it well enough. I—might be prevented.' His voice sounded flat and expressionless, unlike his usual vivacious tones.

Verity bit her lip and studied him doubtfully. 'What do you do for the rest of the year, Alain?'

He shrugged. 'Oh, travel about a bit. Paint a little. Go to the theatre sometimes . . . It depends.'

'You could, you know, be a very fine professional artist if you put your mind to it.'

He shook his head, still standing with his back to her and staring out at the panorama of the mountains. 'No, I couldn't.'

'Nonsense! You have talent to spare, and the money to support yourself until you became known. Why shouldn't you?'

'No time.'

'But you must have plenty of time . . .' Verity began, and then broke off. He'd said that before, or something similar. He seemed obsessed by the passage of time.

He turned round to face her. His face seemed even paler than usual, and she noticed that there were dark smudges beneath his eyes. 'Verity, do you think well of me?' he asked seriously.

'Yes, of course I think well of you. I regard you as a friend.'

'You might not always,' he said. 'Not always think well of me, nor always see me as a friend.' He walked to the table and touched the portrait lightly with the tips of his fingers, as though physical contact with it formed some kind of living communication between the work and himself. 'Verity, I want to say something to you. Don't ask me to explain it. Just listen, and remember. It's important. This drawing, or any other piece of my work as an artist, it represents the best of me. It's the only good thing in me. The rest is rotten—right through—mind, body and spirit. Forget all that, if you can, and just remember the portrait, will you?'

He wheeled away abruptly and walked out before she could reply.

'Yes,' Matt agreed. 'It's a very good portrait. It's a good likeness, and it's well done.'

'Is that all you can say?' Verity demanded, irritated by his apparent lack of enthusiasm.

'What do you want me to say? That you're pretty? Yes, you are.'

'Pah!' she exclaimed in exasperation. '*I* think Alain is a very fine artist.'

'Very well, I agree. The boy has talent. In fact, he's a very clever young fellow, in more ways than one!' Matt turned up and down the room, and stopped by the portrait to glower at it.

'And what is that supposed to mean? You sound as though you don't like Alain.'

'Not a great deal, no. And I don't like his friendship with you,' he told her bluntly.

'Jessica doesn't care for him either,' Verity said. 'I don't know what you both have against him. Why shouldn't he be my friend?'

Matt sat down, stuck his legs straight out in front of him and glared morosely at his own stout boots. He'd spent the best part of the day shut up with Sir Miles. After that, to clear his head in the fresh air and escape from four walls, he had gone for a long, lonely tramp in the hills. It helped him to think. Now, in early evening, about an hour before dinner, he'd returned and called by Verity's room. He'd come 'to see how she did', as he explained it, after her disturbed night. In reality his reason was simply that he hadn't seen her all day. He'd found her sitting in front of young Bernard's drawing and gazing at it in a manner he could only described as rapturous.

He made no secret of the fact that he was highly annoyed. He was out of sorts anyway, because he and Sir Miles were no nearer deciding what to do about the *Dreadnought* papers and the elusive spy-ring. It was not the only mistake he'd made last night. He'd come prepared to find Verity refusing to talk to him, because of his lamentable and ill-received offer to establish her. What he'd found was Verity prepared to talk endlessly about Alain Bernard. She seemed to have forgotten his own proposition altogether. In other circumstances, he would have been pleased at this. He was anxious to forget it himself. But he wasn't pleased to find himself pushed out by young Bernard.

'You'd be unwise to put your trust in that young fellow, Verity.' There he went again, sounding like someone's grandfather. Blast!

'Oh, indeed? I should put my trust in *you*, perhaps?' The grey eyes snapped at him.

'Don't talk to me like a ruddy governess!' he snorted. 'I'm long out of the schoolroom.'

'Indeed you are. You've moved on from doing what the governess tells you to putting suggestions of your own to her.'

So she hadn't forgotten . . . and he wasn't forgiven.

'I told you, I'm sorry if I offended you over that. It wasn't my intention, and I wish to hell now I hadn't said anything about it!' Matt snarled at her.

'Then you might at least be gracious about Alain.'

'The devil I will!' he shouted. He pulled himself together. This was ridiculous. He was beginning to sound jealous. 'See here, Verity, whether what I say is well received by you or not, it's meant in good faith and because I—I mind what happens to you. You can have as many youthful admirers as you like, all drawing your portrait, writing poems about you and carving your initials on tree-trunks, for all I care! But young Bernard is an exception.'

'Why?' Verity challenged him.

Matt drew a deep breath. 'For a start, you *are* aware he's a German citizen, are you?'

That took the wind out of her sails. Obviously she hadn't known it.

It took her a moment to assimilate the idea, then she said suspiciously, 'He's a Frenchman—he told me so.'

'Ah, he thinks of himself as French, no doubt. Many would agree with him, especially in France! But the fact is that he comes from Alsace, and since the Franco-Prussian War of 1870, Alsace has been German.'

'Well, then,' Verity said with dangerous calm, 'I can't see what difference that makes. After all, your friend Karl Hable is an Austrian citizen. But *he* feels himself to be a Czech, and you support him. What is the difference between his situation and Alain's?'

'The difference is Germany,' Matt said bluntly.

'Next you will be telling me you think Alain is the sinister master-spy who stole the *Dreadnought* papers!' She waited for Matt to deny this, and when he didn't, but sat silent and obstinate before her, she added, 'Well, do you?'

'I have no proof,' he said doggedly. 'But it wouldn't surprise me if he hadn't a hand in it.'

'You know,' Verity said in the voice of one reaching a decision, '*you* have a lot in common with your friend Renzo Giulini. *He* doesn't like Jessica, for no better reason than that she married his father. You don't like Alain, because he is my friend. Perhaps I ought to tell you . . .'

Verity was unable to resist the temptation to shock Matt Burton out of his solid, entrenched superiority. Sitting there, every bit as obstinate as Lady Frensham had said he was, he put Verity in mind of a battle-scarred medieval castle, portcullis down, drawbridge drawn up, moat filled and secure in its own invincibility. A few well-chosen words would breach those walls!

'Alain asked me to marry him.'

'*What?*' Matt yelled. He jumped out of his chair as if he'd received an electric shock. 'Young whelp! I'll knock him into the middle of next week! When did he do this? Verity! You didn't *accept*?'

'No, I didn't. Oh, do for goodness sake sit down, Matt, and behave yourself! It's no use getting so cross. It doesn't impress *me*. And don't make threats against Alain. I won't have it.'

'Oh, my, we *are* a governess this evening! You'll be sending me to bed without my dinner next!' Matt told her sarcastically.

'How you go to bed, and with whom, is not my concern, Mr Burton—just so long as it isn't with me.'

There was a silence. 'And what makes you think, Miss Lyndon, that your undoubted talents in other fields extend to the bedroom?' he asked with grim politeness.

'Possibly they don't. But you were certainly prepared, last night, to find out.'

Matt leaned forward and rested his arms on his knees, his hands lightly clasped. 'Shall I tell you what I think,

my dear? I think you're *afraid* to come to bed with me.
Oh, not because it would be immoral or degrading, or
anything like that. But because, Verity, you might just
find yourself enjoying it.'

'Is that what your other lady friends have told you?'

Matt uttered a sound between a growl and a snort, and
strode out, slamming the door.

CHAPTER EIGHT

THE FOLLOWING day saw Jessica still 'indisposed'. Verity suspected that the indisposition was more than a little tactical. Renzo Giulini was still prowling ferociously about the hotel, looking like one of his Renaissance ancestors, plotting to poison or garrotte his enemies. Jessica had barred herself in her room, on the assumption that even he would not dare to burst in and confront her in her bed. Verity was not altogether sure about this. But she had a morning free, and a great deal troubling her mind, so she laced up her strong shoes and set out to walk into Interlaken on her own.

She wandered for a while in the narrow streets and pleasant open spaces of Unterseen, the old quarter where the monks had founded the original community 'between the lakes' of Brienz and Thun, which had grown into Interlaken. She leaned on the bridge over the river and watched the clear, cold water rushing past, while above her loomed the dark-green, densely wooded slopes of the Harder Kulm.

Everyone looked happy and prosperous and no one appeared to have a serious care in the world. Life had a well-organised look about it: everyone had a place in the order of things. Everyone, from the wealthy foreign visitors to the industrious Swiss shopkeepers who made a living out of them, wore a contented, almost self-satisfied air. It was an air of permanency.

But, according to Matt, this was a way of life which had a sword of Damocles hanging over it. Switzerland might be at peace, but all round her, throughout the rest of Europe, the first very faint war-drums were beginning to sound, and the sands were shifting beneath the social order. Yet any one of the foreign ladies and gentlemen promenading in the streets, riding by on horseback or driven past in open carriages, had he or she been asked, would have declared Matt's fears quite preposterous. Perhaps they were preposterous. The royal families of Europe from St Petersburg to Berlin and London were linked by blood, one extended, but closely connected, family. Kings and emperors, assorted princes, archduchesses and regal dowagers, all went happily yachting together in the summer, exchanged family gossip and married their children off, one to another. The idea that their governments might fall out was inconceivable, not while overweight, rakish Teddy, dear, ineffectual Nicky and neurotic but happily-married Willy remained the best of friends, despite the odd squabble.

Verity turned her back to the Harder Kulm and set off towards the hotel. But on the edge of town she stopped at a wide, grassy park, to sit on a bench under the trees, and survey the magnificent panorama of the distant mountains. A permanent backdrop no artist could have bettered, they could not be ignored and yet they had become familiar to her. The dumpy Schynige Platte rising to the left in the foreground, behind it the range upon range of mountains climbing ever higher to the towering summit of the Jungfrau directly ahead, clear against the forget-me-not blue sky. Far to the left, and not visible, lay the mountain that so much fascinated Matt, the Eiger, the Ogre's mountain. Verity was glad she could not see it. Its sinister reputation made it a mountain apart, and the further away and the more hidden, the better.

She took out the picture postcard of Lake Brienz she had bought, and balanced it on her knee to pencil a message to Jack. She would have to wait until she reached the hotel and had access to pen and ink before she could write in the address and post it, unless she retraced her steps to the Post Office, which she could not be bothered to do. But there was no urgency. It was the second card she'd sent him from Switzerland, and the third card altogether, including the one from Paris. That had been an artistic if luridly coloured affair, depicting a floating damsel in shapely draperies suspended in mid-air between a pair of playful butterflies. Jack was more likely to have looked closely at that one than he would be to study this blameless view of Lake Brienz. She had not, of course, heard from him, but that was not surprising. Jack was no great letter-writer—unless he wanted money. Verity wondered, with a pang of conscience, how he was making out. Optimistically, she hoped that, spurred on by the prospect of starvation, he had found himself a new job. More pessimistically, and with greater realism, she supposed he'd descended on some unsuspecting acquaintances and was cheerfully sponging off them. That was Jack's way.

When she returned to the hotel and asked for her key, it struck her that the manager greeted her a little furtively.

'Ah, Fräulein Lyndon . . .' He dithered over the pigeonholes which held the keys as if he'd forgotten her number. Finally selecting it and pushing it across the counter-top towards her, he whispered hoarsely, 'Sir Miles Frensham would be obliged, Fräulein, if you would call by his suite.'

'Yes, of course,' Verity said, puzzled, taking her key.

'Thirty years,' said Inebnit gloomily. 'Thirty years in the hotel trade, and my father before me . . . And *now* such complications!' He vanished into his office, still muttering to himself.

As Verity approached the Frenshams' sitting-room, she heard the sound of several voices, as if some kind of meeting were in progress. She knocked on the door, and the shrill barking of Princess Detkine's Spitz answered.

The door flew open and Matt appeared, with an aggressive set to his jaw. The Spitz was yelping shrilly behind him. An expression of relief crossed his face at the sight of her. 'Oh, there you are at last, Verity! Where've you been?'

'In town. What on earth's happened?' she asked as she walked into the room.

Jessica was not there, presumably still locked in her bedroom against Renzo. But both the Frenshams were present, Sir Miles looking mildly embarrassed. Princess Detkine overflowed a chair in the middle of the room. She was clad in plum-coloured velvet, and her cheeks reflected her favourite colour. She appeared perfectly happy. The Spitz leapt from her lap and ran to Verity, bounding about, grinning, its little pink tongue lolling.

'Verity dear,' said Lady Frensham, effortlessly taking charge. 'You are not to be alarmed and *not* to worry. Something very odd has happened, but no doubt the explanation is simple and we shall sort it out in a few minutes. Now just sit down there. Miles!'

Sir Miles cleared his throat and looked yet more embarrassed. He threw his wife a look as if to ask, 'Why me?', then turned to Verity.

'Good morning, my dear. Sorry to drag you in here for such a—a piece of nonsense. The fact is, it seems that when the chambermaid was tidying up in your room this morning, she came across this.' Sir Miles put his clenched fist on the table-top. 'A drawer was open, the girl says, and she went to close it and saw it lying inside, in full view, according to *her*.'

Sir Miles opened his hand and a ring set with a large cluster of emeralds rolled out of his palm on to the table-top. 'It's one of the Princess's here, one of the three taken the other night.'

'Yes,' said Princess Detkine happily. 'It is my ring.'

There was a silence. Verity, conscious of all eyes on her, awaiting her reaction, felt a burning flush creep up her face to her hairline. 'But—But I know nothing about this? How could the girl have found it in my room?' The full implication of what had happened broke upon her, and she gasped, 'But *I* didn't steal it! Matt, *you* don't think?' She turned to him appealingly, desperation in her eyes.

'No, of course not!' he said swiftly. He took hold of her hand and clasped it tightly in reassurance. 'Calm down, Verity. It's a very rum business altogether. But the one thing we are all sure of is that *you* know nothing about it.'

Princess Detkine beamed kindly upon them all. 'Of course it was not Miss Vera,' she pronounced. 'Miss Vera is a lady. Ladies do not take rings.'

'I agree,' said Lady Frensham, 'but Miss Lyndon's Christian name is *Verity*.'

'That is what I said,' the Princess nodded portentously. 'I shall now tell you who took them,' she informed them.

They all turned startled and enquiring looks upon her.

'The chambermaid,' said Princess Detkine simply. 'In these cases, it is always a servant. As soon as it happened, I said to myself immediately, "Marfa Alexandrovna, my dear, it is the chambermaid",' and Princess Detkine sat back and surveyed them all with owlish affection.

'That's as clear a case of "crooked elbow" as I ever saw,' said an exasperated Lady Frensham to Verity, in a low voice. 'I always suspected that woman drank. Her face is the same colour as her gown.'

The Princess leaned forward awkwardly in her rigid stays, and picked up the ring in her pudgy fingers. 'Only think,' she said with a sentimental sigh. 'My dearest Andrei gave me this ring. Ah, he was so handsome then.

He had such fine moustaches.' She pushed the ring on to her finger with an effort, scooped up the Spitz, and rose to her feet. 'The matter is closed!' she announced graciously. She waved her plump hand at them all in a kind of benediction, and swept out majestically.

'I'm afraid the matter isn't closed,' said Sir Miles regretfully, when Princess Detkine had departed. 'But be assured, Miss Lyndon, *no one* suspects you. It is obvious that someone put the ring in your room, with the intention that it should be found there. The questions to be answered are: Who? How? And why?'

'The thief became alarmed,' Lady Frensham said decisively. 'All those gendarmes asking questions. If you ask me, the thief tried to sell it, and couldn't. It's far too distinctive. All that Russian jewellery is so flamboyant, *barbaric*, somehow. So he—or she—decided to get rid of it.'

'But why in *my* room?' Verity cried.

'Mischief-making,' said Lady Frensham sagely. 'Trying to throw us all off the scent.' She surveyed her, and added in a kindly tone, 'My dear child, you look fit to faint. Such a horrid shock. Let me take you along to your room and you can lie down for a little before lunch.'

'It's all right,' Matt said quickly. 'I'll take Verity to her room.'

Lady Frensham bridled alarmingly and opened her mouth to object, but her husband said hastily, 'Yes, yes, Matt. Off you go.'

'I hope you know what you're doing, Miles,' said Lady Frensham darkly, when Verity had left, supported on Matt's arm. '*I* am trying to preserve that poor girl's virtue. *You* seem set on making a present of it to Matthew Burton!'

'Oh, I think we may trust Matt to look after Miss Lyndon,' Sir Miles said calmly. 'With a little luck, something good may yet come out of this whole sorry mess.'

'Put your feet up,' Matt ordered, shaking out the pillows and propping them against the bed-head. 'Come on, don't argue!'

Verity obediently sat on the bed and put up her feet, and Matt sat down on the far end and unlaced her shoes for her.

'Matt, this is awful . . .' she whispered. 'I thought Inebnit gave me a strange look when I came in. Everyone will think . . .'

'No, they won't!' He dropped the shoes on the floor with a clunk.

'They *will*, Matt! But I didn't take those rings, or the other thing, the watch. I *couldn't* have done!'

'Of course you couldn't,' he said soothingly, marking her flushed face and agitated tone.

'Matt, you're not listening to me. Do, please, listen!' Verity struggled upright on the pillows. 'You know how much noise that dog of Princess Detkine's makes. But the night the sneak-thief entered her bedroom, it didn't make a sound. I know the Princess is a heavy sleeper—in fact, she snores. The whole corridor can hear her, especially when she's had a glass or two. But if the Spitz had done more than growl, she'd have heard it, I'm sure. She dotes on that dog. Now, if it had been *me* in her room that night, the dog would have barked, because I had just arrived in the hotel and was a total stranger to it. So, whoever it was, it was someone the dog knew and recognised. And that means it was someone already resident in the hotel.'

'Like young Bernard,' Matt said quietly. 'He arrived before you. I've noticed he makes a great fuss over that dog. I saw him yesterday afternoon out in the garden throwing an old tennis-ball for it.'

'Alain? It's *always* Alain! According to you, every theft committed in this hotel is committed by poor Alain. You would not only have him a spy who takes secret government papers, but have him a jewel thief as well!' Verity cried accusingly, her hair falling forward over her face in her agitation. She pushed it back angrily.

'That's because I believe the two incidents are connected!' Matt said firmly. He saw he had momentarily attracted her curiosity, and hurried on before she could return to the attack. 'Now, listen to me. I'm sorry if you don't like some of what I say, and if, eventually, I'm proved wrong, I'll go and apologise to Bernard personally. But I don't think that will prove necessary, because I've a nasty feeling I'm *not* wrong.'

'But . . .' said Verity, but he took no notice.

'Ask yourself something. Don't you think there was something very odd about this one single night's work by a jewel thief? No other thefts have been reported on any other night, before or since, either in this hotel or in any other. If he is a genuine sneak-thief, he's not going to get rich! Believe me, no ordinary thief took them. Our spies did. Those two thefts that night were intended to confuse and distract us from their real object and intention. What's more, the very presence of "a thief" in the hotel ensured that Sir Miles would place anything of value in the hotel safe overnight—where our cracksman was able to locate it easily. It's the Frensham emeralds all over again. The loss of Detkine's rings, and the gold watch of the old fellow upstairs, were no more real thefts than the Frensham burglary was!' He sat back and waited for her response.

'I suppose Alain just dashed across to London and robbed the Frenshams as well?' Verity said sarcastically.

'Why not? He had the opportunity. He *was* in London that weekend. I saw him myself, though he didn't see me. He left immediately afterwards, and was on his way to Switzerland while you and Jessica were terrorising the fashion houses of Paris.'

'What?' Verity gasped.

'He didn't mention to you, of course, that he was so recently in England? No, I thought not.'

'Neither did you tell me you'd seen him there!' she countered.

'I had no cause to, till now. Whoever put the ring in your room, my dear, did so quite deliberately. That requires opportunity. Young Bernard bribed the chambermaid, on his own admission, yesterday morning, to let him in here and leave him alone to arrange the portrait.'

'*No!*' Verity said furiously. 'Alain wouldn't do that —not to me!'

'You are supposing Alain to be a free agent. But it's possible that he takes his orders from someone else. More than one person is involved in this, Verity. There are at least two of them. They work as a team, but are never seen together publicly.'

Verity put up both hands to halt him. 'Just a moment, Matt. Why should anyone, Alain or any other of your German spies, want to incriminate *me* in this way?'

'Think, girl! Inebnit still doesn't know his safe has been opened, because I re-fastened it. But the thieves know they've taken the papers, and must realise we've discovered the loss by now. So, at a time when we should be co-ordinating our efforts to track them down, they sow dissension and suspicion among us, and leave us all squabbling with each other and not even sure whether we can trust one another. I believe that, whoever they are, they knew *you* were with me when the loss of the papers was discovered. How they know it, I don't know —yet. But *someone* spies on us. Your admirer, Alain, he has a penchant for hiding in corridors to see what he can see and overhear, doesn't he? He's a great watcher of other people, that gentleman. An artist, you know, can sit and stare and make notes and sketch as much as he likes. No one thinks it odd. As a cover, it's almost as good as mountaineering!'

Verity put her hand to her throbbing head. Everything whirled round and round in a hopeless jumble. It all sounded so plausible, and Matt so obviously believed it. Worst of all, she could hear Alain's own voice, in this very room, telling her. 'All the rest of me is rotten . . .'

But could Alain really be so base? Could he have behaved so badly towards her, when she had admitted him to her friendship, and after he'd drawn her portrait with such loving care?

'I don't know what to think of it,' she said miserably. 'I—I like him.'

Matt glanced away from her and asked soberly, 'Very much?'

'I'm not in love with him, if that's what you mean. I just *like* him. He's amusing. I know he watches people and speculates about them. But that's because he's bored, and he has a wicked sense of humour. Perhaps he hasn't told me everything that I should have liked to know about him. But why should he? I haven't the right to interrogate him. What sort of a friend does that? All you've said of him is true, but *none* of it makes him a criminal.'

'Don't fall in love with him, Verity,' Matt said. 'Love lets you down. I was once in love with Jessica. Believe me, there's no pain like that of being betrayed by someone you love.' Before she could reply, he took her hand, patted it, and said briskly, 'Try and rest a little. I'll sort it out. Not a soul believes you really took the wretched things.'

Verity sighed. 'They're all very kind and say not. But until they find who did, there will always be a suspicion hanging over me, Matt. It's human nature. I'd feel that way myself. After all, I thought *you* were a thief once, on just circumstantial evidence. This is worse. The ring was found here.'

'And far too easily. If you'd taken it, you'd have hidden it well, not left it openly in a drawer.'

'Inebnit and the chambermaid will tell all the other guests. They will tell the police,' she said dully.

'They will *not*. I've seen to that. Inebnit wants no scandal, and likes you, anyway, and agrees it's odd. The maid has been well paid to keep her mouth shut.'

'Oh, Matt . . .' Verity said hopelessly.

'Dearest girl, don't take it so to heart!' he murmured. 'In my line of business, odd things happen all the time, and this is by no means the strangest. You know, this may well prove our conspirators' fatal mistake. I'm frankly astonished they've done something so clumsy. It's out of character. They are usually so prudent. So far, we've had no tangible clue, but now the field is considerably narrowed down. The front-runner is your friend Alain—so beware of him!'

Matt cupped his hands round her face and turned it up towards him gently. 'Cheer up.' He leaned forward and kissed her mouth, at first lightly, and then his grip grew tighter and the pressure of his lips more demanding.

Verity experienced a sudden pang of fear, and tried to thrust him away. He released her abruptly as he felt her begin to struggle, and said vehemently, 'You don't have to be so damn scared!'

'I'm not scared!' (That wasn't true.) 'But I am very worried, and I don't know what to do or what to believe.'

'At least,' he said curtly, 'believe that these are very dangerous people, Verity.'

He stood up and began to pace up and down the little room with his hands in his pockets, while she watched him, trying to understand the expression on his face.

At last he stopped at the foot of the bed. 'What I'd

like, Verity, is to know you were safely away from here. You wouldn't consider, I suppose, going back to England now, at once?'

'You know I can't do that,' she protested. 'What about Jessica?'

'Drat Jessica!' he said fiercely. 'If ever there was a woman well able to look after herself, Jessica is such a one. See here, I admire your loyalty to her, but it might not be the deciding factor. Personal safety comes first.'

There spoke a man, thought Verity with a sigh, who never had to depend utterly on his salary for an income. When Jessica spoke of Matt's modest means, or Matt himself said, 'I'm not a rich man', what both of them meant was that he wasn't a *very* rich man. His private income was limited, but it remained a respectable private income. It would enable him to keep *me*, she thought, if I'd agreed to let him set me up.

'Listen to me, Mr Burton!' she said suddenly in a firm voice, and he looked at her in surprise. 'I don't like what is happening here—of course I don't! But you talk as if I could please myself, and I can't.'

'If it's a question of money—and *don't* interrupt me!—I know you need the salary Jessica pays. I also know you don't like my suggesting I help you in any way. But, confound it, these circumstances are exceptional! If you'll agree to go back to England, I'll take care of any expenses involved, and I'll arrange . . .'

'*No*, Matt! I told you so before!'

'I'm *not* asking anything in exchange!' he almost shouted at her.

'No, not now, but you will,' she said frankly. 'Sooner or later.'

Matt expelled his breath with a hiss of impatience. 'You don't have much faith in me, do you?'

'Isn't it true?'

'If I say "No", you don't believe me. If I say "Yes",

I'm a self-confessed roué. It seems there's nothing I can say that would satisfy *you*!' he growled at her. He glowered at her for a moment and then burst out, 'I've apologised once and I'm not going to apologise again! If there's one thing I can't abide, it's being moralised at by dowdy little prudes who fancy they have a right to tell a man how to behave!'

'And *I*,' said Verity angrily, 'dislike having disreputable propositions made to me by men who fancy not only that they are entitled to make them—but have the conceit and self-importance to fancy themselves wronged if their wretched offers are refused!'

'I do not consider myself either conceited or self-important!' he yelled at her. 'I thought I was being rather generous!'

'You did *what*?' she exclaimed.

Matt was scarlet in the face with suppressed emotion. 'I don't know why I trouble myself with you. If I listened to you, you'd turn my world upside-down! I'd be in a sorry mess! And for what? For a self-righteous little prude of a governess like you!'

Verity leapt up off the bed, grabbed the astounded Matt by his sleeve and hustled him bodily towards the door. 'Get out of here. Get out this minute, do you hear?'

'Let go of me, woman! I'm not going to be hauled about by a slip of a girl!' he roared at her, stopping obstinately in his tracks and trying to disentangle his sleeve from her clutching fingers.

'This is my room,' she retorted, her hair falling over her face in abandoned locks. Her eyes sparkled at him and her cheeks were flushed with anger. 'Get out and don't come back!'

'Oh, my,' Matt said softly, and at the sudden change in his tone, she looked up in alarm and hastily released his sleeve. 'You really don't like it when I tell you

you're a little prude, do you? Well, let's see how you like this!'

He caught hold of Verity in a grip from which it was impossible to escape and crushed his mouth fiercely on hers in an uncompromising demand for submission. There was nothing she could do to escape from that bear-like embrace, and submit to it was what she was forced to do, prey to a host of turbulent and frightening sensations. But as soon as she was able to draw breath, she gasped, 'Let me go!'

'Why? Because you don't like it? I think you do . . .' he replied, still keeping her imprisoned against his chest.

'*Of course I do* . . .' thought Verity miserably, in a moment of truth. 'I'm not different from any other woman. I have feelings. I find you attractive . . .'

To her horror and dismay, despite herself, an unwished little sob rose up in her throat.

'Oh Lord, don't do that!' he said hurriedly, disengaging his arms and stepping back to free her. 'I'm going, anyway.'

'*Now!*' came from Verity in a muffled voice, as she hunted in vain for a handkerchief. She sniffed loudly and said, 'Oh, bother . . .' because she couldn't find one.

'Here,' he said resignedly, producing a capacious man's linen handkerchief and pressing it into her hand. 'Wipe your eyes, do, and don't snivel. It always makes women look such fearful hags. They wouldn't do it, if they knew how they looked.'

'I can't help it!' came furiously from the depths of the handkerchief.

'Oh, all right. If it makes you happy, I'll confess that I'm a bully and a blackguard and I frighten innocent maidens out of their wits!' Irritably, he added, 'And why can't women blow their noses properly? Stop dabbing at it like that.'

Verity crushed the handkerchief into a ball, and said in a strangled voice, 'I'm all right now.'

'I'm not!' he said, and stamped out.

Left alone, Verity sat down on the pillows despondently. She had no desire to go down to lunch. As Jessica was lunching in seclusion, it would have meant going down alone, to sit in self-conscious isolation. But in any case, she wasn't hungry. The pain gnawing at her stomach was one of unhappiness, and her mind whirled with a jumble of thoughts and emotions. She felt she could truly trust no one, and that now, no one trusted her. Perhaps not even Matt, in his heart of hearts, no matter what he'd said. He knew her to be heavily dependent on her modest salary, and he knew about Jack, and his insatiable demands for financial support. Why should a young woman in such circumstances not be tempted at the sight of so much expensive jewellery, left lying about, as if of no consequence? She was, after all, a former governess, a lesser breed. Her standards could be expected to be different, lower. One didn't offer marriage to such a woman—one offered a discreet address and an annuity.

This time, it was true, he'd offered help, free of undesirable conditions. But she couldn't accept it. 'Not because I don't care for him,' Verity thought sadly. 'But because I'm terribly afraid that I do.'

When did caring become loving? She didn't know. She felt her ignorance almost painfully. It was just possible she was falling in love. It wasn't love as she once imagined it, as something rather frail and delicate, to be nurtured like a hot-house bloom. It was love which was physical and robust and almost animal in its passions. To love someone like that, and not to be loved by him in the same way, would be intolerable.

A rapid, urgent rapping at her door roused her from these gloomy thoughts. 'Verity!' Alain's agitated voice

called through the panels. 'Verity? Are you there? Let
me in!'

She dreaded facing him, but it had to be done, and got
over with. She slid off the bed and opened the door.

Alain burst in, his black hair flying and a wild
expression on his face.

'Verity!' he grasped her arm. 'What is going on? I've
just met the Princess in the corridor. She pushed a
hideous ring like a cabbage under my nose and said
something about finding it in your room!'

'Yes, the chambermaid did find it in here,' Verity said
as calmly as she could. 'I didn't steal it, Alain. Someone
put it in here.'

Alain pushed his hands through his untidy hair so that
it looked wilder than ever and burst out passionately.
'Of course you didn't take it! It's an unspeakable thing
for anyone to do! How dare . . .'

Alain broke off. He was so angry, his fury so real.
Surely it could not be faked?

Verity felt her heart rise. Matt was wrong about
Alain. But she had to be sure. 'You didn't have anything
to do with it, Alain, did you? Tell me the truth.'

'*I?*' He stared at her incredulously. 'Dear God,
Verity! I wouldn't do such a thing to *you*! You are the
only person I care for!' His voice rang passionately.

'I'm sorry, Alain,' Verity said contritely. 'I didn't
really think you had, but Matt Burton thinks . . .'

'That man!' he exclaimed furiously. 'Matt Burton?
Only a few days ago, you were telling me you believed
him a thief! Now, apparently, you take his word that *I*
am! What about him? When did you become so convinced he was above suspicion? What has suddenly
made him into a saint?'

'Nothing! Alain, I've said I'm sorry, and I truly am,'
Verity begged him. 'Don't be angry with me. I'm so
confused. I don't think you're a thief—and I don't

believe, now, that Matt is, either. But who *did* put the ring in my room?'

Alain's face was of alabaster whiteness, and the two red spots staining his cheekbones glowed a fiery crimson. 'I'll find out . . .' he said hoarsely. 'I swear it, Verity. I'll get to the bottom of it. I—I may be able to do that. Only give me a little time. Not today, I can't do it today . . .'

His voice broke off in a choked splutter and he turned quickly aside, dragging out his handkerchief and clasping it to his mouth, his shoulders shaking.

'Alain?' Verity asked anxiously. When he didn't reply, only shook his head, she ran to the wash-stand and hastily poured out a glass of water. But by the time she had taken it back to him, the coughing fit had subsided. Pearls of perspiration rolled down his face, but he muttered, 'I'm all right . . .' and crumpling the handkerchief into a ball, thrust it hurriedly into his pocket so that she should not see it.

But he was not quite quick enough, and she had been alerted. She had glimpsed the tell-tale scarlet patches on the white linen.

'Oh, Alain,' Verity said softly and in great sorrow, a sorrow so heavy it seemed to weigh on her heart, like a hand pushing it down. She set down the glass of water, and put both arms round him and hugged him, as though he had been a child. 'You should have told me,' she whispered. 'I did wonder—but you kept insisting you were all right. You should have told me the truth. It wouldn't have made any difference to our friendship.'

'It makes a difference to *me*,' he said bitterly, and without warning, put his hands over his face.

She had never seen a man weep. She had always thought it was something only women did. Now she found it incredibly moving, as if, even in the loneliness of his despair, something inside her suffered pain in sympathy with him. It lasted only a moment or two. Alain took his hands from his face, pushed back his hair and said woodenly, his features set in a cold, white mask, 'We won't talk about it any more, Verity.'

'No, Alain,' she whispered, and felt that terrible aching void inside her which comes of longing to console, when no consolation on earth can be given.

Verity went down to dinner that evening, because the Frenshams had kindly invited her to join them at their table. She was a little afraid that Matt might be there, too, but he was nowhere to be seen. Anything was preferable to sitting in this crowded dining-room. But the noise of chattering voices, the clink of china and the hustle-bustle of the waiters helped in a kind of way. It was all so normal. For a moment, she could almost believe that everything was, after all, all right.

'And how is Jessica this evening?' enquired Lady Frensham.

'Still indisposed, but hoping to be up and about tomorrow,' Verity said cautiously. Depending, of course, on whether Renzo still haunted the lobby, meditating vengeance and demanding the return of his family jewels. But she couldn't tell the Frenshams that.

'Young Herr Hable came down from Grindelwald,' Sir Miles told her. 'I fancy they've gone off to some *Bierstube* or other, he and Matt.'

So that was where Matt was, enjoying his liberty and the beer and sausages in the company of another climber. She wondered why Sir Miles had made a point of letting her know.

She declined their invitation to join them at whist after dinner, and made her way upstairs. But as she turned into the corridor, she became aware of a tremendous commotion, shouting voices and a crashing of solid objects, all coming from behind the door of Jessica's bedroom. Verity seized her skirts in both hands, raced down the corridor, and burst into the room.

Jessica, in a clinging silk wrap, sat on the dressing-table stool, as cool and beautiful as an iceberg, only her snapping eyes betraying that, like the iceberg, there was much more seething beneath the surface.

Renzo Giulini rampaged about the room like a man possessed. He had dragged out all the drawers and tipped them up, scattering delicate French lingerie across the floor. Jessica's gowns had been wrenched from the hangers in the wardrobe, and even her shoes lay in a heap in the middle of the floor. Renzo's face worked with rage. He hardly seemed to know what he was doing.

'Ah, Verity,' said Jessica drily in greeting. 'You remember Count Giulini, don't you? If you recall, he described himself earlier as *"not* a violent man"! I should describe him as a very stupid one. I have told him there is nothing here, not so much as an earring, but he insists on searching everywhere.'

Her cold, taunting voice acted like a goad on the enraged Renzo. He leapt towards Jessica, seized her shoulders and shook her like a terrier with a rat. '*Where* are they?' he demanded hoarsely.

'Count Giulini!' Verity cried loudly. She ran forward and forced herself bodily between Renzo and Jessica. 'For goodness sake, remember where you are, and think what you are doing!'

Renzo released Jessica and stepped back, panting. 'I *will* have them!' He pointed a shaking finger at Jessica, and then turned and flung himself out of the room.

'Are you all right?' Verity asked her employer anxiously, surveying the wreckage with dismay.

'Goodness,' said Jessica, straightening the silk wrap which Renzo had dragged from her shoulders. 'Oh, yes, perfectly all right! Don't worry about all this,' she

gestured at the clothing scattered about the room.
'Maddox will clear it up.'

'I'm going to tell Inebnit he's to bar Count Giulini
from the hotel!' Verity said strongly.

'Oh, no, my dear, quite unnecessary!' Jessica turned
to face the dressing-table mirror and cupped her chin in
her hands. 'Renzo is a madman,' she said dreamily. 'But
very attractive, don't you think?'

'Jessica!' Verity cried, aghast.

'Oh, don't be so narrow-minded. You're twenty-
seven, not seventeen! You must have discovered the
facts of life along the way. You have to admit he's a fine
figure of a man, and such a passionate nature! Really,
Verity, don't looked so shocked. Or perhaps you prefer
pale, artistic souls like young Bernard? I have noticed
that many very independent women do. Like George
Sand, making a fool of herself over Chopin. I've always
preferred rugged men, myself, but there . . .'

She spun round neatly on the stool. 'When I first set
eyes on Renzo, I thought him attractive. In fact, if I'd
thought he would have married me, I'd have thrown
over Gianni straight away. But there was no chance of
that. It's the sisters, you know. You haven't met *them*.
Dreadful, plain girls, all black veils and grumbles. A
regular Greek chorus. So then I saw how it was. Renzo
was surrounded by the wailing harpies, all demanding he
find husbands for them, but poor, dear Gianni was
desperate to marry me. So I settled for Gianni, after all.
I couldn't have the young man, so I took the old one,
there!'

Renzo was right in calling his stepmother an adventuress, Verity thought. Jessica was hard, clever, unscrupulous. No wonder Renzo's actions were tinged with
desperation.

Jessica was smiling at her own reflection in the mirror,
and said in the same dreamy voice, but now imbued with

a deep, malicious satisfaction, 'Poor Renzo, he'll never touch one piece of his miserable family heirlooms ever again.'

There was little Verity could say, in the face of such an attitude, though a great many strong thoughts invaded her head which were better not expressed. Telling Jessica she would seek out Maddox to tidy up, she went out.

When Maddox had been despatched, grumbling, to repair the havoc wrought by Count Giulini, Verity went down to the lobby and knocked on the door of the manager's office.

'Something *else* is wrong, Fräulein?' Inebnit asked her apprehensively.

'Do you happen to know whether the Italian gentleman has left?'

Inebnit smoothed down the fringe of hair which surrounded his shining bald dome, and said gloomily, 'Yes, Fräulein, about five minutes ago.'

'I should be obliged,' Verity told him, 'if you would tell me immediately, should he return.'

'I shall tell you, Fräulein Lyndon. I also tell you, never *never*, in my entire career as a hotelier, have I experienced such a summer! This is—or was—a quiet hotel, a respectable establishment. I am a respectable man, and a respected one, here in Interlaken. And this summer, in my hotel, I have thefts! I have guests who take *dogs* into the dining-room. I have mysteries, stolen rings hidden in people's rooms, and now I have a madman, an Italian nobleman, who terrorises my staff and gives me not a moment's peace! I am not anxious to see Count Giulini return. If he comes, I promise you, Miss Lyndon, you will be the first to know it!'

Inebnit bowed stiffly, and firmly showed her out.

Outside the office, Verity stood for a moment, lost in thought. It was unlikely that Renzo would return that night. She sincerely hoped not, as poor little Inebnit seemed at the end of his tether. She went to the front door and peered out cautiously, half-expecting to see Renzo roaming round outside, meditating his next move. But there was no one. It was not yet quite dark, the last moments of a summer evening. The sky was a luminous ultramarine blue, dotted with the twinkling diamonds of stars, and dominated by a great silver moon. A lover's sky, an evening to walk beneath the star-strewn canopy. Verity was loath to return to the turmoil upstairs, and pushing open the door, went out.

There were a table and some chairs by the entrance, beneath a tree. She sat down and breathed in deeply the cool, clean evening air. A faint hum of noise came from the hotel, guests in the public rooms chatted, Princess Detkine's Spitz yapped, and from the rear came a clatter of crockery, as the staff washed up the huge stacks of dinner dishes. The hotel used a splendid dinner service, decorated in blue and gold on white, with the hotel name discreetly tucked into the frieze of swirling tendrils and stylised leaves. The dinner plates were a foot across, and the soup tureens looked big enough for witches' cauldrons. The guests here wished to live in the style to which they were accustomed, and that meant lavishly.

'Are you waiting for me?'

Verity gave a start. Looking towards the hotel façade she had failed to mark Matthew Burton's approach from the road. His solid form loomed up out of the darkness, his footsteps crunching on the gravel. It was much darker now than when she had come out. The last remnant of day had fled, and the moon reigned supreme, like a great silver Chinese lantern in the sky. A night breeze blew softly against her cheek and ruffled her hair.

She said awkwardly, 'No, I was watching for Renzo Giulini, in case he came back.' With the light from the hotel reflected on his face, she saw Matt raise his eyebrows enquiringly, and explained hastily, 'He was here earlier, and burst in on Jessica in her bedroom, which was most improper and quite inexcusable.'

'Oh, Jessica can cope with the occasional male visitor to her bedroom,' Matt said drily. He put his crumpled felt hat on the table, and pulled out the chair opposite to her and sat down. 'So, you disapprove of Renzo, do you?'

'I can't say I like him much, though I understand how angry he feels. I suppose he was cheated, if his version of the story is correct, of course!' she added, out of loyalty to Jessica.

'Given the choice of believing Jessica or Renzo. I'm inclined to accept Renzo's version of events. But my advice to you, Verity, is to let well alone. Jessica and Renzo are both capable of handling their own affairs. I'd say, they were pretty evenly matched. Don't meddle. It's a family squabble.'

Verity flushed in the darkness, and said sharply, 'I've no intention of meddling! I've already made clear to the Count that I shan't help him. But I don't want him bursting back in here tonight. Poor Inebnit is in a terrible state.'

'He won't do that. Renzo gets a little overwrought at times, but he's a shrewd fellow and sensible—and a fine climber.'

'Is that how you judge everyone?' she asked bitterly. 'By their mountaineering skills? How is Herr Hable, by the way?'

'Very well, and fretting to get on with the Eiger climb. Sir Miles told you I was with him, I suppose?' Matt paused. 'You've no objection to my smoking out here?'

'No, none!' Verity sounded her surprise. 'I didn't know you smoked. Alain does, which I'm sure he shouldn't . . .' She broke off, fearing to betray his secret.

But Matt said dismissively, 'Cigarettes! No, thank you. I'm a pipe-smoker. I've been coming out here of an evening, and smoking a pipe of tobacco before turning in. Smoke keeps the midges away.' He dug into the pocket of his jacket and produced a tobacco-pouch, a briar pipe and a box of matches.

Verity watched him go through the ritual of filling the pipe and tamping it down, lighting it and drawing on it. The scent of the tobacco filled the air with an aroma like that of a fine old brandy. 'I don't know much about him at all,' she thought, 'not really. Only that he likes mountains and his independence, nothing about the ordinary things of his life.'

'Where do you live, in England, Matt?' she asked suddenly, overcome by her curiosity.

'I've a couple of rooms in London. They suit me. A bachelor's rooms, not elegant, but comfortable, a place to keep my books.'

'Who looks after you?'

He rubbed the end of the pipe-stem across his chin, and said, 'No one, really. The landlady keeps the place clean. I eat out, at my club, anywhere. I'm away a lot, so I don't need more than that.'

'It must be nice,' Verity said reflectively, 'to be able to please yourself.'

Matt said nothing. The truth was that he'd always thought so, too. He'd always considered his life as ideal a one as a man could reasonably hope for. But, put like that, as she had put it, it suddenly sounded, to his ears, a selfish existence, inward-looking, self-protecting. Describing his domestic arrangements to Verity, they sounded more than simple, they sounded sterile, non-productive, more like a life sentence to solitary confinement than true independence. Yet it was the very basic simplicity of their nature which appealed to him. Bother the girl, she unsettled him, disturbed his tranquillity, upset his preconceived notions. Yet, despite this, he found himself thinking, 'At this rate, I shall end up an eccentric old buffer living in a couple of rooms, turning out to lunch at his club with a lot of other old fellows, boring each other silly with their reminiscences of their youth.'

Above their heads, the tree rustled its leaves softly in the night air, as if it were trying to prompt him. Verity was sitting with her elbows on the table and her chin propped in her hands, and he wondered what she was thinking about. Matt tapped out his pipe and asked, 'Do you want to take a turn up and down the road? It's not dark. I mean, we can see where we're going.' He stood up and offered her his arm.

Verity thought, 'I don't know where *I'm* going,' and shivered.

'Unless you're cold, and would rather go in?'

'No, I'd like to walk up the road a little way,' she said, and stood up to take his arm.

It was quiet out in the road, the houses shuttered or with drawn curtains, all the little local shops fastened up till morning. At the corner of the street, light and laughter came from an inn, an old building with over-hanging eaves and window-boxes of geraniums, visible now only as dark smudges. Men's voices were raised in merriment, and there was a strong smell of beer. It was an island of life, real and vibrant, and Verity and Matt, outside in the darkness, were cut off from it and isolated. She felt a desperate longing to join it, to be a participant in life itself, instead of merely an onlooker.

'That's where Karl Hable and I were, earlier,' Matt said.

They passed by the inn, and the voices faded as they walked on in silence. Then he asked, 'You're not really worried about Giulini, are you? He won't do anything stupid.'

'I wasn't thinking about him; I was thinking about Alain,' Verity confessed.

Matt said, 'Oh,' sounding vaguely disconsolate in the darkness.

'Because he isn't well, and makes no allowance for it, tramping over the hills as he does, and smoking . . . And he *didn't* put that ring in my room!' she added fiercely.

'All right, so he didn't,' Matt replied calmly, 'Who did?'

'*I* don't know! I don't want to talk about it, Matt. I don't want to quarrel.'

They had stopped by a fence of iron railings bordering a garden. A tangle of shrubbery grew over it and touched them with leafy fingers. The moon, shining palely above, set herself quietly to weave her spell.

'I don't want us to quarrel, either, Verity,' Matt said quietly.

Verity's heart gave an odd little lurch and the old, familiar panic swept over her. She stepped back, away from him, and said hurriedly, 'Don't, Matt, please!'

'Don't *what*?' Matt demanded with rising anger in his voice. 'Don't touch you, I suppose? Just what did you think I was going to do?'

'I don't know,' Verity mumbled, embarrassed. 'I thought—you might kiss me again.'

'Now that *would* be a disaster, wouldn't it?' came the sarcastic response out of the darkness, making her cheeks burn miserably but unseen. 'Or would it? It's about time you made up your mind about that, Miss Lyndon. If you really don't want to run the terrible risk of some assault upon your virtue, perhaps you ought not to go walking by moonlight with a man?'

'I wouldn't have come if I'd thought you'd—misbehave!'

'*Misbehave?* I'd call it behaving naturally!' Suddenly Matt stepped round her and threw out his arms, one either side of her and grasped the railings. 'Right, Miss Lyndon, you can scream if you want.'

Trapped between his muscular form and the iron railings, the trailing fingers of foliage snatching at her hair, Verity pushed energetically but in vain at his chest, and threatened furiously, 'I will, if you don't let me go!'

'Try it . . .' Matt offered softly.

Verity caught her breath, and froze into immobility.

Matt gave a little snort of disgust and took his arms away, freeing her. 'The worst I could have done was to steal a kiss. I'm not likely to rip all your clothes off in the middle of the road! As it happens, I didn't lure you down here to kiss you, so you're quite safe.'

Rallying at the barbed quality of his tone, she thrust aside her humiliation and snapped, 'You brought me here because you have something to say to me, I suppose. Then say it, Matt, and we can go back!'

The moon scudded across the sky and hid discontentedly behind a cloud at seeing her efforts wasted on the two below. Matt felt there were a dozen things he wanted to say, or half-wanted to say, but they were all pushed aside by a sentiment of baffled frustration.

'Do you know what I'd like to do now, Verity?' he demanded in a low, harsh voice.

'No . . .' she replied apprehensively, her alarm returning. She edged a little further away.

'I'd like to grab hold of you and shake the living daylights out of you. But I won't, so stop trying to climb into that hedge! I warned you about young Bernard, getting yourself emotionally involved with him, as you so obviously are! You're going to get hurt!'

'It's no business of yours! As it happens, I'm *not* emotionally involved with him, and I've told you so. If you don't believe it, I can't help it. I *like* him. He's a friend, and a sick man. You don't like him, I suppose, because he's an artist, and doesn't go scaling mountain peaks, and isn't built like a brick wall!'

'Nobody ever told me I was beautiful!' Matt said hoarsely. 'Not even when I was a baby, I believe. But people don't generally accuse me of being stupid, as well! *I* know Bernard's lungs are done for! Do you think I haven't seen similar cases before? Switzerland is full of Alain Bernards. Not every consumptive is lying on a couch, looking pale and interesting and surrounded by doctors. It's a disease which takes people in different ways, and one effect it has is to—to heighten activity, especially creative activity! Think of all those consumptive artists, musicians and writers in their garrets! The mistake you're making, Verity, is to confuse a natural pity for the boy's condition with *liking* him, and the result is that you're getting sentimental over him.'

'I'm *not*!' she argued furiously.

The moon was sulking obstinately behind her cloud now, refusing to show her face.

'You are, Verity! Put your sympathy on one side and try and judge him objectively, will you? Do you really like the way he behaves?'

'He's always behaved well towards *me*!' she said coldly.

'Ah, we are back to that, are we? Well, I'm not going to keep apologising for anything I've said or done, my dear. I'm not so convinced that you did mind so much.'

There was a long silence. Then Verity said firmly, 'I should like to go back to the hotel, Mr Burton.'

Matt sighed and muttered. 'Oh, damnation . . . Look, Verity, I didn't mean to make you angry tonight. I just thought that, if we walked down here a way, where it's quiet, I could try and warn you about what *I* think is a mistake you're making.'

There was genuine regret in his voice and Verity felt her annoyance melt away. She heaved a sigh. 'I'm not cross, and I do know you mean well. I just wish you wouldn't criticise Alain all the time without any real evidence for what you say of him. Very well, he was in London. He has a right to travel about as he wishes, without its signifying anything sinister.'

'I won't say another word against him. I don't want to discuss the wretched fellow anyway!'

The moon ventured out hopefully and cast her pale, enchanting light over them. Matt lifted his hand and touched Verity's hair briefly, and then took it away. 'Yes, we'd best go back—you're right.'

There was a note of resignation in his voice that left her feeling strangely comfortless.

They walked back to the hotel, past the brightly lit *Gasthof* with its promise of carefree company. The night porter was already on duty, and shut the door behind them, turning the key.

'*Gute Nacht!*' he said politely.

'Good night, Verity,' Matt said soberly. 'Things will look better in the morning, sort themselves out—they usually do.'

She did not want to meet his eye, and only muttered, 'Good night!' before running upstairs.

CHAPTER NINE

ANYONE TEMPTED to believe that Jessica would be sufficiently alarmed by Count Giulini's threats to remain in embattled seclusion for the rest of her stay was proved wrong the following day. The Contessa emerged from her bedroom, to all appearances refreshed and confident, and announced that she meant to spend the morning with Lady Frensham, and dressed accordingly.

Verity had to admit that her employer was an exceptionally beautiful woman and, as she contemplated her, her own heart sank for reasons difficult to explain. Jessica wore a white dress with a train, and a violet sash round her well-corseted waist. A deep V-shaped frill of exquisite lace frothed on the bosom of the gown, her fair hair was swept up in an intricate series of intertwined locks and curls, and atop it all rested a large white hat, swathed with tulle and decorated with bunches of violets. She pulled on her gloves, gave a shake to her parasol to make its frills hang neatly, and announced, 'I don't need you, Verity. Run along now!' in a coolly dismissive voice.

Then she swept out, leaving Verity alone and depressed in the room. She went to the cheval-glass and surveyed her own reflection forlornly. After a moment, a more obstinate expression crossed her face. She put her hands on her hips and turned first one way and then the other, looking critically over her shoulder at her reflection. Well, her figure was as good as the Contessa's, *and* didn't need so much tight-lacing to bring it into shape. But plain, practical clothes disguised rather than enhanced her trim shape, and as for her hair . . .

Verity caught up handfuls and tried to arrange them to give different effects. Perhaps Maddox, if asked, would condescend to put up her hair for her, as a favour. She stood for a moment in an agreeable day-dream, and then shook herself. What was the point of all this? To attract Matthew Burton? That was the last thing she wanted to do.

'The last thing!' she repeated, aloud, to her reflection in the mirror, as if it would dare to argue with her.

Jessica had descended to the ground floor, swept past the bowing Inebnit, giving him a gracious nod of recognition as she did so, and emerged into the dappled sunlight of the garden. Several couples were already there, walking slowly round and gossiping. Jessica put up her parasol and surveyed the idyllic scene thoughtfully. Right in the middle of it, a burly, forthright figure sat at a table under a tree, alone, an open book in his hand. If he was reading at all, it was very slowly, for he hadn't turned a page in several minutes. Jessica crossed the grass to him in a rustle of petticoats, and said, 'Good morning, Matt.'

Burton looked up, startled, and got to his feet, looking not altogether pleased at the interruption. 'I didn't see you, Jessica,' he said briefly.

'No—very unobservant of you! You have the most frightful manners.' Jessica closed the parasol with a snap, and took the chair opposite him. Matthew sat down again and eyed her a trifle warily.

'And what is that very interesting book,' she enquired archly, 'which takes up your attention so completely?'

Silently he turned it towards her, so that she could read the title.

Jessica made a *moue* of distaste. '*Climbing in the Swiss*

Alps. Really, Matt, didn't anyone ever tell you that enthusiasts are very boring company?'

'You don't have to seek my company out, Jessica,' he said calmly.

'That *is* very rude!'

'You've just told me I've no manners.' He glanced up, his blue eyes resting shrewdly on her. 'You look very elegant today. Is that to impress me, or to strike awe into the heart of Renzo Giulini?'

'Don't talk to me of that brute Renzo . . . And *don't* flatter yourself I mean to impress *you*, Matthew dear. In fact, I'm waiting for Emma Frensham.'

He grinned briefly at her. 'I've always said that women titivate to impress one another, and not some poor luckless male, as they pretend.' His grin faded. 'Where's Verity?'

Jessica twitched her slim shoulders. '*I* don't know. I've given her the morning free. I've no idea what she does.' Her fine eyes glittered mockingly at him. 'She's very friendly with that young French artist.' She saw the displeasure cross his rugged features, and asked directly, dropping all pretence of banter, 'What do you see in her, Matt?'

'Who says I see anything?' he countered.

'I'm not a fool, Matt dear. Of course you do. You hang on her every word, and your eyes watch her all the time. A man of your age, too, and your experience! Obviously something about the girl fascinates you, but I'm truly puzzled as to what it can be. She's such a little mouse.'

'She's a very nice girl, and sensible,' he said shortly.

'Really?' Jessica raised an arched eyebrow. 'Then you won't achieve what *you* want, will you, Matt dear?'

'Which is?' he demanded, a touch of anger in his voice. Seeing the smile on her lips, he added brusquely, 'You're imagining things.'

'No, I'm not,' Jessica said waspishly. 'And I won't be made a fool of, Matt. Remember that.'

'Don't threaten me,' Matt said gently. 'I owe you no explanation for anything I do.'

Jessica inclined towards him in the peculiarly rigid fashion, straight from the waist, which tight-lacing dictated; her face shaded by the tulle and violet decorated hat was set in hard, brittle lines and her fine eyes snapped dangerously. 'I won't be displaced in any man's affections by my own paid companion! No woman would stand for that!'

'I have a certain regard for you, for old times' sake, Jessica, but I'm not in love with you, my dear, not any longer. And you were never in love with *me*. Let's be clear about that, at least. I shall always acknowledge you to be one of the most beautiful women I've ever met, but I know from sad experience that beneath that lovely exterior beats a heart of solid granite. Permit me, as an old friend, to offer you a word of advice. Beauty and a good figure will always attract a man. Mother Nature, I dare say, ensuring that the species continues to reproduce itself *ad infinitum*. If Darwin had chosen to explore that avenue of experience, he wouldn't be such a pompous bore and his writings wouldn't send me to sleep. However, Man being a reasoning animal, once the physical nature has claimed its due, he then begins to look for something else in the object of his attentions. I would suggest, Jessie, you worry less about what is fashionable, and more about developing some truly womanly qualities.'

He had to admire her for the fact that she didn't turn a hair, at least not visibly. 'You really are a perfect swine, Matt,' she said sweetly. 'I do so hope you have some really ghastly accident on one of your mountains. I shall come to your funeral. I do look really well in black. Am I to understand that that dowdy little nonentity I employ is awash with these womanly qualities? She's always struck me as the perfect governess.'

'I've no wish to discuss Miss Lyndon with you, Jessica. She's a fine girl, and I'd expect you, as her employer, to look after her.'

She ran the tip of her tongue across her upper lip in a way which, despite himself, set the old Adam stirring within him. 'You'll never have her,' she said in a quiet, vicious little voice. '*Never*, Matt, do you hear? I'll see to that!'

In a split second, before he'd even had a chance to react, her manner changed entirely. The air of grace and charm returned, and she rose elegantly to her feet.

'Here comes Emma Frensham. Do excuse me, Matt!' She put up the parasol, twirled it provocatively, and swept away across the grass with the same seductive swirl of skirts.

He watched her go, thoughtfully.

Verity had been so concerned for Alain that, finding herself free, she sought him out. She found him, sketch-folder under his arm, clad in his linen jacket and disreputable hat, preparing to set out on an artistic expedition.

'I was going to walk part-way up the Harder Kulm,' he said. 'I didn't suggest you come, as I thought you might not want to, not with me.'

'Alain,' Verity said patiently, 'I've told you I'm sorry about what I said yesterday. If you can't forgive me, then say so. But please don't sulk.'

Alain shrugged and nodded, screwing up his eyes and regarding her speculatively. Then he scratched the bridge of his nose with a crayon and asked, 'What about the Contessa?'

'Spending the morning with Lady Frensham. I'm dismissed to my own devices.'

'She thinks the English milady better protection

against the fire-breathing Count than a closed bedroom door?' Alain chuckled. 'Well, come along. Strong shoes, mind! The Harder Kulm is *steep*.'

On their way out, they passed, unseen, by Jessica and Matt, deep in conversation beneath the tree. Alain glanced at his companion, but Verity was staring straight ahead.

The ascent was very steep. Verity wondered at the wisdom of Alain making this climb, even part-way, but she didn't dare to question it aloud, knowing how angry this would make him. He seemed reasonably well in himself this morning, yet at the same time a cloud seemed to hang over him. Once or twice he was quite abrupt with her, as though his mind ran on some other matter and he found her chatter an annoying distraction.

Half-way up, he said, 'Far enough for today!', and they stopped and sat down on a fallen tree-trunk. The panorama of Interlaken, the valley beyond it and the further mountains was spread out below them. Alain propped up his sketch-board and began to work, cigarette in mouth, the blue smoke curling into the pine-scented morning air.

Verity sat quietly, watching him for a while, and then got up and began to wander about in the trees, picking up pine-cones and oddly shaped twigs with the vague intention of making an arrangement of them back at the hotel. Away from the path, it was not easy going. Underfoot, a dry carpet of shiny pine-needles offered little support. They slid treacherously beneath her weight and once or twice she slipped, and had to grab at a tree-trunk to stop herself sliding helter-skelter down a steep bank. No wonder Alain had said that unwary walkers often broke their ankles up here. Without difficulty, one could break one's neck!

She had climbed down a steep incline, by sitting and slithering, and arrived in a gully at the foot. Birds flew up at her intruding presence as she searched about for items for her arrangement. The more she thought about it, the more she liked the idea. She would set it in cork, and if Alain would lend her some paints, even colour some of the stems. It would make a striking, if unorthodox, display. She was so pleased with the idea that she decided to go back and tell Alain about it. But when she turned, she found that the climb up the slope was more difficult by far than the climb down. There were few reliable handholds, and the mulch of leaves and needles gave way, so that there were no toeholds at all. She slipped badly twice, and slithered back, scraping her hands painfully.

Verity said 'Bother!' aloud, and looked about her. Alain was out of sight, further up the slope, probably twenty-five or thirty yards away, but possibly even more. She had been pottering about for quite fifteen minutes, all the time moving further away from him. But she needed him now, to reach down a hand from the top to help her to climb out of the gully.

'Alain!' she called twice. Her voice echoed in the trees, absorbed and distorted by them, the birds rustled in the branches, but no Alain came. Verity experienced a sudden pinprick of fear. It seemed so very silent and lonely up here. The trees were dark, unmoving, unfriendly observers of her plight. She tried walking some way down the gully and re-attempting to scramble out at a different point, but with no more success. She was perspiring profusely now, covered with dust and dry leaves and beginning to feel desperate.

'Well, you have got yourself into a fix!' said an amused voice above her head.

'Oh, Alain!' she gasped in relief, and looking up, saw his face grinning at her. 'I'm stuck.'

'So I see. Don't try and climb up in a straight line, go diagonally. See this tree over here? Make for that.' He crouched down on his heels and stretched out his hand. 'Come on, try and reach my hand, and I'll pull you up.'

Somehow, following his advice and directions from above, she managed to scramble to within reach of his hand, and grasped it firmly with the greatest relief. He hauled her up, scrabbling inelegantly, until she was almost level with him, and then, quite suddenly, the pull he was exerting on her arm relaxed. Verity gave a little cry as she found herself, though still holding his hand, marooned, clinging to the hillside near the top of the rise. She looked up into his face questioningly, alarm in her eyes.

'If I were to let you go *now*,' Alain said softly, 'just look and see where you'd finish up.'

Verity glanced over her shoulder. Her diagonal progress had led her clear of the entrapping gully, but left her at the top of a particularly steep drop, without trees to block her descent, a clear, slippery, handhold-less chute, which would precipitate her down at ever-increasing speed, scraping against rocks and débris, to a narrow stony ledge a hundred feet or so below. She took a deep breath. The terrible fear of falling, of finding herself helpless as when she had plunged from the catwalk at the gorge, swept over her. She felt the perspiration on her body run cold, and her heart begin to beat frantically.

'Don't, Alain. Please!' she pleaded. 'It's not *funny* —pull me up, I'm scared!'

He looked down at her white face turned up towards his, and he hesitated; she was sure of it. It was an odd little moment, and then he gave her a hefty tug which brought her, gasping, up level with him and enabled her to scramble at last to her feet.

'Thank you!' she panted. 'But you ought not to have teased me like that. It was really dangerous. I could have fallen straight down again.'

'Yes,' he agreed, and shook an admonitory finger at her. 'So let that be a lesson to you. I warned you about the Harder Kulm. Don't go wandering off. Stay by me.'

Disconcerted at his reproof and still unnerved by her experience, she followed him to where his sketch-folder and drawing materials lay on the ground, and as he gathered them up, she said accusingly,

'You did frighten me, Alain. At the top of such a steep slope, you should have known better. I dare say you meant to teach me a lesson, but I might have been killed! You shouldn't have fooled about like that, when I had hold of your hand. Very silly *you* would have looked if you'd had to go back to the hotel and tell them I was lying dead on the Harder Kulm!'

'Oh, no one knew you came out here with me,' he said casually. 'I needn't have told them anything!' He smiled at her.

Verity left Alain in town and made her own way to the hotel, sunk in thought. The lift was out of order again, and a young man in a blue overall was tinkering with it industriously, making a great deal of noise but not much progress. Inebnit hovered over him, looking very put out. She set off up the staircase, and on the first mezzanine, found her progress barred by Matt's large and solid form.

'I've been looking for you,' he said. 'Where did you get to?'

'I went for a walk.' She hesitated momentarily, 'With Alain.' Matt wouldn't like that, she thought, and he didn't.

His bushy eyebrows crinkled alarmingly in a forbidding scowl, and he said aggressively, 'I told you to beware of him! Where did you go?'

'To the Harder Kulm.' She walked resolutely past

him, but she was not to escape so easily, and he fell into step beside her as she climbed the stairs.

Something in her face and manner must have alerted him, because he asked more quietly and less aggressively, 'What happened?'

Verity tried to say, 'Nothing much', in a light tone, but the words came out with a horribly flat ring to them.

'Come along to the Frenshams' sitting-room,' Matt said grimly. 'We need to have a word in private.'

She followed him along the corridor unhappily, and when they were alone, faced him defiantly.

Ignoring the challenge of her grey eyes, he asked bluntly, 'No nonsense, now, out with it! What did he do?'

'He didn't seize me passionately in a sudden onset of emotion, if that's what's worrying you,' she said, bridling.

'Believe me, Verity, that is *not* what's worrying me. If Bernard wants to hold your hand and whisper sweet nothings into your ear, he can do so with my blessing!' She flushed. 'But that's not what he did, is it? So why don't you just tell me what he did do?'

Verity unpinned her hat to gain time, and surveyed it thoughtfully. In fact, she felt an impulse to confide in Matt. She needed someone else's opinion, even someone as prejudiced against Alain as Matthew Burton. She turned and saw him leaning against the wall, arms folded, immovable as a granite statue, his blue eyes following her every move.

'I'm quite possibly making something out of nothing, Matt, only something a little odd did happen. I got stuck in a sort of big ditch, through my own fault, and when Alain was pulling me up out of it from above, I thought, just for a moment, he was going to let go of me. I mean, let go deliberately. If he had, I should have rolled straight down right to the bottom of the Harder Kulm. Just at the point where it happened, there wasn't a thing to stop me.' She paused, but Matt said nothing, waiting. 'But he didn't let go, after all,' Verity concluded with false briskness. 'So it didn't matter. He was cross with me because I'd wandered off, and he meant to punish me, to give me a fright.'

'And that's all?' Matt asked coolly.

'Yes, of course! Now that I tell you about it, it does sound silly. A fuss over nothing. He wouldn't really have done it.'

He remained silent, and his silence was the most damning answer of all. Verity turned away from him and went to the window. In the garden below, Jessica and Lady Frensham were sitting in the shade of the trees. Waiters circulated with glasses of lemonade and cups of coffee. Lady Frensham was gesturing widely as she described something, and Jessica was fanning herself with her little oriental fan. Verity couldn't see her face beneath the tulle and violet hat, but from her attitude and languid movements she looked bored.

Verity glanced round the rest of the garden, half-expecting to glimpse the solid but elegant form of Renzo Giulini, skulking in the bushes. He wasn't to be seen, but it was unlikely he'd given up his objective.

Matt stood watching her slim-waisted figure in her drab grey walking-dress, which gave her an almost puritan look. Her chestnut hair was coiled into a knot on the top of her head, and the sunlight falling through the window struck auburn depths in it. Matt said, 'You know, I'm anxious that nothing—no accident—should befall you.'

Perhaps it was the conversation he'd had that morning with Jessica which had unsettled him; he didn't know. But he did know that, watching Verity now, he felt again those physical stirrings that were so difficult to ignore. It

was that damn awful grey dress. He wanted to tear it off.
He wanted to shout, 'For goodness sake, you're a
beautiful girl with a lovely body, why don't you buy
yourself some pretty clothes?' No wonder that young
imp Bernard wanted to draw her portrait. Probably it
wasn't all he wanted to do.

Verity couldn't see him, but an atmosphere had entered the room which communicated itself to her in some
subtle, primeval way. Perhaps it was the very faintest
vibration in his voice.

'It's kind of you to worry about me so much,' she said a
little shakily.

'No, it isn't kind!' he said vehemently. 'I'm not *kind*.
I'm not some benevolent old uncle watching over you!
I—I'm interested in what happens to you, becomes of
you . . . I'm not, not bargaining with you. I think you
need some help.'

'I'm not an object of charity!' Her voice was louder,
with a jarring note in it akin to pain.

Matt walked across to her and gently put his hands on
her shoulders. 'Verity?' He felt the shudder run through
her slender body beneath his touch. 'You don't forgive
me,' he said soberly. 'But what I said the other night
—stupid though it was, as I readily confess now—I said
with the best of intentions.'

'Intentions to do what? Take away what few shreds of
self-respect I had left? How could you ever think, Matt,
that I would agree to—to such a thing?' Her averted face
was pale, and he saw her lips tremble.

'You think I don't respect you, but that's not true!' he
protested. 'I admire you, possibly more than any woman
I've ever met. You're proud and independent and
courageous . . . I don't want to take any of that away
from you! All right, perhaps my intentions were not
entirely selfless! But, for pity's sake, Verity, at least they
were human! You're a very attractive woman. Yes! I

have a normal man's reactions! You can't, surely, blame me for that?'

'Yes, I do blame you,' she said with suppressed fury.

'For what? Letting you see the impression you'd made on me? For being honest about my feelings? Or was it because I made you see yourself differently? Made you face feelings you wanted to keep hidden away?' Suddenly he added in a stronger tone, 'Confound it, turn round and look at me, Verity! You're not afraid to look me in the eye, are you?'

He wrenched her round towards him. She looked up and cried out, 'No, I'm not afraid!' and found herself caught up in his powerful embrace, unable to say any more, as his mouth closed over hers with fierce possessiveness. Struggling to free herself, she stumbled against the sofa, and, caught off-balance, fell back on to it beneath him.

Panic swept over her, and she turned and twisted in his grip like a wild thing, kicking and striking out at him blindly. As she scrambled away, he tried to restrain her, and his fingers closed on the bodice of the grey dress, just as she wrenched it from his grasp. The little pearl buttons that fastened it had not been designed to withstand this kind of rough treatment, and gave way. The front fastening parted, and the entire bodice sprang open, baring one shoulder and her chemise.

For an awful moment, as his fingers touched her bare skin, she really believed he would use his superior strength to take what he wanted, and instinctively she cried out in rising hysteria, 'No, no!'

'Stop that, Verity, stop it!' his voice ordered loudly, forcing itself through the fog of blind panic which enveloped her. He grasped her arms and shook her violently. 'I'm not going to—to do anything to you against your will!'

The panic subsided, and Verity stared into his angry face, close to hand.

'For heavens' sake!' he exploded. 'What kind of a man do you think I am?' She gulped and found no reply, and he released her and said curtly, 'Do something about that dress!' indicating her partially disrobed state.

As her fingers tremblingly refastened the buttons, he got up and walked away to the further side of the room. When he judged her calmer, he turned to face her. He had controlled his anger, and now gave her a sardonic look of his blue eyes.

'You'll be glad to know that I shall be out of your way for a day or two,' he said coldly. 'So you won't have to fear I shall be pressing unwelcome attentions on you.'

'You're going away?' Verity looked up quickly, her alarm sounding in her voice.

For a moment, he almost said, 'Ask me to stay, and I will!' But immediately he thrust the thought from his mind. He needed to get away from here. He was losing his grip on the situation. He needed to get the girl from under his skin. There was only one place for that. The one place to which he always took his problems, and which always reduced them to seeming insignificance —the mountain

'Yes,' he told her. 'I came to climb a mountain, and if I don't climb it, people will start to ask why. I can't afford that. Anyway, Karl Hable is fretting. So he and I go up to Grindelwald tonight.'

'I see,' Verity said in a flat little voice.

'You'll be all right,' he said roughly, because he wasn't sure it was true. 'Stay in or near the hotel. Keep away from young Bernard, and if anything odd happens, anything *at all*, tell Sir Miles or Lady Frensham, *at once*, do you understand?'

'Yes, Matt,' Verity said, and he thought she meant it. He hoped she did.

'Well, then,' he growled. 'I'd better leave you. I've matters to arrange.' He went out, and the door slammed after him.

That afternoon, just after lunch, the weather broke at last. The stifling heat that had been building up for two weeks was shattered by a roll of thunder and a brilliant diamond-white streak of lightning. Verity stood at the window, heedless of the danger, and filled with the wild exhilaration of the storm, as the magnificent drama in which the skies hurled great bolts of lightning at the mighty Jungfrau was played out before her fascinated eyes. A true battle of the gods and the Titans, monsters locked in mortal combat, and Man, who so fondly imagined himself to be the conqueror of the earth, reduced to a pitiful and insignificant creation, clinging to the surface, at the mercy of the elements.

After the thunder and the lightning came the rain, lashing down in torrents. A thick mist descended, and before long the lofty mountain was lost from view, as if it had been suddenly wiped from the face of the earth.

Towards tea-time, the rain stopped. Jessica was resting on her bed, saying thunderstorms gave her a headache, and Verity put on galoshes, armed herself with an umbrella, and went out for a walk.

Everywhere was wet and shining, as if newly washed down by an army of maids, and smelled fresh and clean. As she passed the gateway of a near-by restaurant, she almost collided with a man coming out. They jumped apart, and the stranger bowed correctly, and said, '*Entschuldigen Sie, bitte, Fräulein.*'

Verity stared at him with justifiable curiosity. He looked so much like the popular caricaturists's idea of the Prussian officer, with his cropped, military haircut, walrus moustache and—yes—duelling scars!—that she almost laughed.

Hastily she said, 'It was my fault. I'm sorry.'

'Ah, an English lady?' he said in guttural tones, and bared a formidable array of gold teeth at her. To her alarm, he fell into step beside her. 'You like to walk, Fräulein? It is much cooler now, after the rain.' He breathed deeply and declared, 'Ah, the mountain air. It revives the constitution! You are a frequent visitor to this country, Fräulein?'

'No, it's my first visit,' she said, disliking his travesty of a friendly smile and wishing the wretched man would go away.

'Then you must profit by it,' he said amiably.

Verity didn't know why, but something in these last words rang as if they held some double meaning. The two of them had reached a crossroads, and, apparently, the parting of their ways.

'We go different paths, Fräulein. Permit me, before we part, to present myself. Major Stein.' He bowed again, with portly dignity, and clicked his heels. 'I, too, am a great walker. No doubt our paths will cross again, dear young lady. I am sure we have much in common.'

On this enigmatic note he wheeled away as if on parade, and strode briskly off, his boots clattering on the road surface.

'How very extraordinary . . .' Verity mused. The strange meeting had unsettled her, and she decided to abandon her walk and turn back. But so preoccupied was she with what had happened that, when she reached the hotel, she failed to see Count Giulini's elegant form standing in the gateway, and did not hear him until he had spoken to her twice.

'Is something wrong, Miss Lyndon?'

Verity surveyed his dapper figure and concerned face with some embarrassment. 'I'm so sorry, I wasn't trying to ignore you. But something very odd did just happen, and I was quite taken up with it.'

'You have some troubles?' He raised his dark eyebrows. He had the large, liquid brown eyes of the South, and they seemed filled with a genuine concern. 'I am able to help, perhaps? You see, I have always been one son in a family of daughters. I have the most sympathetic ear for the troubles of ladies.'

Despite her lack of spirits, Verity had to laugh. 'You are very kind, Count Giulini, but I won't bore you with my problems. You have your own. Tell me, how do your affairs progress?'

He grimaced and made a wide gesture with his hand. 'Poorly. My stepmother refuses to divulge the whereabouts of the jewellery, and I await your confirmation, Miss Lyndon, that it is indeed in her locked jewel-box. As to what condition it is in—well, since she will tell me nothing at all, I am in no position even to guess at that. I begin to fear that, however hard I try, I shall not gain access to it. She is a formidable woman.'

'Anything capable of causing such upset and misery as these jewels have done is perhaps better left where it is?' Verity suggested.

He smiled at her. He was really quite a pleasant young man, probably no more than twenty-eight or so. Now that he was no longer in a towering rage, she found her former dislike of him fading rapidly, despite her obligation to be loyal to Jessica.

'You are possibly right, Miss Lyndon.' He glanced towards the hotel. 'I've just been to call on Matt, and wish him well. As you probably know, he's going up to Grindelwald tonight, and hopes to make the Eiger climb tomorrow.' Renzo cast a shrewd, professional eye up at the grey sky. 'It's poor weather for climbing. All that dry weather will have loosened the rock. Now we shall have mist and rain, which is worse. He should wait a day or two. Matt agrees with me, I fancy, but Karl Hable is impatient and has to return to Vienna shortly. Matt has put aside his better judgment, I suspect, in order to oblige Hable. They will certainly attempt it.' He noticed how pale she had become, and added, 'Do not be alarmed—they are both highly experienced mountain men. You have, perhaps, some interest in Matt?' He smiled at her.

Verity coloured and said, 'You find that unsuitable, perhaps?'

'Unsuitable? In what way? No, Matt needs someone like you . . . but he doesn't know it.' He bowed. 'It was very nice to see you again, Miss Lyndon. Goodbye.'

He set off up the road, and Verity went slowly into the hotel. In the lobby, a pile of objects by the desk caught her eye, and the sight of them sent her heart plummeting to the depths. They were mundane and ordinary objects enough, certainly here in Switzerland: haversack, once green and now faded to a greyish hue, an ice-axe, a coil of thick rope and a pair of sturdy boots.

She sat down on a chair by them and awaited the arrival of their owner. He came running down the stairs a few minutes later, and stopped in some surprise when he saw her.

'Well, Verity! Are you standing guard over my kit? No one is going to steal *that*!' He grinned at her cheerfully.

How happy he was. Released for a day or two from tiresome official duties, he was going to do the only thing he really cared to do—climb. Yet the grin revealed the chipped tooth, and that recalled the circumstances in which it had been damaged—on the Eiger, two years ago, in an avalanche that had almost swept him from the mountain.

'Are you leaving now?' Her voice sounded oddly disembodied, falsely calm and composed.

'Yes, going up to Grindelwald tonight. Karl and I will have to get up at three in the morning, you see, to hike over to the foot of the mountain and be ready to climb as soon as it's daybreak.'

'It's very dangerous, isn't it?' she asked him soberly. She had not meant to say it, but the words forced themselves out.

Matt hesitated and avoided her eye. He dropped down on his heels by the haversack, and opening it up, thrust his climbing-boots inside. As he rebuckled the straps with deft movements of his strong, capable fingers, he said, without looking up from his task, 'Yes, it's a dangerous sport. But the risks can be reduced if you know what you're doing. Karl and I are both experienced climbers. Lots of people have climbed the western slope since Barrington did it. Karl and I were half-way to the summit, two years ago, and know the route. Last year he and I climbed the Wetterhorn without mishap.'

'I met Count Giulini outside. He thinks the weather is too bad.'

Matt shrugged his broad shoulders. 'It could be better. But, you know, the weather hereabouts can change suddenly. You've seen that for yourself. Maybe, tomorrow, it will clear.' He paused in his task, and his eyes gained a faraway look. 'To be high on the mountain, on a fine clear day, with the world far below, there's nothing like it . . . And it's like nothing I can describe to you.'

Verity said obstinately, 'Suppose it doesn't clear. What if it rains?'

'Then we may call it off. Rain makes all your kit so damn heavy, boots weigh a ton each and the rope is almost impossible to handle. I'm more concerned about visibility. No one wants to be blind up there.' He glanced up at her now, at last. 'Worried about us?'

'A little,' she confessed.

'Don't be. A grizzled old cat-a-mountain like me is notoriously hard to kill. Besides, Karl Hable is a good

fellow with all the virtues *I* lack. He must have at least
one angel on his side.' He paused and looked into her
pale, set face. 'And perhaps I have one on mine, eh?' he
added softly.

'When will you be back?'

'Day after tomorrow. See you then.'

Suddenly he sounded brusque, as if he wanted her to
go, to be out of the way. Verity saw that Sir Miles had
come downstairs, and stood up.

'I hope you have a good day's sport. I'll see you
—later.' She held out her hand. 'Good luck!' she forced
herself to say briskly, and managed it with only the
barest tremor in her voice.

He took her hand briefly, dwarfing it in his broad,
brown leathery palm, and gave it a squeeze. 'Good girl!
Behave yourself. Get Giulini to take you into town. He's
an entertaining chap when he's not obsessed with long-
lost heirlooms!'

Verity nodded, said 'Good evening' to Sir Miles, and
hurried away upstairs.

'Just come down to wish you well, Matt,' Sir Miles
said, his eyes following Verity's retreating figure. The
girl was upset—didn't want Matt to go, but wouldn't
dream of asking him to stay. Burton, confound the
fellow, probably hadn't even noticed her distress,
nothing but the wretched mountain on his mind.

But Sir Miles was wrong. For as he shook Matt's hand,
he was surprised to hear the other say, a little awkwardly, 'You will look after Verity for me, won't you,
sir?'

'Good heavens, my dear chap!' Sir Miles exclaimed.
'Don't worry about that! The girl won't come to harm in
the next twenty-four hours.'

'I meant,' Matt said, in a cool, competent voice, 'Look
after her if I should . . . If anything should happen to
me.'

Sir Miles put his hand on the other's broad shoulder, and said quietly, 'Yes, Matt, of course. My word on it.'

CHAPTER TEN

THE NEXT morning, Jessica curtly dispensed with Verity's company again, without explanation. The Contessa seemed even more irritable and capricious than usual. Maddox bore the brunt of her ill-humour, but Verity came in for her share and wasn't sorry to be free of the Contessa for a few hours. She did wonder, uneasily, whether Jessica's bad temper was in some way connected with Matt, or perhaps Renzo's presence was wearing her down. The Italian had abandoned the direct approach for a policy of silent observation, so that Jessica declared crossly, 'I cannot turn left or right, but it seems I must find him before me. Wretched young man!'

Released, Verity went downstairs. The large public lounge was empty but for an elderly gentleman scanning a week-old copy of *The Times*. Even the Count wasn't there, for once. She sat down in a far corner, and propping her chin on her hand, stared disconsolately out of the window. It was still dull, and overcast. She could not help wondering if, at the higher altitude of Grindelwald, it was raining, and if so, whether Matt and Karl Hable had called off their climb.

It all depended on how the outlook had seemed at daybreak, on the lower stages on the West slope. Verity consulted the little fob-watch pinned to her crisply starched white cotton blouse, and saw that it was just on eleven. If all had gone well, the two climbers were about half-way up, having covered the easier lower slope and with the difficult part yet to come. They were now out of touch with all human life, and no one would know, until they returned, how the day had gone.

Verity tried to picture the mountain, and the two men clinging to its rocky flank a insignificant as flies on a wall. How puny a creature was Man, compared with the mountain, with all its changing moods and variety of climate, which took the climber from an alpine summer at its foot to the eternal winter at its summit, over thirteen thousand feet above sea-level.

A shadow fell across her, and she was startled to see Alain, his face pale and set. He took a seat opposite, uninvited. Verity tried to smile at him in the old, friendly way but, despite herself, the smile would not come, and her cheeks reddened guiltily.

'You avoid me,' Alain said, without greeting her. It was not a question, but a statement. His long fingers plucked nervously at a fringed cushion. 'Are you still angry with me because I frightened you? Or do you no longer trust me?'

'Is there any reason why I shouldn't trust you?' she managed to reply lightly.

He hunched his shoulders and made a wry grimace. 'Why ask *me*?' he said bitterly. 'Why not ask Matthew Burton, since his word is always to be taken in preference to mine?'

'Don't talk that way, Alain,' she said swiftly. 'It's as if . . .'

'As if I were jealous?' His mouth smiled, but his dark eyes remained sombre. 'Well, I am. Shouldn't I be? He has his health, he has you . . .' He leaned back and surveyed her. 'I have a little piece of theatre, you know, which I rehearse in my mind. One day, who knows, I shall work it all up into a real play—if I have time . . . which, I suppose, I haven't.'

'What is it about?' Verity asked awkwardly, moved by the bleak resignation with which the last words were spoken.

'Oh, about you, and me, and *him*. *He* is the villain, of

course, and I dispose of him at the end of Act IV. So—he's gone to climb his mountain, has he, today?' He glanced at the window. 'He's chosen bad weather for it.'

'Don't!' she interrupted, in a voice ragged with suppressed tension.

Alain's dark gaze flickered to her face. 'It would hurt you if something were to befall him? No, don't answer!' He scrambled to his feet in a sudden burst of energy. 'I don't intend to sit here and talk about Burton. Oh, there is someone asking after you at the reception. Stay there, and I'll send him in here.'

'No, Alain, wait!' Verity called after him, because she didn't want to see anyone else. But it was too late, and he was already walking rapidly away in his light, quick manner.

She fully expected him to direct Renzo Giulini into the lounge, but it was quite a different figure which appeared, and glanced around enquiringly, before catching sight of her and coming jauntily over.

Verity grasped the arms of her chair and gasped, 'Jack!'

For a moment, she stared at him in pure disbelief. Reason told her he could not be here, yet her own eyes told her he was. He stood before her, solid and real, looking both highly amused at the expression on her face, and a little apprehensive, as well he might do. He was clad in a sporting outfit of knickerbockers and a Norfolk jacket, which suited his slim, well-proportioned figure. He carried a cap in his hand, and, for some reason, a pair of goggles. Now he flopped down on the armchair where Alain had sat and stretched out his long legs, grinning at her. He looked as pleased as he'd done years ago, as a small child, when he'd played some particularly ingenious and successful practical trick on her.

'You look as though you've seen a ghost! But it is

me—I'm here. Pinch me, if you like.' He held out his arm teasingly.

But Verity had got over her initial surprise, and rallied. 'How did you get here?' Suspicion entered her heart. 'What are you *doing* here? Where did you get the money?'

He looked hurt. 'That's not much of a welcome! Fine loving sister you are. I thought you'd be pleased. I planned to give you a surprise.'

'You've certainly done that!' she said grimly. 'Tell me all of it, Jack. The truth, mind! Who gave you the money to come here?'

Jack dropped his cap and goggles on the floor by his chair, already making himself at home in his usual untidy fashion. He pushed back the lock of fair hair which fell over his forehead, and said smugly, 'You might not have any friends, Ver'—but *I* have!'

'Your friends are all as worthless as you are!' she said coldly.

'Sour grapes!' He pulled a face at her. 'That's where you're wrong. I'm a sociable fellow, and I make friends with the right people.'

She drew a deep breath. 'All right, whom are you sponging off now?'

That annoyed him. Like most of his kind, he liked to be well thought of, without having done anything to earn respect. An aggressive look entered his handsome, discontented face. 'No one! I told you, I've got friends! If you must know, I ran into Toby Cavendish in the Strand. He's just come down from Oxford, where he did fearfully well, got his rowing Blue, and so on.'

'I'm surprised young Toby did so well,' Verity said shortly. 'He never seemed to me to have enough brain to pass examinations. All he ever did when he was at his parents' home was shoot pigeons.'

'And try and seduce me on the stairs,' she thought in addition. 'But that's neither here nor there!'

'Oh, exams!' Jack said dismissively. 'I don't think he bothered much with those. Toby's not got much be- tween the ears, you know, but a chap would have to be a frightful swot to go passing exams, and Toby isn't that. He is a cracking good shot, though, and a splendid amateur jockey at point-to-point, and a fine all-round cricketer, too.'

'And a dissolute young cad with the makings of a first-class bore . . .' thought Verity. Aloud, she asked suspiciously, 'And how does Toby find his way into all this? Jack, I warn you, Mrs Cavendish has always been very kind to me, and I won't have you embarrassing her family! What's more, she's a friend of Lady Frensham, who is also staying here, so please be careful!'

'Fair enough,' he said a trifle too nonchalantly. 'As I say, I ran into Toby, and we went off to have a drink together to celebrate his coming down from Oxford . . . and he told me about this uncle of his. Well, it seemed the uncle was in the Diplomatic, in Paris. He's a crusty old bachelor, but a great amateur sportsman in his day. Toby's always got on well with the old chap because of that. So, the uncle wrote to Toby, that if he'd come over to Paris, he—the uncle—would buy Toby a motor-car! Imagine it, just like that!' Jack looked momentarily wistful. 'So there was Toby, all set to go over to Paris, pick up the new motor and go touring round Europe. Thing was that he didn't fancy doing it all alone. I told him you were in Switzerland, and he said why not come along with him as far as Switzerland, and he'd drop me off here.'

'You mean,' Verity interrupted, speaking very slowly and carefully, 'that Toby Cavendish has met the bill for all your expenses, from England to here?'

'Trust *you* to put it like that!' Jack said sullenly. 'Well, yes, in a way. But I was doing him a favour, too. He needed me. To start up a motor, you know, is a damn difficult thing. It's much easier if there's two of you, one to crank the starter handle and one to adjust the levers —and coming over the hills, I kept the brakes from seizing up, with a wet rag. It was jolly hard work, I can tell you. But, you know, Ver'—'his eyes took on a dreamy look '—it's marvellous fun. The motor-car is a wonderful thing. The horse has absolutely had its day, you know. Another fifteen or twenty years, less maybe, and I bet you won't see a single nag on the streets of London.'

'That's all very well!' Verity said sharply, dragging him back from his roseate dreams of a future dominated by the horseless carriage. 'But where's Toby now?'

'Gone on to Vevey, where he's got some sort of girl cousin at finishing school. He's got the idea that he can climb over the wall and see her. No use ringing the front-door bell, of course, because the girls aren't allowed men visitors, except brothers. Cousins not excepted.'

'And left you here penniless, I suppose? I don't have any money, Jack, and don't know how long this post will last—so don't look at me to fund you!'

'I don't depend on your charity,' he said resentfully. 'Toby lent me fifty pounds.'

'*What?*' Verity gazed at him in horror. 'Oh, Jack, how could you? How will you repay it? *I* can't!'

'Oh, plenty of time to worry over that,' he said comfortably.

That was Jack, ever the same. Somehow, someone always footed the bill, and he never worried that one day a rescuer might fail to come along. Now he was here, and she would have to introduce him to the Frenshams . . . and to Matt.

Matt. But Matt had already met Jack. Verity's heart

sank. At the same time, she thought, 'Thank goodness Matt is away! I'll have to try and get rid of Jack before he comes back, or, at least, try and get it into Jack's head that he mustn't tell any of his foolish stories.' She leaned forward earnestly.

'Jack, listen! It's *important*. Someone is here who knows you. Matthew Burton, he's a very well known alpinist.'

Jack brightened. 'Of course he is! I've met Burton, up in Scotland, last year.'

'Yes, *and* told him a whole rigmarole of nonsense, which he hasn't forgotten!'

Her brother had the grace to flush. He bit his lip and muttered, 'Awkward.'

'Awkward? Is that all you can say? It's humiliating! Jack, you *lied* to him.'

'No, I didn't,' he defended himself. 'I may have exaggerated a bit—but a chap's got to keep appearances going for himself. Burton will have forgotten.'

'Oh no, he hasn't. He isn't the sort of man who forgets. I've warned you over and over again about playing at being an independent young gentleman, Jack. You're not. You're an unemployed clerk.'

Jack's handsome face reddened angrily. 'I'm not, confound it! If father hadn't lost every last bean, we'd be in clover now. I'd be like Toby, riding around in my own motor!'

'Father *did* lose everything, and you're not like Toby. Listen to me, Matt's gone up to Grindelwald . . .'

Whatever else he might be, Jack wasn't slow-witted. A gleeful smile creased his face, and she realised too late she'd made a fatal mistake in referring so unthinkingly to Matt by his Christian name.

'First-name terms, is it?' His grin broadened. 'Don't say you've decided to play your cards right at last! Must be the mountain air. Is that what you've been doing, holding hands with Burton? Where is the Contessa, anyway?'

'She is about somewhere, and, Jack, she is not going to be pleased to see *you*. When Matt Burton gets back, you're not to say one word to him which isn't the plain, unvarnished truth. What's more, there is *no* romance, so don't imagine there is!'

'He's got expectations of a baronetcy,' Jack said shrewdly. 'Don't be stupid, Ver'. If there's no romance yet—make one!'

'Men who are heirs to baronetcies don't marry penniless governesses or companions.'

'No . . .' he conceded. 'But he might set you up. Don't look so fierce, Verity. It's quite respectable. I mean, quite *permanent*—like being married, almost.'

'*Jack!*' she gasped incredulously. 'How could you even think such a thing, let alone say it? You're my brother, for heaven's sake!'

But Jack's handsome face hardened obstinately in a way she hadn't seen before. He glanced quickly and furtively at the old gentleman slumbering beneath his *Times*, and leaned forward.

'Now you just listen to me for a change, Verity! You're always telling me what to do, and telling me I'm a dreamer like father, and not practical. So now I am being practical, and trying to think for both of us!'

Seeing his sister's expression, he had the grace to turn slightly pink.

'Of course I don't damn well like the idea! But you're twenty-seven, and you aren't likely to meet too many fellows like Burton now! You've had your chances, and wouldn't take them! You could have had Toby, if you'd wanted. He told me on our journey here how keen he was on you at one time, and how you turned him down. You could have got Toby to marry you if you'd cried a bit and looked helpless. He's that sort of chap. Burton won't come up with marriage, of course, but he's got one hell of a reputation with women, and if he's interested, you're mad to throw away an opportunity like it. Just tell me, what's the alternative? Are you going to keep grinding away teaching snivelling brats to spell, or trotting behind some spoiled woman, running errands and putting up with every whim and fancy? The older you get, the harder it's going to be to keep going from job to job. You've got no security, no savings, nothing!'

'I might have had more, had I not had to fund *you* all these years!' Verity burst out.

'All right, so you have. I work as a clerk, but I'm no good at it, and I don't see why the devil I should be. How would you like to spend all day from eight-thirty to six-thirty standing over a dusty desk without even a break for lunch? At Benson's we were supposed to eat our sandwiches as we worked, and if a chap wanted to follow a call of nature, he had to ask permission to leave the room like a blasted schoolboy! The Head Clerk even timed him! You've always grumbled at me for not sticking it out, but I'd like to see you stick out a job like that! I know about Burton. The uncle, the one he stands to inherit from, has an estate down in Hampshire or Dorset or somewhere. It's good farming land, and when Burton inherits, he'll be able to live comfortably off his rents. He's a decent chap, and he'll look after you. If he does decide to marry someone else—as I suppose he will one day, to get an heir—he'll settle a decent sum on you to take care of things. We'd *both* have security, you and I, Verity—and you can believe me, it's the only security you're ever likely to get!'

'I won't be his mistress,' Verity said furiously, 'and he knows it!'

'You mean he's already asked?' Jack sat back and gave a low whistle. 'You turned him down, I suppose.

You *would*! For crying out loud, Ver'—come to your senses, will you?'

'You're my brother, Jack, and I've always loved you,' Verity said quietly. 'I've always known you were work-shy, and a liar, and spendthrift. But I never realised before how thoroughly despicable you were, deep down inside. I used to think I'd forgive you anything. But no longer. I'll never forgive you this, Jack. Never.'

He looked away from her level gaze. 'It's not that I don't care about you, Verity, of course I do. You've always been a brick. But I'm not going to say I could have done more, because I *couldn't*, can't you see? I'm just useless at holding down a job. Just think about it sensibly, will you? And abandon those high-minded principles of yours. You told me I couldn't afford to play at being a gentleman. Well, *you* can't afford to stand on your dignity, Ver'. Independence is all very well, if you can afford it. We can't—neither of us. People like Toby and Matt Burton go through life having whatever they want, because they can pay for it. And if Burton wants you . . . Good grief, woman! Society women chase after Burton! You should see 'em! You don't seem to realise what a catch you could make.'

'I don't want a catch,' Verity said fiercely. 'I want my self-respect. I don't want to be ashamed to see my own face in the mirror every morning! How about you, Jack? Are you content with yourself?'

Exasperated, he struck the arms of the chair with the flat of his palms. 'Devil take it, Ver'! You—You make such a fuss about it all.'

'That's right, Jack, I do—and I shall continue to do so,' she told him calmly.

He threw himself back in the chair and eyed her thoughtfully. She was a good-looking girl, and he'd always been proud of having such a handsome sister. Her hair was a pretty colour, and now she was wearing it differently, not scraped up in that old way, but just tied back with a ribbon, she looked younger and not so much like a governess. She had on some sort of blue walking-skirt, with an inset of pleats at the side, secured neatly by a strap and button. She looked healthy, the outdoor sort of girl, which wasn't fashionable in London but was just the sort to take Burton's eye. Just as she'd taken Toby's. The sort who wouldn't insist on a chap dressing up in a stiff collar and white gloves, but be happy to go off and live in the country and take an interest in country pursuits.

In fact, she was even prettier than he remembered her. She looked different, somehow, more feminine. She'd lost that schoolroom air, even though she was in a temper at the moment. But he was used to that.

Jack chewed on his lower lip and cast about for a way round the rock wall of an obstacle she'd put up. His conscience didn't trouble him, he was far too self-centred for that, but he hadn't liked the way she'd spoken to him, or the things she'd said. It was all so blasted *unfair*! She'd had her chances. She could have had Toby, mutton-headed, muscle-bound chump that he was, but a generous, good-natured chap who'd have been a first-rate brother-in-law, never refusing to lend a chap a few guineas.

Casually, he asked, 'Where is Burton now? In Grindelwald, you say?'

'Yes—no. I mean, he went there last night, but he's gone climbing today.'

'Back here tomorrow?'

'Yes.' Verity caught her breath. 'Jack!'

'Oh, calm down!' He gave her his youthful, endearing smile, the one which melted old ladies' hearts and made them tell each other what a dear boy he was. 'I'm not going to play Cupid, for goodness' sake!'

*   *   *

'You see?' Karl Hable called down, after he had hammered one of the long masonry nails purchased in a Grindelwald ironmonger's store into the rock. 'I told you it was a good idea to bring these.'

Matt, several feet below him on the mountain face, grunted. They climbed on several feet more until Hable reached a narrow rock ledge, and there he perched, like a benign and happy mountain troll, waiting for his partner to come up and join him.

When Matt's head appeared, Hable said cheerfully, 'Lunch time!' and as Matt squeezed on to the ledge beside him, he broke a bar of chocolate in two and handed over one half courteously.

They munched on it, perched on their crag like a pair of eagles. Wisps of vapour floated past their noses. It was cold, clammy, and a sharp, unpleasant wind blew across the face of the mountain. The valley was lost in the mist. Matt craned his neck round at a seemingly impossible angle, and peered at the face above. The summit, too, was lost in a swirling, opaque veil.

'The weather is worsening by the minute, Karl. This muck blowing in our faces is part mist, part rain and part ice. In an hour everything will be soaked—clothes, boots, ropes. We'll be carrying dead weight. We'll get up there all right, but getting down again will be a dickens of a job, and neither of us wants to spend a night on the mountain. We should go down while we can still see a hand in front of our faces. Try again tomorrow.'

'Absolutely not!' argued Hable through his chocolate. 'I've been sitting around in Grindelwald for two weeks, waiting for you. All that time it was too warm and too dry, and look . . .' He tapped the rock behind him. 'It crumbles, flakes away. Now I get you up here, and the weather changes and the visibility is against us. I can't stay in Switzerland indefinitely. I have to go back to Vienna.'

'I don't *want* to turn back, Karli. I'm trying to be prudent. Another chance will come in two or three days. You can wait that long.'

'Ah,' said Hable darkly. 'By then you'll be too busy trying to make a conquest of Miss Lyndon, no doubt.'

'Unlikely,' Matt said dourly. 'And you needn't make me sound like a blasted Don Juan. What about you? Do you never have woman trouble?'

'I am engaged to be married,' the young lawyer said primly. 'There is a correct way and an incorrect way, and the incorrect way always gets you into trouble!'

'The same goes for mountains,' Matt said promptly. 'Bad conditions are the wrong way. We're going down!'

Before Hable could answer, there was a faint clatter from near at hand that made them both turn their heads sharply. A single stone rolled down the mountain face from above, out of the mist, and bounced off the rock into the void below. It was followed by a shower of small stones and grit. These increased until a hail of flying stones flew past their faces. Both men had scrambled to their feet, and were flattened against the rock-face, trying to protect themselves from the barrage of stones. At that moment a sound like the emptying of a large bucket of rubble echoed out of the mist above their heads, and Matt shouted the single warning, '*Rockfall!*'

'What do you mean, your *brother* is here?' Jessica said.

'I'm sorry, Contessa. I wasn't expecting him. He just arrived.'

'Well, he must amuse himself and not get under my feet. It's bad enough that I'm plagued by Renzo without I must have sundry relatives of yours appearing at every turn. Keep him out of my way.'

'You can be sure I'll do that!' thought Verity.

But, alas, it wasn't to be. When they went down to dinner, Jack was hovering by the dining-room door and, as luck would have it, the Frenshams also chose that moment to arrive. There was nothing for it. Verity had to introduce Jack all round.

Jessica deigned to recognise him, but remained cool. However, Jack was on his very best behaviour, and he knew how to be charming. He made such a favourable impression on the Frenshams that Sir Miles suggested amiably that they should all dine together.

They trooped into the dining-room and waited while the waiters hurriedly rearranged the tables to accommodate the larger party. Verity took the opportunity to give Jack a warning look, and, as they sat down, reinforced it by kicking his ankle just in case he should overlook her warning. But she needn't have worried. Jack was being pleasant, cheerful, obliging and engagingly modest. Lady Frensham had visibly warmed to him, and Sir Miles seemed to show a cautious approval.

A pang of misgiving touched Verity's heart. Whatever Jack did, it was disturbing. He was so untrustworthy that the more she saw him making a good impression, the greater the doubt in her mind as to his true intentions. He was a handsome young man, and this was the milieu he loved, among the rich. He was so totally at ease in this dining-room, and his relaxed gestures, his aristocratic features and diffident smile were all working their charm above the china and crystal. Several ladies at other tables were glancing curiously at the newcomer. Verity did not know it, but opinion was almost equally divided among them as to whether he was the heir to an English dukedom, or an Austro-Hungarian arch-duke, travelling incognito.

Jessica, to be true, ignored him completely and addressed her remarks exclusively to the Frenshams. Verity knew Jack must be disappointed, but she was glad to see it, all the same. The last thing needed to complicate an already complex situation was for Jack's charm to work its wiles on the Contessa. But Jessica was not likely to forget that the personable young man was her companion's brother, and by tomorrow, Verity was fairly sure, every other lady in the dining-room would know it, too. Jessica would see to that.

Dinner was nearing its conclusion, and Verity was already mentally giving thanks for its having passed off so uneventfully, when the Head Waiter appeared at Sir Miles's elbow and whispered confidentially into his ear.

It was a trivial incident, and not such a very unusual thing, but for some reason the sight of the Head Waiter's earnest face, and something indefinable in the man's manner, filled Verity's heart with a sense of foreboding. She tried to tell herself that the message could concern almost anything, from a corked wine to urgent telegrams from London, and there was no reason at all why it should concern Matt. Yet intuition whispered into her ear in a cold, certain little voice, 'It's Matt. It's bad news.'

Sir Miles nodded and looked up at the circle of silent faces watching him: Jessica's serene; Verity's pale and tense; his wife's—her instincts alerted by thirty years of marriage—calm, and prepared to take charge if need be, in whatever crisis had blown up; and lastly Jack's, curious and faintly wary.

Sir Miles crumpled his napkin and dropped it on the table. He stood up, bowed slightly and said, 'Excuse me for one moment, won't you? Someone is asking for me in the lobby.'

He walked out at an unhurried pace, as Jack whispered to his sister, 'What's up, Verity?'

She shook her head and pushed her plate away from her. Lady Frensham leaned across the table and said comfortingly, 'Whatever it is, dear, Miles will take care of it. I dare say it's only the Embassy, or the Admiralty, or some such body. They never think one is at dinner, but send their wretched telegrams at the most awkward times.'

Verity hardly heard her. The chatter round her seemed dulled and distant to her ear. The whole dining-room and its occupants were veiled in a gauze-like haze.

Sir Miles was coming back, his face serious. He put a comforting hand on Verity's shoulder, and although he addressed himself to Jessica, she knew his words were intended for her.

'Now, you are not to be alarmed, my dear. But Count Giulini has called to tell us that he has received a telephone call from an acquaintance in Grindelwald, to say that Matt and Herr Hable have not yet returned to the *Gasthaus* where they spent the night, although they were expected an hour ago. They are not yet seriously overdue, so don't take fright, but, of course, it's getting dark.'

Verity did not let him finish, but jumped up from the table, clutched her skirts in both hands and ran through the room, past the astonished diners. Jack muttered, 'Excuse me!' and hastened after her.

As she burst into the lobby, her eye fell on a young man in casual clothing and strong boots who was about to leave it. For a second she did not recognise the normally elegant, white-suited Renzo Giulini in this new guise, but then she called loudly in an anguished voice, 'Oh, please, Count, wait!'

Giulini spun round at the sound of her voice and hurried back, looking so different now in his well-worn jacket over a knitted pullover, and with his olive-complexioned face serious yet so kind. He grasped both her hands tightly in his.

'Dear signorina, you must not be afraid. Perhaps it is only a mistake, and some small matter has delayed them. But I am going up to Grindelwald myself now, and I will then know exactly what has happened, and if . . .'

He broke off, and eyed her apprehensively.

'Please,' Verity begged in a choked but tolerably controlled voice. 'Please tell me the truth.'

'I do not know the truth, signorina, believe me. Only that Matt and Hable have not returned, and a farmer from the pastures below the mountain came to Grindelwald to report seeing a large rockfall high on the mountain, and to ask if any climbers had been up there.'

'Avalanche?' Verity whispered, frozen with horror.

'A careful scrutiny of the mountain was made by telescope but, alas, the visibility was so poor that little could be seen,' Giulini went on. 'It does not mean that there has been an accident, but there is a possibility, of course, and I won't lie to you. If they don't return, I shall set out myself at daybreak tomorrow with a rescue party, to see if—if an injured man is to be brought down the mountain.'

Or a dead one, or two dead bodies . . . thought Verity. If they were lying helpless and injured now, how could they hope to survive a night of exposure on the mountainside?

Giulini raised her hands to his lips and kissed her fingers. 'Dear signorina, you will not lose heart. I swear it to you, I, Renzo Giulini, shall not give up until I am *sure*!'

Sure that no one remains alive to be brought down.

'Thank you,' Verity said quietly. 'Thank you, Count Giulini, and please take great care yourself. That you should be lost, too, is not what Matt would wish.'

He gave her a brief, taut smile, and hurried out of the door.

Inebnit, a small, disconsolate figure by the desk, said pessimistically, 'A man should not tempt his luck twice.'

Behind Verity, Jack drew in his breath and muttered, almost inaudibly, '*Damn!*'

She heard him, and she understood with a deep and

bitter disgust what his comment signified. He had begun to build his hopes on a possible liaison between his sister and Matthew Burton, and now it was probable that Matt Burton was dead.

Verity turned slowly round to face her brother, and hissed, 'Get out of my sight, Jack!'

In the face of so much scorn and anger, and the despair and wretchedness in her eyes, he did not even attempt a reply, but took himself off without a word.

CHAPTER ELEVEN

NOT CARING what Jack did, and unable to face returning to the sympathetic and curious stares in the dining-room, Verity ran upstairs to her own room and, shutting the door, leaned her burning forehead against the panels.

Much as he had wanted to climb, Matt had not been happy about the weather conditions. Why, oh why, had he not persuaded Karl Hable to wait another day? If Matt is dead, she thought now with harsh realism, what shall I do? I couldn't stay here in Switzerland, even if it means giving up my post. I couldn't bear to look out every morning and see the mountains, and remember how much Matt loved them . . . and how much I loved him. Because I do love him, and now there's no pretending otherwise.

Verity pushed herself away from the door, and went to open the windows to let in the breeze. But, at that moment, there came the sound of rapid steps outside in the corridor, and her door burst open as Jessica stormed in.

The Contessa was obviously in a towering rage. Her fine eyes gleamed viciously, her cheeks were flushed, and her bosom in the low-cut dinner-gown heaved with her rapid breath. The diamond pendant on the swell of her white breasts rose and fell, glittering in the electric light.

'Well, miss?' she demanded. 'And what is this be-haviour supposed to mean? Since when do you flounce away from the dinner table without *my* permission, and barricade yourself up here to sulk?'

Many things had happened since she had entered Jessica's employ, and Verity had withstood any number of snubs and criticisms, bouts of ill-humour and petty vindictiveness. But now, at this dreadful time, Jessica had taken the fatal step too far.

Verity met her eye and retorted, 'I'm sure the Frenshams understood. As to what *you* feel about it, Contessa, I neither know nor care! I am sure, however, that I don't need your permission to withdraw from company at a time like this.'

Jessica gasped, and then darted forward, her lovely face twisted and distorted with venom. 'You fast little hussy! So this is all because of Matt, is it? I suppose you fancy yourself in love with him? I knew it! I knew that self-contained, quaker-like exterior of yours was just a sham! Why, ever since that wretched day at the gorge, when you contrived that stupid accident, you've done nothing but throw yourself shamelessly in Matt's way. Perhaps you fancy he will be stimulated by high-motivated decency to offer you some sort of disinterested protection? Poor little Miss Lyndon,' Jessica went on mockingly, 'all alone in this cruel, cruel world! I think you'll find, my dear, that Matt's motives are far less high-principled. He was always a practical man, and will expect some tangible return for his investment!'

'As I listen to you,' Verity burst out, 'I begin to wonder if you aren't a little crazy. I was nearly *killed* at the gorge, for goodness' sake! How or why should I contrive such a thing?'

'Nevertheless, you've made it painfully clear to every single person in this hotel, including the Frenshams, that you've decided to imagine yourself in love with Matt and have set your cap at him accordingly. Running from the dining-room like that, *and* flinging yourself on Renzo's charity—I suppose you fancy Renzo might also fall to your charms and replace Matt, should he finally have broken his neck. Pah!' Jessica turned in a swirl and rustle of taffeta and sat down in the armchair. 'What men see in you, I can't imagine. You haven't the slightest bit of style. I suppose . . .' Jessica put her head on one side and surveyed her companion critically, 'I suppose you make them feel like knights in shining armour, rescuing a poor little damsel in distress!'

'I barely know Count Giulini!' Verity snapped.

'And Matt? How well do you *know* him?' Jessica retorted.

'Matt could be *dead*!' Verity cried in fury and pain. 'And you sit there and haven't expressed a word of anxiety about him. He is, or was, your lover! At one time you were even going to marry him!'

'Matt is married to the mountains!' Jessica said coolly. 'I found that out long ago, and now you're finding it out, Verity.' She gave her companion a cruel little smile. 'If the mountain has finally claimed him, there's a poetic justice in it. I'm not going to shed tears for Matthew Burton. Of course I regret his loss—if he *is* lost. But I have one consolation, Verity dear, and that is, if he's fallen victim to an avalanche, at least, try whatever tricks you like, you'll never have him now. So you'll have to turn your attentions elsewhere, and try to capture some-one else. There's young Bernard, but he's coughing his lungs up. However, there's plainly money in the family, and he might just *marry* you—which is what you're really after, isn't it? I've been watching you—and watch-ing poor Matt grow more and more frustrated at your continuing virtuous refusals. But if you think that simply saying "No" is going to prompt him to offer marriage, you are very wrong. He's too shrewd, and too fond of his liberty. And if Matt's gone, and you decide to try for Renzo, you haven't a chance. *He* will marry to keep the aristocratic blood-line pure. All those continental noble families breed with one another, like racehorses. That's why they're riddled with all manner of inherited weakness and disease, including certifiable insanity! No, your best choice is Bernard, because he's a sick man, and sick men tend to act rashly. With him you may just achieve what you want, Verity!'

Verity pressed her lips tightly together, walked briskly across the room to the astonished Contessa, and stooping, slapped her roundly on one rouged cheek, the crack echoing in the room.

Jessica recoiled before the blow slightly, but made no reply. Perhaps she was simply too astonished.

'Someone should have done that long ago,' Verity told her. 'I regret it's had to be me, but I won't stand by and be insulted, and certainly, Contessa, not by a hard-hearted, vicious-tongued and petty-minded woman like you!'

'You'll pay for that,' Jessica whispered hoarsely in a voice totally unlike any Verity had heard her use before. 'You little slut, you'll pay—see if you don't!'

'I'm not impressed by your threats, Contessa,' Verity told her. 'And I'm more than glad that our association is now at an end.'

Jessica rose slowly to her feet, the marks of Verity's fingers still clearly visible on her skin. 'If and when you cease to be employed by me, Miss Lyndon, *I* shall inform you of the fact,' she said icily. 'You undertook to make this Swiss visit with me, and I hold you to your undertaking. I have *no* intention of releasing you so that you may run round defaming my character and behaving as you wish. You remain my companion, until I dismiss you as such. In the meantime, you will conduct yourself in a suitable manner. You will cease mooning over Matthew Burton. You will pack that attractive but worthless brother back to England, and you will have no further contact with Renzo Giulini. And, incidentally, I dare say he's asked you to help him recover my jewellery. In future you will not have access to my jewel-box. I've learned that, while I was recently indisposed, Princess Detkine's ring was discovered in this room—*your* room!' Jessica indicated the room in which they stood. 'Light-fingered servants are a bane, and I cannot be taking risks with my own valuables!'

'I have taken nothing!' Verity said furiously. 'And how the ring got here is a mystery. Nor am I a servant!'

'I pay you—it's the same thing,' Jessica shrugged.

Verity drew a deep breath. 'No one, except you, has even suggested that I stole the Princess's ring.'

'I really have no interest, Verity, in whether you took the wretched thing or not. But until we know who *did*, you seem to be the most likely candidate, and I shall take care of my own jewels myself, out of simple prudence. You may tell Renzo that.'

Verity walked to the door and opened it wide. 'You've spoken your mind, Contessa. I've no intention of listening to any more. I'd be obliged if you'd leave.'

Jessica rose, appeared about to speak, but then apparently changed her mind at the warlike gleam in Verity's eye. She swept past her companion and out.

Verity undressed slowly and climbed into bed. She was emotionally drained and physically exhausted, but she was sure she would not sleep. However, nothing would be gained by sitting up. Count Giulini would do all that could be done, and with this poor consolation, she switched off the light. For a long time she twisted on the creased pillows, seeing Matt's face before her in the darkness, recalling every word of his and every touch, and whispering his name aloud into the night.

Exhaustion overtook her at last, and she fell into a restless doze in which her brain, still feverishly active, threw up a series of jumbled pictures, as if a magic-lantern show had gone crazy and muddled all the scenes which should have been in a logical sequence. Now they

appeared as tormented nonsense, which her mind tried
in vain to sort into some kind of order. In a wild dream,
faces flickered out of the gloom, and voices called to her:
Alain's impudent smile, which turned into Major Stein's
array of gold teeth, Lady Frensham wearing her ostrich-
feather hat and Jessica's cold beauty. Jewellery, in
glittering heaps, lay scattered around, while she tried to
gather it up all in vain, and Renzo stood by, shaking his
head sorrowfully. Voices called to her, and eerie sounds
echoed in the darkness. Finally she heard Matt's own
voice, calling, 'Verity? Verity!'

'Verity!' The voice sounded near at hand and very
real, whispering urgently into her ear. A hand was
shaking her shoulder.

She came awake and gave a gasp. It must have been
just on dawn, and a faint grey light was beginning to
permeate the gloom. A figure knelt by the bedside, and
bent over her. She struggled upright, stretching out her
hand, and her fingers touched the unshaven stubble on a
man's chin. She whispered 'Matt?' incredulously, and
then 'Oh, *Matt*!' and threw both arms tightly around him
and burst into tears.

'Don't, Verity . . .' His voice sounded extraordinarily
weary, and his hand fumbled at her hair. 'Don't cry,
come on, please . . .'

She forced back her sobs and whispered, 'I thought
you were *dead*. Giulini said there had been an avalanche
on the mountain, and you and Karl hadn't come back.
Oh, Matt, I was so frightened. Are you really all
right?'

'Yes, rockfall,' Matt said in a tired voice. 'All that dry
weather . . . I—I'm all right.'

His voice gave her the clue. She froze in his arms and
asked, hardly daring, 'And Karl?'

'Injured—not dead. I had to bring him down. It took a
devil of a long time. When we got nearly down, Giulini

and a rescue party with lanterns, searching the base of the mountain, found us both.'

'How badly hurt is he?'

'Split his head and cracked some ribs . . . Smashed his left hand and has lost a couple of fingers.'

'But—But he'll recover?' She had not understood the implication of what he had told her.

Matt said, in a suddenly fierce voice, 'You don't understand, Verity! Karl has lost two fingers, and perhaps three! Don't you realise what it means to a climber to lose fingers—the grip of one hand? It means he never climbs again! What good is a climber without his hands?'

'Yes, of course . . .' Verity whispered, appalled. 'I wasn't thinking.' She stretched up her own hand and brushed it consolingly over his cropped hair. 'I'm so sorry, truly.'

'Well, that's the way it goes,' Matt said resignedly. 'I wanted to get him down alive—he's got a girl in Prague and is getting married in the autumn . . .'

'*She* won't be sorry he'll never climb again,' thought Verity. 'Whoever she is, Hable's girl, she would never have asked him to give it up, and she'll share his grief, now it's forced on him—but she'll be glad he won't ever run the risk again.'

She could see the faintest outline of Matt's face and features in the lightening dawn. They looked harsh and drawn, unutterably weary.

He muttered hoarsely, 'Giulini said you were worried . . . so I came back. I wanted to tell you myself that it was all right.' Suddenly he threw his arms round her and clasped her to him. 'Oh God, Verity, I thought, if we didn't get down, I wouldn't ever see you again!'

'But it's all right now,' she whispered. 'It's all right now, my darling. You're here, with me . . .'

Matt expelled his breath in a long sigh and released

her, throwing himself back on the pillows beside her. After a moment he murmured indistinctly, 'I'm all in . . .' and, after that, neither moved nor spoke.

'Matt?' Verity whispered, after a few moments, bending over his apparently insensible form.

Deep, even breathing was the only reply. He had simply fallen asleep from exhaustion, passing effortlessly into unconsciousness. Verity hesitated. She could try and wake him, but it might not be easy. On the other hand, he couldn't stay here, until the chambermaid came with the hot water in the morning. She compromised. He might wake of his own accord, as easily and suddenly as he had dropped off, in a half-hour or so. She pulled the coverlet over him and lay down beside him, aware now how much the waiting and worrying had drained her mentally and physically. Despite intending to stay awake, she fell asleep, too.

The tap of the chambermaid on the door, signifying the arrival of the hot water, awoke Verity later in the morning, and sent her scrambling out of bed and to the door before the girl could open it.

'Thank you—please, just leave it outside!'

She waited until the girl's footsteps could be heard retreating, and then opened the door cautiously, just enough to drag the water-jug inside. She carried it to the wash-stand, and looked over to the bed.

Matt was still fast asleep, sprawled in a tangle of crumpled bedclothes. She didn't want to wake him, but was afraid that Lady Frensham might take it into her head to call and ask after Verity. For all her kindness, discovering Matt Burton in her protégée's bed was not calculated to call forth favourable comment from that capable matron.

Verity called out softly, 'Matt!' and put her hand on his shoulder. When he didn't answer, she gave him a quite hefty shove, but she might just as well have pushed at a marble slab. He only muttered in his sleep and twisted away from her, rolling over and dragging the pillow with him, over his head. It was hopeless. Not only would it be difficult to wake him, it seemed almost cruel. Verity sighed and went back to the wash-stand to make her own toilet, and to dress. When she had finished, she bent over Matt's recumbent form again, but he was still slumbering soundly.

'My goodness, he does need a shave,' she thought, quite irrelevantly. 'I wonder he doesn't grow a beard.'

Each room was thoughtfully provided with a printed card that said 'Please Do Not Disturb' in three languages. Verity let herself out of the room, closed the door softly, and hung the notice prominently on the handle. Then she went down to breakfast.

'Ah, Fräulein Lyndon!' exclaimed Inebnit as she appeared at the foot of the stairs. 'Such good news! Mr Burton has returned, very early this morning, while it was still dark. He is not hurt. But there was an accident, alas, and the other gentleman was injured.'

'Thank you, Herr Inebnit,' Verity said. 'I'm—very pleased to hear Mr Burton is safe.'

'Such good fortune,' Inebnit said severely. 'He has indeed been most lucky. But my staff and I are all very happy to see him safe.'

The Frenshams were at breakfast, but Jack was nowhere to be seen; nor Jessica. Verity greeted them before either could speak, and said hastily, 'I've just seen Inebnit!'

'Got the glad news, eh?' said Sir Miles heartily. 'Blessed fellow gave us all the fright of our lives. I've told him it's time he thought about giving it all up and leaving it to younger fellows. All's well that ends well, I suppose. Pity about young Hable.'

'Yes . . .' Verity glanced about the dining-room.

'You haven't seen my brother this morning, by any chance?'

Both shook their heads. 'Probably sleeping in,' said Sir Miles. 'Turn up for lunch, I don't doubt.'

Jack had not slept in, but breakfasted in his room. He had no intention of seeking out his sister just yet, not until he had formulated his plans, and she'd had time to cool down. At the moment, he'd just get sent off with a flea in his ear if he so much as said 'Good morning' to her.

Jack went out on his balcony, his breakfast finished, and an attempted badinage with the maid who took the tray away doomed to failure through lack of a common language. Alone, and oblivious of the splendid view, he lit a cigarette. The weather was better, he was aware of that, and he was pleased. A good clear day brightened up the whole atmosphere of the place and put everyone in a better mood. With luck, the news the Italian fellow had brought last night would prove to be only a wild rumour. The chances were that Burton would turn up, safe and sound. The chap was built like a rock crag himself, and Jack could not imagine that he could be easily despatched into the next world.

One thing of which he was certain was that whatever Verity had *said* to him yesterday, the plain fact was that she cared about Burton, and was even in love with him. She wouldn't have carried on the way she had the night before if she weren't.

Jack felt a momentary stir of an emotion akin to jealousy, and it was mixed with alarm. Of course, he'd been urging her for years to try and catch the eye of someone like Burton, but now that it had really happened, he didn't feel entirely pleased. He hadn't reckoned on her actually falling in love. Until now, for all his imperfections and her frequent scoldings, he knew he'd been the only man in her life, the only one for whom she cared. Now it was different. She cared for Burton, and probably far more than for Jack. Hence his jealousy, and his unease. Until now, he'd always played on the strength of her affection for him, knowing that, however badly he behaved and however angry she was, he'd win her round in the end. Now he could no longer be sure of that.

It all depended on Burton. If Verity cared about the fellow, and if Burton was still interested, despite lack of encouragement, some arrangement might yet be arrived at, beneficial to all three of them. He would give Verity time to have her breakfast and get back to her room, and then he'd go along, eat humble pie, wheedle her into forgiving his stupid lapse last night, and see if he couldn't talk her into reconsidering Burton's advances. Hang it all, they'd never get another chance like this one, and he wasn't going to let it go; certainly not just because Verity had principles!

Jack, who had never been troubled with principles, had never understood how they could influence anyone else. So it was that, a little while later, when he judged Verity would have finished her breakfast and returned upstairs to prepare herself for whatever the morning's activities were to be, he set out for his sister's room. As he approached it along the corridor, he saw the 'Please Do Not Disturb' notice hanging on the door, and paused to consider what it meant. Verity was no slug-a-bed, and unlikely to be sleeping. The notice had certainly been put there, in a fit of pique, to keep him, Jack, away. Jack scowled and his mouth set obstinately. She must have got over her anger by now, and he would show her that he wasn't to be got rid of by means of a cardboard notice. He approached the door with a brisk step and stretched out his hand to knock.

Even as he did, there was a click, and it swung open,

and Matthew Burton stepped out into the corridor. For a second the two men stared at one another, then Jack, all colour drained from his face and his mouth hanging open in surprise, exclaimed faintly, 'You!' A little foolishly, he added, 'You're back, then!'

Immediately his brain sprang into feverish activity. Burton hadn't been involved in any accident. The Italian had told them a pack of nonsense. The mountaineer had returned, and gone straight to Verity's room. The 'Please Do Not Disturb' notice told the rest of the story. Jack almost whistled aloud in disbelief. To think that he'd been taken in by Verity's protestations, when all along . . . But Burton had foolishly allowed himself to be caught here, by his mistress's brother, and Jack was determined Burton wouldn't get out of it easily, not without paying a high price. And he himself was in a position to name that price—now!

Jack drew himself up and demanded stiffly, 'Where is my sister?'

'Not in there, if that's what you're thinking,' Burton said. He turned and reopened the door behind him.

Jack pushed past him unceremoniously into the room and stopped, baffled, at finding it empty. There was no sign of Verity—but the tumbled bed was still unmade, and Burton, who had followed him back into the room and shut the door behind them, had an unshaven, just-out-of-bed look about him.

'Sir,' Jack said loudly. 'I should like an explanation of your presence in my sister's room!'

A glow of triumph spread over him, and he had to fight to prevent the glee from sounding in his voice. He had Burton trapped. What would the fellow do? Try and deny everything, or come up with some feeble excuse? To Jack's considerable discomfiture, Matt did neither.

'Would you, indeed?' he said mildly. 'Well, lad, you're not going to get one.'

Jack flushed angrily, but hesitated. Burton was several inches taller, quite a few pounds heavier, and considerably fitter than he was. Nor did the mild tone deceive him. A sleeping leopard presents a relaxed, even indolent air. It is not on that account to be discounted as harmless. What was more, Burton stood between Jack and the door.

'Verity is my sister!' he began. 'I didn't come along here expecting to find *you*! You can't expect me not to ask why you're here.'

'I'd expect most brothers to ask,' Matt agreed. 'But not *you*, Jack, my boy.' He sat down and surveyed him with his sharp blue eyes, which made Jack shuffle his feet uneasily on the carpet, and recalled horribly to his mind his days at school when he'd been summoned before the headmaster. 'Since when,' asked Matt in that same mild, dangerous tone, 'have you had such a deep concern for your sister's welfare, or care twopence what she did?'

'Now, look here . . .' Jack began hoarsely.

'No!' The mild tone had vanished, and the voice was curt, angry and brooked no opposition. 'You listen to me. You haven't lifted a finger to look after your sister for years. You're a useless young layabout and a smooth-tongued trickster. I'd tell you you ought to be ashamed of yourself, but you haven't sufficient intelligence or natural decency for that. So don't ask me *my* business!'

Jack ran his tongue along his dry lips and cast about for a new approach. 'All right, fair enough!' he said —and the reply was unexpected enough to make Matt raise his eyebrows in surprise, and wait in silence for his next words.

A measure of confidence returned to Jack, and showed in his face, manner and voice. He felt he had regained some of the initiative he had lost at the beginning of their conversation.

'See here, I'm not asking you your business. Nor am I going to accuse you of ruining Verity or any nonsense like that. Verity's old enough to know what she's doing. But, looking at it frankly—man to man . . .'

Matt's bushy eyebrows met in an incipient scowl, but Jack ignored the warning signal.

'The decent thing to do would be to put it all on some sort of regular basis. I don't mean marriage, of course. I'm not naïve enough to think you'd find that idea acceptable—dare say your family wouldn't wear it, either. But, well, there are alternative arrangements.'

His voice died away, and a note of uncertainty echoed in the final word. He didn't much care for the way Burton was looking at him.

'I ought to punch you on the jaw,' Matt said calmly, and Jack took a hasty step out of reach. 'I would do—if I hadn't already made such a suggestion to Verity which, thank God, she turned down! Someone ought to have been on hand *then* to take a crack at me. Damn it, boy, if you had an ounce of spunk, you'd do it now!' Matt's voice grew louder in irritation.

'Now, look!' Jack said hastily. 'I'm not one for fisticuffs . . .'

Matt stared at him with undisguised contempt. 'I'll bet you're not! You reckon to talk your way out of trouble. But, this time, you've talked your way into it. You miserable, conniving little coward—I ought to thrash you, but I can't be bothered. Right!' Matt got to his feet and towered over Jack, who scurried to the door. 'Now I'll tell you something you won't like to hear, but which you'd better listen to carefully. Your days of sponging off your sister are over; finished for good, do you hear me? If I ever find you've taken so much as a shilling off her in future, you'll have me to deal with, do you understand? I'm not a kindly, soft-hearted fellow, so you won't be able to bamboozle me as you have done

that poor girl for years. I say this, in case you're entertaining the wild idea that *I* might be a soft touch for the
occasional loan. *You* are going back to England. There's
a train timetable downstairs. Ask Inebnit. I'll give you a
letter to a friend of mine in London who may be able to
offer you a job. If he does—take it, and stick to it, Jack
my boy. Believe me, it's the first and last piece of help
you're going to get from me.'

Jack stared at him wildly, like a trapped animal. 'I owe
Toby Cavendish fifty . . .' He broke off.

'I'll pay it—and you can pay me back over the period
of a year.'

'W—What are you going to do now?' Jack faltered,
as the mountaineer's burly form moved purposefully
towards him.

Matt rubbed his bristly chin. 'I'm going to get myself
a shave, lad,' he said, and walked out, leaving Jack
dumbfounded.

Verity had chosen not to return to her room, leaving
Matt time to awaken and vacate it before she ventured
near it again. She could not help wondering if he would
remember, among other things, the term of endearment
that had escaped her in her joy at seeing him safe.
However, later in the morning, as she was hurrying
along the corridor, she heard Matt call her name. She
stopped with a bundle of the newly arrived English
newspapers in her arms, and waited for him to join
her.

For a man who had had a near-miraculous escape on
the mountain, he looked remarkably hale and hearty.
He'd bathed and shaved and changed his clothes, and
only a purple bruise above one eye, and hands scraped
raw, betrayed his narrow brush with death. He took her
firmly by the arm and said purposefully, 'Come along to
the Frenshams' sitting-room.'

'Jessica's waiting for the papers and the post,' Verity said.

'Jessica can wait! It will do her no harm.'

The sitting-room was empty, and rather wishing one or both of the Frenshams was there, she sat on the very edge of a chair and waited for Matt to speak.

He sprawled back on the sofa and spread out his arms in a comfortable way. 'Why didn't you wake me up and throw me out?' he asked without preamble.

'You were so tired.' Verity avoided his eye. Remembering the agonising hours of waiting and not-knowing through which she had passed, she exclaimed, 'I—*We* were all so worried about you!'

'To tell you the truth, I was pretty worried myself for a bit,' he admitted wryly.

Verity said sadly, 'Poor Herr Hable.'

'Yes.' Matt paused. He leaned forward, resting his arms on his knees and clasping his hands loosely in the way she knew so well. Then he said, 'I've seen Jack.'

Verity's heart plummeted. It was inevitable that the two men should meet, but she'd hoped to keep them apart a little longer.

'I wasn't expecting him,' she said dully. 'He cadged a ride in Toby Cavendish's new motor-car.'

'Young Toby has a motor? Fellow's got more money than sense. What were you planning to do, Verity?'

'You mean, about Jack? I don't know. He depends on me. He always has.'

Matt studied his scratched and scraped fingers and broken nails with elaborate unconcern. 'Actually, the lad's decided to go back home.'

'He's *what*?' Verity stared at him, open-mouthed. 'Oh, if only he would! But you're wrong, Matt. He won't go, not yet anyway.'

'I do assure you I left him consulting the railway

timetable back to London.' He saw her eyebrows pucker as she puzzled over this.

'But what made him change his mind?'

'Oh, I think he realises that this isn't the best place for him to be.'

'It's your doing, Matt,' Verity said frankly, 'and I do thank you, but . . .' She paused and bit her lip before bursting out, 'You didn't lend him any money, did you? Because you won't get it back!'

He grinned at her, the chipped tooth gleaming. 'Won't I just? I'm not so stupid, my dear, that I'd put ready cash into young Jack's slippery fingers! I'll pay young Toby the fifty Jack borrowed, and Jack will pay me back a little at a time. It's arranged. An acquaintance of mine will give Jack a job in London, and I'll make sure he sticks it out. Well, look a trifle more cheerful about it than that! I thought you'd be pleased.'

'I am pleased, Matt, and grateful—but, most of all, I'm pleased you're safe. Nothing seems important compared to that, not my troubles, anyway.'

'Ah? Something happened while I was away?'

'I had a quarrel with Jessica,' she admitted, 'about —well, never mind—but I'm afraid I hit her.' She eyed him a little apprehensively.

'You did what?' he exclaimed incredulously, and then burst out laughing.

'She was so horrid and I was so worried . . . Despite that, she refuses to let me go, and I'll have to stay here in Switzerland with her.'

'Hmm,' he said, frowning. 'That's a pity—because I'm more than anxious you should leave.' He saw a shadow pass over her face, and went on, 'Perhaps there's something I should tell you. Accidents can always happen on the mountain, and this one was unforeseen. But someone took great care to ensure that if we had an accident, it would be a bad one. The reason Karl was so

much more badly hurt than I was that the rope broke
when it should have held him. I brought the rope back,
and this morning I examined it. It was frayed—and not
through wear and tear. Someone had made a good job of
weakening it. I checked that rope myself a few days
back, so whoever did it, did it just before we went up to
Grindelwald.'

'You're thinking of Alain again, aren't you?' Verity
said quickly.

'The rope and my other equipment lay unattended in
the lobby for the best part of an hour. Anyone passing
through could have tampered with it easily enough. Our
spy friends want me out of the way—and you, too,
Verity, perhaps.'

Verity jumped up and exclaimed energetically, 'Matt,
I have to know who those people are! I know you suspect
Alain, but you're not sure and you have no proof. I want
to trust him, but I have to listen to you. It leaves me so
confused that I don't know what to do, or what to think.
It was because I was so unsure and suspicious that up
there, on the Harder Kulm, I was ready to believe for a
moment that even poor Alain might do me some harm!
I've *got* to find out the true identity of these—these
agents of yours. I have to find proof!'

'With a little luck, after tonight, we'll have proof,'
Matt said calmly. He stretched and grunted as sore
muscles protested. 'Keep it to yourself, but Sir Miles and
I have set up a little trap with the aid of Inebnit. It's an
outside chance, but keep your fingers crossed, and our
quarry may just walk into it.'

'How do you mean?' she asked.

He hesitated imperceptibly, but then explained,
'Well, our friends think themselves safe. They don't yet
know we might be on to anyone of their real identities.
Oh, Alain Bernard may think I suspect him of being
light-fingered in the way of other people's jewellery, but

he has no reason to suppose I yet connect him with the *Dreadnought* papers. In fact, if I think his interest is in the jewels, that would seem to leave him in the clear. As for—as for his accomplices, as far as *they* are concerned, that's a total mystery to us. Sir Miles received an important coded telegram today. It's a dummy, of course, faked by our Embassy. Never mind, Sir Miles has stashed it in Inebnit's safe, and it's my belief our agents will try to get their hands on it. They'll want at least to read it, take note of its contents and send them off to Berlin for decoding. I think the prize is so great that they'll take the risk tonight. They can't leave it later, in case Sir Miles sees fit to dispose of the telegram tomorrow.'

'But how will they know it's there—that Sir Miles has received it?'

Matt gave her a dry smile. 'I've taken care of that —but I won't tell you how, until I see how things turn out! If I'm being a complete fool, I'd rather you didn't know it. I'll be hidden downstairs tonight. Inebnit has kindly organised the emptying of a conveniently located broom-cupboard. You'll see, our friends will put in an appearance. I fancy the night clerk is in for another sound sleep!'

'I want to be there,' Verity stated.

He shook his grizzled head. 'Not a chance! These people are dangerous, for goodness' sake. If they're cornered, they'll do anything to break out—and that includes kill.'

'They might kill you,' she said soberly. 'They failed on the mountain, but they can try again.'

'I shall be armed, and I hope to have the advantage of surprise.'

Verity shook her head obstinately. 'You must understand, Matt. I have to be there and see the truth for myself. If—If it is Alain, I want to know. I'm coming too.' She tilted her chin defiantly. 'Anyway, you can't stop me! I shall come downstairs and hide.'

'All right,' he acquiesced. 'So I'll take you spy-hunting with me. But you'll be under *my* orders, my girl, and you'll do exactly as I say!' He eyed her shrewdly. 'No arguing or trying out any little plan of your own! I'll call at your room around eleven-thirty. People will be going to bed. Jessica will probably have shut the door against Renzo. If you're not averse to being shut up in a broom-cupboard with me for an hour or two, be ready. It's going to be hot and uncomfortable, and you're going to have to put up with my close proximity.' A grin tugged at the corner of his mouth. 'But it won't be worse than having me sprawled out all over your bed!'

Rain had set in later, when Matt tapped at Verity's door, monotonous heavy rain, which made the hotel and its occupants seemed as enclosed and beleaguered as Noah's Ark. The establishment was already in darkness and slumbering as they made their stealthy way down the stairs. Princess Detkine's snores reverberated gently along the corridor of the second floor, and the Spitz squeaked and twitched in his sleep, reliving in his dreams an encounter with the hotel cat.

'The lift is still out of order,' Verity whispered.

'I should hope so!' he returned, 'after all the trouble I took to put it out of service! We are hunting rats, you and I, When you flush out their nest, you block up their bolt-holes first. Once our quarry goes into that office and opens the safe—there will be no escape.'

He had certainly been right about the cramped quarters afforded by the broom-cupboard. Verity was pressed against his muscular frame in an unwished proximity, which she hoped would not give him any ideas. But she had overlooked his determination to see through the task he'd set himself. The breaking of the spy-ring alone occupied his thoughts. He settled himself in a corner to wait with a seemingly endless patience, which she tried, none too successfully, to imitate.

Her legs ached, her back ached, her neck had a crick in it. The air was warm and stuffy and smelled of wax polish, dust and dirty wash-rags. Time seemed to have no meaning, as if they'd been there years and still had years to wait. Claustrophobia overcame her, and she fell to wondering if this was what those condemned to be walled up alive in the Middle Ages had felt, only far, far worse for them. Packed against him like this, in the darkness, she remembered how he had held her that night he'd climbed through her balcony windows. That, too, seemed so long ago now, and so much had happened in between. Would they really solve the mystery tonight?

Unwarily, she moved slightly, trying to ease her cramped muscles, and Matt's hand tightened warningly on her arm. But then she heard it, a faint sound from outside in the lobby. Someone had come downstairs and was moving about.

The lobby clock had struck midnight, it seemed an eternity ago, and now, without warning, it struck one, so loudly and clearly that Verity started. The butterflies already fluttering about her stomach turned to a cold, hard, nauseating grip of fear. This was the reality. Whoever was out there had the capacity to be a killer.

The lobby clock's metal voice faded. The person was near the desk. She could imagine whoever it was, stooping over the unfortunate night clerk in his drugged slumbers, and checking that he was insensible. There was a creak of a hinge. Someone had gone into Inebnit's office.

Verity shook Matt's arm, wondering why he didn't dash out and apprehend the intruder, but he breathed almost inaudibly into her ear, 'Let them open the safe . . .'

The two or three minutes seemed interminable. But, at last, Matt gave the door of the cupboard a little push. It opened easily on its newly-oiled hinges (another contribution by Inebnit to the night's work), and they stepped out of their prison into the further dark.

With difficulty, Verity's eyes adjusted to the gloom. The window curtains were drawn, muffling the rain-drops beating against the panes. Only moonlight filtered in, through the glass panel above the main doors. A feeble light gleaming on the mezzanine of the staircase did little but illuminate the immediate treads beneath it.

The night clerk's head was pillowed peacefully on his arm, and the door of Inebnit's office stood ajar, a faint yellow glow showing beneath it. Matt and Verity approached cautiously and Matt put out his hand to signal her to keep back, and out of a possible line of fire.

Then he threw open the door of the office. Verity had the barest glimpse of the figure crouching by the safe, a slim, boyish figure in a jacket and trousers with a tweed cap pulled down over its face, obscuring the features. Then the figure doused the lamp by its side and they were all left in darkness.

'The light switch!' Matt exclaimed, and Verity fumbled desperately for the switch inside the door. Her frantic fingers found it, and pressed. Nothing happened. She tried again.

Matt, in the darkness, was grappling with the intruder and seemed to have fallen over some piece of furniture. He was cursing loudly.

Verity gasped, 'The electricity's failed again!'

As she spoke, the intruder tore free of Matt's grasp and bolted towards the door, cannoning into Verity, who blocked it. Both recoiled, half-winded, and then the intruder leapt at her. Verity tried to hold on, and at the same time defend herself. Her fingers closed on a sleeve, but it was torn from her grasp.

Now they were all out in the lobby, hunters and pursued, by the stairwell. The night seemed full of fists and squirming bodies.

'Someone's thrown the ruddy main switch!' Matt gasped, from somewhere near at hand. She heard him moving by the stairwell, seeking the main electric switch located beneath it.

At the same time Verity heard a scrabbling by the hotel's main doors. The intruder was attempting to make an escape. She had no time to pause and think. She threw herself forward and flung her arms round the slim form. The other whirled with a low snarl, and a set of steel-strong fingers clasped Verity's throat.

She tried to wrench her assailant's arms away, but the fingers maintained their murderous grip with a frenzied strength. The pressure on her windpipe was unbearable. Noises buzzed in her head, and coloured lights flashed before her eyes. She knew she was being slowly and remorselessly strangled, the life squeezed out of her. Alain, she thought despairingly, was finishing the job he had lacked the courage to do on the Harder Kulm. It was her last conscious thought. The coloured lights, the pain, the remorseless pressure and the pounding of the blood in her ears increased until blackness enveloped her.

Without warning, a light brighter than all pierced the black veil. The murderous hands around her throat were torn away. Verity staggered back and fell to the ground, drawing deep, rasping, pain-wracked breaths through her bruised throat. She could hear Matt's voice, seeming to come from a great distance, calling desperately, 'Verity, Verity! Dear heaven . . .'

The mist cleared. The light remained, because it was the electric light which he'd managed to restore. Verity, sitting on the floor of the lobby, opened her eyes to see

Matt's worried face leaning over her, and his strong arms were supporting her.

'Verity?' he gasped anxiously. 'For pity's sake, are you all right?'

She managed to nod, and then her gaze, as it cleared, fell on the huddled form in the tweed cap by the door. 'Oh, Alain,' she croaked hoarsely, the words tearing at her bruised throat. 'How could you . . .?'

Matt, following her gaze, said wearily, 'No, *not* Alain. *He's* over there by the stairs, unconscious. Sorry, Verity, I had to knock him out. I didn't like doing it to a sick man, but he was between me and the main switch, which he'd thrown to help *that one* escape.'

He took his arm from Verity's shoulders and got to his feet to walk over to the huddled figure by the door.

'But who is it?' Verity whispered painfully.

Matt stooped and caught at the tweed cap, tearing it off. The mass of ash-blond hair, which had been piled beneath it, fell down in tangled curls.

'Oh, Jessica,' Matt said sadly. 'Did you really think that, once I had begun to suspect, I'd ever let up till I could prove it?'

CHAPTER TWELVE

'WELL,' MATT said, 'our conspirators are under lock and key, but for how long is another matter. Jessica has engaged a good lawyer, and the German Embassy has already sent along a gentleman with a walrus moustache and duelling scars, loudly demanding Alain Bernard's release.'

'Major Stein,' Verity said knowledgeably. 'We've met.'

Matt heaved a sigh of exasperation. 'I wish you'd tell me these things, Verity, and not try and manage everything yourself! The most irritating thing is that we still don't know the whereabouts of the *Dreadnought* papers. Jessica denies all knowledge, and treats us with all the injured disdain Marie-Antoinette had for her gaolers. Alain Bernard appears to find the whole thing amusing. Your acquaintance with the duelling scars was most irate when it was suggested *he* might know anything about it. The culprit is not likely to own up, and they seem to have disappeared. Perhaps the Admiral of the Atlantic is already studying them over his breakfast coffee?'

He shrugged, and added, 'As for your friend Alain, the Swiss government is anxious to preserve its neutrality and privately would probably be more than content to turn over Bernard to the Prussian Junker. To be honest,' Matt admitted in a burst of candour, 'I'd prefer it, too. The lad should be in a good sanatorium, and a prison hospital would be no substitute.'

'I want to see him,' Verity said quietly.

Matt shook his head and murmured, 'No, Verity, don't do that to him. He really cared for you. It's the one thing about which he didn't lie. Remember him, as a friend. It's what he would wish.'

'Remember . . . this drawing . . . The rest is rotten . . .'

Verity looked down at her tightly clasped hands, and asked soberly, '*Did* he put the ring in my room?'

'No, Jessica did—and for reasons quite unconnected with the *Dreadnought* papers, after all. My mistake. I knew it had been done deliberately, but didn't realise why.' Matt looked faintly embarrassed. 'Jessica was jealous of you. She was hiding out on the balcony the night I—foolishly outlined a certain proposition to you, which you, quite rightly, refused. She saw us, and she thought . . . Well, Jessica's a woman who gives up nothing to which she believes herself entitled, by right, neither the Giulini heirlooms, nor me.' He drew a deep breath and hurried on, 'Alain was furious about it. He knew she'd done it, because she'd taken the ring from him. But she'd shut herself up in her bedroom that day, and he couldn't get at her to force the truth out of her, or her reasons.'

Verity thought she could understand his exasperation.

'By the way, when I saw young Bernard, he was very insistent that *you* should have his folder of sketches. He said you'd take care of them properly. He was quite agitated about it. I suppose his art means a great deal to him. He insisted I go to his room immediately I returned to the hotel, collect his sketch-folder before anyone else got to it, and put it personally in your hands. I was to tell you that it's his parting gift. I brought it along and put it somewhere. Ah, here it is . . .'

Matt, who had been looking about him in the Frenshams' sitting-room, retrieved Alain's folder from the table and handed it over to her.

Verity took it in silence. It was such a familiar object, and conjured up a picture of Alain as clearly as if he'd stood here before her, in this room, in his linen jacket and battered hat, a cigarette in his fingers and his eyes screwed up against the light as he studied his subject. She smoothed the surface of it with the flat of her hand, and said soberly, 'If you should see him again, please thank him, and—and tell him, I'll always take the greatest care of it. I—know what it represents to him.'

She looked up at Matt, and exclaimed emotionally, 'He could have been a great artist, truly! Why? Why did he throw it all away? And for a country he doesn't even consider his own.'

Matt nodded. 'Yes, a pity. The cards were pretty well stacked against him, though. He didn't lack money, and might have made more of an effort if he had done. But he's the son of well-to-do, indulgent and generous parents, one of those attractive, sickly children whom people pet and spoil. He never learned sufficient self-discipline to harness his talent into something. You know the sort of thing, you were a governess. No rough-and-tumble of school for him, he must have a private tutor because of his delicate health . . . Later on, the consumption that took hold of his lungs wrought its own effect on his mental attitude, a febrile brilliance and a reckless irresponsibility born of despair. Perhaps he did the whole thing out of devilment? Perhaps, Alsace being occupied by Germany, threats were made against his family? I dare say we'll never know the truth. He laughed at me when I asked him why he'd done it, and asked me, "Why do you climb mountains?"' Matt gave a rueful grimace.

They were interrupted by an imperious knock at the door. It flew open, and the agitated, white-suited form of Renzo Giulini bounded into the room, his face flushed and his dark eyes shining.

'Matt! Oh, good day, Miss Lyndon.' He waved his panama hat vigorously at them both. 'I trust you're recovered? I always knew my stepmother would stop at nothing.' He whirled round to Matt again. 'You must help me, and you, Miss Lyndon. Straight away, it's imperative!'

'Calm down, old chap,' Matt said soothingly. 'What's happened now? Jessica's in custody, and the jewel-case is in Inebnit's safe. Nothing's going to happen to it for the time being. It won't be spirited away.'

'But that's just it!' Giulini flung both arms in the air in frustration. 'Signorina . . .' He addressed himself earnestly to Verity. 'I have taken your advice, and instructed lawyers to proceed for me against my step-mother in the matter of our family heirlooms. She's trapped here in Switzerland and I have a golden chance! This time she can't run away from me. My lawyers are attempting to get the jewels impounded until such time as a court delivers its judgment on their ownership.'

'Excellent!' Matt said approvingly.

'Only if the jewels *are* in that box!' Renzo exclaimed. 'Matt, Miss Verity—I *have* to see into that box. I don't want my lawyers wasting my time and my money trying to impound jewels which aren't there! You *must* open that box for me! I swear I won't do anything against your wishes. I only want to see the items with my own eyes. Miss Lyndon, you must understand. Matt?' Renzo turned to Matthew and held out his hand beseechingly.

'It isn't any good,' Verity objected. 'I still haven't got the key. We can't force it open! Anyway, I can't take the responsibility. I *am*, in a way, responsible for Jessica's belongings while she's —away. In theory, I'm still em-ployed by her.'

Renzo Giulini looked alarmingly as though he might burst a blood-vessel. His face was scarlet with emotion and his neck bulged over his stiff collar. He had tears in his eyes. He grabbed Matt's sleeve and burst out, 'Matt

—you are an expert in the matter of locks. It would be a simple matter for you to open the box.'

'What?' Matt looked at him in amazement. 'Good grief, man! Are you trying to put me in gaol with all the others?'

'But I'm not going to *take* anything, Matt. I give you my word, on my family honour, I swear! All I wish to do is check the contents. You cannot—either of you—in all decency, refuse! You shall be present, both of you, also Sir Miles Frensham, if you wish.'

'No,' Matt said hastily. 'Leave Sir Miles out of this. If I'm sure of anything, I'm sure he wouldn't want to know we'd even discussed such a thing! Confound it, Renzo, it's highly irregular, to say the very least!'

'And you, Matt, you talk to me of irregularities? When did you ever worry about such things?' Renzo challenged him, unaware of Miss Lyndon's deepening flush.

'What do you say, Verity?' Matt asked her. 'It's not an unreasonable request in the circumstances. Poor Renzo here has got a point, even if he's making it as though he's taken complete leave of his senses.'

'*You* can be calm about it,' Giulini exploded. '*I* cannot! This is my one chance to check the contents of that box.'

'He *is* to be trusted, I suppose?' Verity whispered. 'He won't just—just grab the jewels, stuff them in his pocket and run?'

Matt chuckled. 'I shouldn't think so. He's emotional, but not crazy.' He raised his eyebrows. 'Well, do I open that box? I'm game, if you are.'

Renzo and Verity stood and watched Matt pick the lock of Jessica's jewel-box.

'This is awful,' Verity hissed. 'I feel—I feel like a criminal. Oh, do be quick about it, Matt! Then Count

Giulini can look at the jewellery and we can put it all back. I shall be glad when it is impounded. It's a thorough nuisance, all of it. I'm sorry if that's speaking disrespectfully of your family heirlooms, Count, but that's how I feel.'

'I, too,' Renzo said unexpectedly, 'consider the whole affair a blasted nuisance, but that does not relieve me of my responsibilities, alas.'

'Got it!' Matt said, as a metallic click came from the box. 'Here we go.' He raised the lid in both hands.

Renzo sat down at the table, visibly shaking. He took a jeweller's magnifying eye-glass from his pocket and, with a trembling hand, set out on the table the items to which he lay claim.

Verity and Matt watched in silence. Verity found herself holding her breath and had to force herself to breathe. There they were, the subject of so much passionate dispute: the pearls, cold and beautiful; the snake bracelet with its opulent, pagan beauty; the rings; the earrings of gold filigree . . .

'Spanish workmanship, that,' Matt commented non-committedly, pointing at the filigree work of the last items, his voice breaking the spell and the hushed suspense.

Renzo nodded and said, 'Ah, yes, the Borgia earrings . . .' as if it was the most normal thing in the world that someone should own a pair of earrings which had probably once graced the earlobes of the notorious Lucrezia herself.

Verity shivered. The weather had changed completely from their first days here. Following the storm, the clouds had set in above Interlaken, and a cold, grey light fell into the room. Outside, even the Schynige Platte was lost in mist, and the Jungfrau was modestly hidden in her veil like a nun. But not only the sudden chill in the air sent an unpleasant quiver running through Verity's muscles as she gazed down at the jewellery. She found herself thinking, 'How horrible those things are. What crimes must have been committed because of them! Perhaps there is even blood on them.'

Renzo was still examining the pieces minutely, one by one. After an interminable time, he took the glass from his eye, put the ring with the *Agnus Dei* seal on one side and pushed all the rest together in a heap with a careless —even disparaging—motion of his hand, as if they'd been no more than tawdry fairground trinkets.

It was such an unexpected gesture, and so expressive, that Matt immediately exclaimed sharply, 'What's wrong, Renzo?'

The Count looked up at them. For a moment he seemed bemused. Then he began to laugh, softly and without mirth. Finally he thrust back his chair and, getting up, went to the window. As he passed by them, he pressed the jeweller's eye-glass into Matt's hand, and flung his own hand out at the table.

'See for yourself! Examine them. Oh, the papal ring, that is the original. It's about all. The rest is false— paste—fakes!'

'W—What?' Verity stammered. 'That's impossible!'

'Oh, no, Miss Lyndon,' Renzo said courteously. 'I'm afraid not. It's what we feared. She sold the originals long ago. Damn her, damn her thieving, deceitful, vicious heart!' Renzo's voice cracked suddenly, and he turned quickly away from her.

Matt, who had been quickly examining the pearls and the bracelet, said, 'It's true, Verity. These pearls are certainly paste, and the stones in the bracelet are, sadly, glass.'

'You mean—worthless?' Verity gasped incredulously.

'Oh no, not entirely worthless. This stuff is not without value in its own right. It's all good fake, made by a craftsman. The gold is only rolled gold, of course. These are pretty "costume" pieces, not unlike theatrical jewels. They are certainly not what they purport to be, and their value is a fraction of the real thing. More important, from Renzo's point of view, they are *not* the real things!'

'But—she worried so over them. Every night they were locked up with such care . . .' Verity was still unable to believe it.

Matt smiled appreciatively. 'Yes, Jessica was always clever. Have you never seen a stage magician perform his act? He takes a valuable gold watch from a member of the audience. He puts it into a paper bag and smashes it with a hammer. No one doubts the watch is in the bag, because everyone saw it put there. Therefore, how can the mangled fragments the magician shakes out with an apology be anything but fragments of the real thing? The same with these jewels. You were told they were the real things. They were treated as the real thing, and every night they were put in this box and ceremoniously locked away . . .' Matt spread out his hands in a vaguely theatrical gesture, as might a magician, demonstrating the genuineness of his actions. 'Why should anyone doubt they were real? Why, when the magician offers to saw the lady in half, does the audience not just laugh him off the stage, it's so ridiculous? Because *he* seems to believe it, and therefore they are prepared to suspend disbelief, and believe it, too. The secret of every great and successful lie, Verity, is that the liar must appear to believe it, too, for every second, of every minute. That is how it happens that they sometimes finish by persuading themselves.'

'I always suspected her,' Renzo muttered in a muffled snarl from the window. 'I felt in my bones she'd sold the real jewels.'

'Ah,' Matt told him. 'That's because *you* were shrewd

enough to watch the magician, and not his act!'

'She did it to spite us!' Renzo cried wildly.

'More likely, she just had no money,' Matt contradicted him gently. 'Perhaps you should have given her a share in the family fortune, after all? If she'd known, before your father died, that she'd have an income of some sort . . .'

Renzo shrugged dispiritedly. 'Perhaps. Now, all I can do is to try and track down the buyers, and purchase the items back. It will probably take me years.'

'It matters that much to you?' Verity asked curiously, and with a touch of disgust in her voice.

He glanced over his shoulder towards her. 'Yes, Miss Lyndon, it matters that much. You see, where I come from, it is not the wishes of any one individual which matter, but the duty he owes to the family. I am only one member of the house of Giulini, one of a long line. The jewels outlive us all. They *are* our family.'

'Family,' thought Verity dully. Renzo's life was dogged by his obligation to regain the lost heirlooms, as hers was by her responsibility for Jack.

When the jewellery and its box had been returned to the safe and Renzo had departed to inform his lawyers of the changed situation, Verity and Matt returned to the Frenshams' sitting-room.

Matt threw himself on the sofa and spread his arms out along the back of it in his favourite attitude. He was wearing a crumpled corduroy jacket which had seen better days, but which sat comfortably on his broad frame. Though the lost papers still presented a grave problem, the capture of the two agents had considerably lightened the load on his mind, and it showed in his face. He looked more relaxed, less entrenched and gritty. Verity thought that, in his way, he was a handsome figure of a man, not conventionally so, but in a striking and slightly unnerving way. Even the look of the features, the broken nose and the weatherbeaten skin, put her in mind of some battle-worn Roman general. She had not been surprised to learn, from Lady Frensham, that women were attracted to Matt; there was something so uncompromisingly masculine about him.

He met her scrutiny with a level look of his blue eyes, and asked, 'Well, Verity?'

'I find it hard to take it all in,' she admitted. 'What made you suspect Jessica, in the first place? You—You were so close to her, once.'

'A long time ago!' he said harshly.

'It must have been a very hard thing to accept, that she might be a traitor,' she suggested.

'Harder than having my ring returned, and all my protestations of love thrown back in my face, as she did fifteen years ago?' he asked bitterly.

Verity said, 'You loved her very much,' and felt a cold hand close on her own heart.

'She was very beautiful, vivacious . . . charming. Jessica *can* be very charming, if she's mind to be. I was much younger, and considerably more trusting!' Matt pulled a wry grimace. 'I thought it impossible that she could deceive me, but, of course, she did. Even so, it wasn't I who broke the engagement. She wanted social brilliance, parties, balls, all those occasions when people turn out to be seen, rather than to see. A fellow like myself, who, if he goes to Ascot, actually watches the horses run, well—he's not for Jessica! I doubt she can even understand such a thing. She didn't like the mountaineering, of course, because it doesn't have all the social hullaballoo around it that, say, fox-hunting, or point-to-point racing or even cricket, in its own mild way, has . . . All those tea-parties for the ladies, while the gentlemen sweat it out on the field. The more I climbed mountains,' Matt said suddenly with deep feeling, 'the more I appreciated the freedom it gave me from all *that*!'

His freedom, the ability to go as he pleased and do as he wished. Even his chosen career was an unpredictable and erratic one. He'd never surrender that freedom willingly, never settle down.

Verity was jerked from her reverie by his voice, suddenly exclaiming, almost ferociously, 'But I never thought she had it in her to be a murderess! I'll never forgive myself, Verity, for allowing you to run into that danger! It was my fault entirely. I should never have let you come with me when I sprang our trap.'

'I wanted to come,' she objected. 'This is a hotel. If I wanted to go down to the lobby in the middle of the night, you couldn't stop me.'

'I could have ruddy well tried!' Matt glowered at her, then added mildly, 'I don't want a dead heroine on my hands. I'd rather a Verity Lyndon, alive and kicking, any day.' He smiled at her briefly.

'No, you wouldn't . . .' Verity thought. 'Not on your hands. You don't want me on your hands, dead or alive. You want me tidily taken care of, settled somewhere —comfortably, of course—but off your hands, your mind and your conscience!'

'Why did I suspect her?' Matt hunched his shoulders. 'We knew, of course, that German agents were at work, trying to sniff out all they could about Britain's naval plans. There were any number of incidents, but it seemed to us, to Sir Miles and myself, that one set of agents was at work throughout. Just as the police recognise a common criminal by the way he works, so they had adopted a basic procedure, efficient, and very much their own. I looked for some link, some constant factor among the several which might suggest a person. Being so—conscious of Jessica, I was inevitably aware of her presence. It struck me that she was *always* there, in the background, as a dinner guest, a member of a house-party, a good friend of some politician's wife . . . I began to speculate, almost idly at first. I knew her to be unscrupulous enough, but what motive could she have? Then I enquired into her financial circumstances. She appeared to be a rich woman. She spent a great deal of money, on her clothes, her travels . . . But she had inherited nothing from Giulini by way of money; Renzo assured me of that. She had only the jewellery, which at that time appeared to be still in her possession. As a girl, she'd had no great fortune. Her father was a country squire of modest means. Who, then, paid the bills? I was eventually led to the sad conclusion that Berlin did. When traitors are caught, they talk loudly of principle. But they nearly always do it for money.'

'But you still had only your suspicions, Matt.'

'Enter your friend Alain!' he retorted. 'Now *he* was a different kettle of fish altogether! We knew all about him. We tried watching him, as far as we could, but he's a clever young devil, as slippery as an eel. So I watched Jessica, instead. Much easier; the lady likes to be seen. If I could prove a link between them, I could be sure I was on the right track. Then, in London recently, I did find that vital link.' Matt sat up and leaning forward, rested his arms on his knees, his hands clasped, in the way he had when he was in earnest. 'Oddly enough, Jessica and Alain *worked* well together. But their partnership had one fatal flaw. They cordially detested one another. "When thieves fall out . . ." as the saying goes. So, our two thieves fell out over the failed attempt to gain the *Dreadnought* papers from the Frenshams' town house. Jessica had spied out the land, and Alain did the burglary—but all they got was a set of emeralds they didn't want. They couldn't even sell them to a "fence", in case the things were ever recovered and traced back to them. Do you know what they did with them?' Matt chuckled.

'Alain put them in a packet in a left-luggage locker at Victoria Station. They're still there! Lady Frensham will get them back. But our two conspirators weren't amused. Alain was so angry that he broke a golden rule and made a rare mistake. He made contact with Jessica openly. He went to the St Lambert's hotel and had a flaming row with her. I was watching the hotel and saw him. At last, I *knew*.'

There should have been jubilation in his voice, but there was none, and Verity could understand, only too well, why.

'But someone else saw Alain Bernard, also at the St Lambert's . . .' Matt paused. '*You* did, Verity.'

'I?' she gasped.

'Yes—as you went into the hotel for your interview with Jessica, Alain passed you, running down the steps on his way out. *You* didn't take him in properly. But when you arrived, here in Interlaken with Jessica, *he* recognised you, and was horrified. You could link Jessica with him. You were a possible danger to them, and that put you in great danger, Verity! At that meeting in the St Lambert's, Jessica and Alain had made a hasty resolve to follow the Frenshams to Switzerland. Jessica knew the Frenshams were intending to spend some weeks in Interlaken. She and Alain reckoned that an important man like Sir Miles keeps in touch with his office, even on holiday. Jessica had been a frequent guest at the Frenshams', and knew Sir Miles's temperament and habits well. If she and Alain came to Switzerland, too, Fate might well give them a second chance to seize what they wanted. I dare say that Berlin was not pleased to hear of their sad lack of success in London.' He shrugged his shoulders.

'The journey to Interlaken was typical of their more usual, impeccable, planning. They travelled separately at different times. Jessica went via Paris. On arrival in

Interlaken, she didn't come directly to this hotel, but went first to another. She pretended to take a dislike to the accommodation offered, and came here to find— by a surprising coincidence—her good friends the Frenshams!' Matt said sarcastically.

'Alain struck up an acquaintance with you, originally because he wanted to know if you'd remembered him. You hadn't, and they were safe. But then he . . .' Matt paused.

'Yes, I know,' Verity said, colouring.

'Well, *laissons cela*. On the night they took the papers, Jessica herself took down her jewel-box. That enabled her to check that Sir Miles's brief-case had already been deposited in the safe. She asked for the bookcase key. The bookcase lock is stiff. She couldn't turn the key, and asked the night clerk to go and do it for her. In the few moments he was absent, Alain drugged his coffee-pot. Simple.'

'There's just one thing,' Verity said in some embarrassment. 'Why did you try and climb through her window—although you ended up climbing through mine?'

Matt shrugged. 'She wasn't yet aware at that time that I was in Interlaken. I thought if I found her alone —surprised her—I might be able to persuade her how foolish she was being, or, failing that, shake the truth out of her. I had a stupid notion that she might be frightened enough to confess to it all, once she realised I knew. I—felt, I owed it to her at least to try.'

He fell silent, then added, 'When I did meet her, I realised at once how stupid my idea was. She was absolutely in control, totally confident and bent on her own destruction. Nothing on earth would have swayed her; certainly no argument of mine.

'The morning that Sir Miles received the dummy telegram, we did something to force Jessica into the open. Sir Miles engaged his wife to tell Jessica about "the telegram" that morning, as a friendly confidence. If an attempt were made to get access to it, it would lead directly back to Jessica, the only one outside the Frenshams, myself and you who knew of it. What *we* didn't know was how very angry Alain Bernard still was with Jessica over the affair of the ring. They must have had some kind of row. Perhaps she threw the bungled burglary in London in his face. At any rate, he told her that he wasn't prepared to open the safe a second time; she could do it herself. He'd back her up in the event of emergency, but *she* could take the risk of opening the safe. She knew how to do it, to pick the lock. She wasn't an amateur spy, she was a professional. She'd been trained.'

'What will happen to her now?' Verity asked.

'Her lawyer will get her out on bail. Doubtless, she'll jump it and flee to Germany. The Admiral of the Atlantic will give her a pension. She's earned it, after all. She'll never be able to go to England, or to Italy, and I doubt the French will allow her in. But she can do very nicely in a villa in, say, some pleasant German spa town. She'll probably marry some minor princeling and end up in a castle, if I know Jessica.'

CHAPTER THIRTEEN

ALONE AGAIN in her own room, Verity sat down holding Alain's sketch-folder in her arms, and wondered ruefully what she was going to do now. Whatever happened to Jessica, it was the parting of the ways at last as far as their relationship was concerned. Worse, the parting of the ways, as far as her relationship with Matt was concerned, could not be far away.

'Well, Miss Lyndon, you are out of a job again!' she told herself aloud.

Without employment, penniless and about to lose for ever the only man she had ever truly loved with total commitment. Things could hardly be blacker. There were, however, plenty of British and American families holidaying in the area, and possibly Lady Frensham, always a friend, might be kind enough to enquire among them if they had need of a governess or a companion. Jessica's maid, Maddox, had already found a post with an English lady whose French maid had left for her own country to marry. The swiftness with which Maddox had achieved this transition made Verity suspect that Maddox had secretly been enquiring about a new employer, even before Jessica's arrest. Verity didn't blame her for this, remembering Maddox's dire prediction in Paris. If Jessica treated her survants badly, she could hardly complain if they lacked loyalty.

If Matt were right, Jessica herself was headed for the gentilities of Baden-Baden and Alain for some German sanatorium. Everyone, therefore, was taken care of, except for she herself. Despondency settled over her, but she shook herself and said sternly, 'This won't do!'

Perhaps it was the folder of sketches that made her feel so sad. So much talent, half-realised and eventually thrown away. In giving her his sketch-folder, Alain was effectively saying goodbye to Art. She felt that he had somehow made his testament, and united the only two things for which he cared, his work as an artist, and Verity herself. To take care of these assorted drawings and water-colours was now, for her, almost a sacred duty, a trust. 'Don't fail me, Verity . . .' Alain's voice seemed to be saying in her ear.

She took the folder to the desk, and sat down to untie the ribbon round it and open out the sturdy card cover to reveal the pile of cartridge-paper drawings. She began to pick the sketches up, one by one, studying each carefully, not only for what it depicted, but for what it revealed of the man who had created it.

There were several views of the Jungfrau, and here was the cartoon sketch of the goats which brought to life again so vividly that day in the meadow, when he'd asked her to marry him. She could almost smell the scent of the grass, and hear the buzzing of the flies. What if she'd accepted? Would he have confessed his role as a German agent? Pointless speculation, now. There were two little sketches of her in this folder, of which she'd known nothing. He must have caught her unawares. Matt had been right to describe Alain as a great watcher of people. A natural spy, perhaps; alert, sharp-eyed and elusive.

Here was an amusing, even affectionate, sketch of Princess Detkine's Spitz. The little dog sat, ears pricked, tongue lolling, obviously waiting for its good friend Alain to stop messing about with pencil and paper and throw the tennis-ball again. Beneath it in the pile was a cartoon of the Princess herself, very funny but extremely rude, the poor lady depicted grotesquely as Goya's *Naked Maya*. Verity bit her lip. *That* drawing would have to be destroyed! It showed the unkinder side of Alain's nature, and heaven forbid that it should ever fall into the wrong hands.

Verity pushed it aside and then paused, frowning. She had reached the middle of the stack, and now found herself looking down at a set of quite different papers, printed diagrams illustrating some point of engineering. Attached to them was a screed of printed prose, some kind of report, on crested paper. Turning the sheets over, she examined them carefully.

'Oh, Alain . . .' she said softly.

Was this a last joke? Or a genuine attempt to make amends? Was Alain chuckling to himself even now, imagining how her expression must be as she looked at this unexpected find . . . or was he asking her sincerely, 'Forgive me, Verity . . .?' She would never know. But this, then, was Alain's parting gift to her: the missing *Dreadnought* papers.

'Mary Tudor may have died with "Calais" engraved upon her heart,' said Lady Frensham with deep feeling, 'but I'm sure, if anyone cares to look after I'm dead, they will see *Dreadnought* engraved upon mine!'

'But the papers are all safely back,' Verity ventured to point out.

'Thank goodness. It did nothing for Miles's temper, their being lost like that. So *tiresome*!'

This remark was not, in fact, pronounced with regard to the *Dreadnought* papers, but to the tea-tray that a waiter had just deposited with a flourish on the table between the two women. Lady Frensham flipped aside the lid of the teapot with an expert fingernail, and peered suspiciously into its steaming interior. 'Just as I thought! Hot water and *no* tea. I keep telling them to put the tea *in the pot*, but no, they must always bring a pot of hot water which probably hasn't even boiled, and the tea is in this funny little metal egg . . .'

There was a pause while the unsatisfactory infusion was brewed, and poured.

'A very strange young man, Monsieur Bernard,' recommenced Lady Frensham. 'Such a talented artist. Princess Detkine agrees. She was so thrilled with the study of her little dog which monsieur Bernard did, and you gave her. She said, if she had only known Monsieur Bernard was an artist, she would have engaged him to do *her* portrait.'

Verity sipped hastily at her tea to avoid a reply. In the tea-rooms, the chatter of voices swelled as more and more visitors descended for the sacred four o'clock hour. Waiters were positively racing past with huge slices of chocolate cake and mountains of whipped cream.

Leaning across the table, Lady Frensham hissed in a low voice, 'I shall never understand how Jessica could behave so badly. Such an ill-bred sort of thing to do. I shall never forgive her!' The ostrich-feathers on her hat quivered with sympathetic indignation.

Verity's instinct was to think that Jessica was probably not too worried about Lady Frensham's enmity. But, on the other hand, the social ostracism by polite society, which it implied, would cause Jessica considerable anguish. Little comfort would be afforded by the company of middle-European barons in German watering-places if the distinguished British visitors refused to acknowledge her. Jessica would pay a painful price for her treachery.

'The Russians make very good tea,' said Lady Frensham, and, with those few words, consigned Jessica to perpetual social oblivion.

Verity returned to her hotel room with at least the immediate problem of her future resolved, for the

Frenshams had insisted she remain in Interlaken for a
while as their guest.

Staying on also meant that she might see Matt a few
more times before the final, dreadful parting. Verity
went out on the balcony and leaned on the ledge. The
sun had returned in milder form, and doused the mountains with a soft, golden haze. She almost hated them for
their beauty and the hold they had on Matt. His first
love, his only love, they were his life.

And me? thought Verity sadly. For her, a life without Matt would always be incomplete, as if an artist
had painted a picture intending to people it with
figures, and then forgotten, leaving only an empty
landscape.

'So this is love,' she thought to herself, almost won-
deringly. This is what is was to love: to belong with
someone and to be an unfinished creation without him.
To be in that painful and paradoxical situation where she
resented even those inanimate lumps of rock and ice
which meant so much to him, and yet knew she could
never ask him to give up any part of his independent life,
just for her. Love is sacrifice. It wants to hang on: and it
lets go.

Verity sighed and wondered if the cloud of depression
was ever going to pass or whether it would hang over her
for ever. The visit to the tea-rooms hadn't helped, since
Lady Frensham had insisted that she eat large quantities
of pastry which she hadn't wanted, and now, in an hour
or two, she would be obliged to sit through a six-course
dinner.

Shaking herself briskly, she declared aloud, 'Walk it
off, my girl!' She took off her afternoon dress, changed
into something more robust and laced her strong shoes.
She could walk a little way along the country road
towards the village of Wilderswil, and be back well in
time to change for dinner.

She had not gone far, however, when, to her surprise, she heard the rare toot of a motor-horn, and the chugging of an internal combustion engine. The motor-car was becoming an increasingly familiar sight, but was still unusual enough to warrant stopping and staring, especially here in Switzerland, where the brakes of the day had difficulty in coping with the steep alpine roads. Now Verity turned and saw, proceeding majestically along the road behind her, a huge, prestigious chauffeur-driven Daimler. To her further surprise and some consternation, the imposing vehicle came to a halt by her, and the rear door opened.

'Ah, Miss Lyndon!' Major Stein's guttural tones came from the studded leather interior, and he put his cropped head and bull-neck through the open door. 'I may perhaps offer to take you to your destination?'

'No, thank you,' Verity said coldly. 'I'm out for a walk, and how do you know my name?'

He gave her the sort of smile the crocodile is reputed to give its victims. 'We have a mutual acquaintance, dear young lady.'

Alain, Verity thought with a sigh. But Major Stein was indulging in a pantomime of deep breathing.

'A walk? Ah, yes, so healthy. I, too, shall walk a little with you. You permit?'

He descended from his vehicle with a rapidity she would not have expected from one of his girth and stature, and before she could prevent it, fell into step beside her. The Daimler rolled forward, a little to the rear, the chauffeur keeping a discreet distance.

'We have something to discuss, Fräulein,' Major Stein said affably.

'I think not, Major!' she told him crisply.

'Forgive me, dear young lady, I must disagree.' He was very polite, but there was a firmness in his tone which brooked no opposition. Behind them, the

Daimler followed like a sinister shadow. 'It is the matter of young Bernard's sketch-folder.'

'Yes, I have it,' Verity said calmly. 'And no, I shan't give it up. Alain wanted me to have it.'

'My dear young lady, I don't require you to surrender it. It has, perhaps, some sentimental value for you? But I am possibly interested in some of its contents. Have you—examined—it yet?'

'Yes, and as regards the *Dreadnought* reports, Major Stein, they have been returned to the rightful owners.'

Major Stein sighed. 'Such a pity! It will not affect the long term, Miss Lyndon. Germany will build her own fleet of dreadnoughts, and sooner than Britain expects. But—though I applaud your patriotic gesture—I wish you had thought to contact me first. We could have come to some arrangement.'

Verity stopped in her tracks. 'My employer may have been a traitor, Major, but I am not! I wish you would kindly get back into your motor-car and not trouble me any more!'

But Major Stein was looking past her, at someone who had approached unseen till now, and whose footsteps now crunched on the roadway.

'Ah, Mr Burton, we meet again! You have come to claim the young lady, no doubt? Well, perhaps we shall all three of us meet again some day, eh?'

He beamed his gold smile upon them, re-entered his conveyance and rolled away at a stately pace.

'Come along, Verity,' Matt said, and picking up her arm, linked it through his.

They turned back and began to walk along the road. 'Stein must be out of his teutonic mind, approaching you like that!' Matt said fiercely. 'But he's probably panicking. He must be in trouble with Berlin. Not only did he lose the *Dreadnought* papers, but he's lost Alain Bernard as well.'

Verity looked up at him enquiringly, and he explained, 'Stein knows Bernard returned the papers to you, and so Bernard's fate, should the Swiss surrender him, is uncertain. Bernard's applied to the Swiss government to be allowed to stay here, in a sanatorium, for treatment. As he's a very sick young man, the Swiss seem likely to agree.'

'I'm glad,' Verity said quietly. 'I hope the sanatorium can help him.'

Matt glanced down at her. 'If you still care for him, Verity, I'll understand. I won't like it, but I'll understand it. So, tell me, tell me the truth, please! It will make a difference to what I want to say to you.'

Verity's heart quickened, and she said nervously, 'I never loved him, Matt, not in *that* way. I told you so, before.'

'Yes, I know—but love, real love, is something I've been rather a fool about all my life. I'm thirty-eight, you know, and only just beginning to learn what it really is.'

They had reached the foot of the Rugen, and by unspoken accord, turned aside from the road and began to climb through its leafy glades to the top. When they reached its highest clearing, they sat down on a fallen, mossy log, before the magnificent view it offered.

The mountains had a faint, blue haze on them, as the sun began to sink. Alain would have painted them in their blue veils. Verity unpinned her straw hat and put it on the ground beside her. The sunlight fired auburn embers in her hair, and Matt, looking at her pale, calm, classical features, felt an ache in his heart, and wondered why it had taken him so long to realise what should have been obvious from the first.

'Just before that rockfall came down on us,' he said unexpectedly, 'Karl and I were talking—sharing a bar of chocolate. Karl made a reference to his engagement. He said, "There's a right and wrong way of going about things." I did everything the wrong way, didn't I, Verity?'

Verity fixed her gaze on the panorama of misty mountains spread out, smoky-blue, before them, afraid to look at his familiar, battered profile in case she betrayed her own feelings. 'You went the way you wanted, Matt,' she replied quietly.

But he shook his head vigorously. 'No, I didn't even do that! I wasn't bright enough to know, then, what I wanted. Now I do. I want to marry you, Verity.'

It was very quiet on the hill-top, and the valley showed scarcely a sign of life.

Matt said huskily, 'I love you, Verity. I loved you from the start, but was too stupid to recognise it. I began to realise that what I felt for you was something different, and something special, the evening we talked outside the hotel, in the moonlight, do you remember? I described my life in London to you, and as I was talking, I began to see what an empty and meaningless existence it was, and always would be, unless you were there to share it with me. Even then, it took poor Karl to unlock the final barrier to my understanding. It just came to me, and seemed so obvious, that what I wanted, was for you to be my wife . . . And then a couple of tons of rock came down the mountainside. Great lumps of it were bouncing all round, like bullets and cannon-balls, as if we'd got caught up in a battle. Karl was struck, and went spinning round and down, sliding in among it all, and the rope snapped . . . All the time I kept thinking, "I'm never going to get back down and tell Verity I love her, now" . . . When I did get back, I had to wait until the matter of the *Dreadnought* papers was settled, because I knew they were after me. But I had begun to think that perhaps you did care for me, just a little—

and to dare to hope . . .'

'Don't, Matt!' Verity interrupted in agony. 'I can't marry you. Not because I don't love you, because I do, so very much and far more than you'll ever know. But I can't take from you all the things which mean so much to you—your liberty, and the mountains and just being free. You'd hate me for it one day, Matt, and I couldn't bear that.'

'My dearest love, I do *know* it's time to hang up my ice-axe and boots!' He caught hold of her hands and pulled her round to face him. 'The mountains only give so many warnings, and then they stop fooling with you. I'm getting too old for hanging by my fingertips from rock ledges. Turn me down, because I look like an orang-utang or because I'm a slow-witted oaf who doesn't even know when he's in love—but not for a freedom which can't exist without *you*! There are no paths I want to tread, no peaks I want to scale, and no corner of the earth I want to visit if you, Verity, are not there. Please, say you will.'

She had barely time to answer, 'Yes', before he caught her up in his arms and his mouth sought out hers hungrily. The pine trees whispered above, imbuing the air with their fragrant perfume, as she felt herself respond, mind and body, to the pulsating rhythm of both their hearts.

The sun had slipped out of sight, and the rose-coloured mantle it had thrown across the Jungfrau had darkened to mauve and now purple, as the night crept over the mountains. Verity stood by the window in her night-gown, her loose chestnut curls framing her face, and watched it for the last time. Tomorrow, they were going home to England. The fading colours of the mountain sunset were reflected on her face, and as they merged into the night, so she was left in the darkness, illuminated by the silver moonlight.

She and Matt had been married that morning in the town's Protestant church. It had turned out almost like a family affair, a small assembly of friends lending a cosy intimacy to the little service. Sir Miles had given the bride away, and Lady Frensham had been matron of honour. Even Karl Hable, one eye still closed and blackened, sticking-plaster on his head and his damaged left hand in bandages, had emerged, hobbling, from hospital, grinning and cheerfully defiant, to be best man.

Now that the panorama of mountains was finally lost from view in the blue-black night, Verity closed the window. As she did, she heard a movement from the door, and knew Matt had come into the room. He crossed the floor behind her quietly, and put his arms round her.

'Still gazing at the mountains?'

His voice vibrated in her ear and his warm breath touched her neck. Verity quivered in his arms, and their grip tightened around her in response.

'Only thinking . . . how much you'll miss them . . .'

'I have something better, I have *you*,' he murmured, and stooped to kiss the soft swell of her breast beneath the thin cotton material.

Verity whispered, 'Yes, Matt . . .' turning into his embrace and surrendering herself entirely to him, as he swept her up effortlessly into his strong arms and carried her to the waiting bed.

Outside and high above, the mountains, lords and guardians of the valleys, slept like armoured knights, ready to awake and repel the bold adventurer who would scale their lofty summits. Beneath their mute, protecting splendour, the pine trees moved softly together in the scented night breeze. They whispered their secret to the shining moon, and she stretched out her silver fingers in a gentle blessing and touched the forms of the lovers below, united at last.

MASQUERADE

YOU'RE INVITED TO ACCEPT

2 MASQUERADE ROMANCES
AND A DIAMOND ZIRCONIA NECKLACE

FREE!

Acceptance card

NO STAMP NEEDED	Post to: Reader Service, FREEPOST, P.O. Box 236, Croydon, Surrey. CR9 9EL

YES! Please send me 2 free Masquerade Romances and my free diamond zirconia necklace – and reserve a Reader Service Subscription for me. If I decide to subscribe I shall receive 4 new Masquerade Romances every other month as soon as they come off the presses for £6.00 together with a FREE newsletter including information on top authors and special offers, exclusively for Reader Service subscribers. There are no postage and packing charges, and I understand I may cancel or suspend my subscription at any time. If I decide not to subscribe I shall write to you within 10 days. Even If I decide not to subscribe the 2 free novels and the necklace are mine to keep forever.

I am over 18 years of age   EP22M

NAME _____

(CAPITALS PLEASE)

ADDRESS _____

_____

_____ POSTCODE _____

Loving

Little Heather Fraser had everything she could possibly want, except the love of her father, Jay.

His callousness shocked the tiny Cotswold village, and most of all Claire Richards, whose daughter Lucy was Heather's friend.

When Jay accused Claire of encouraging the girls' friendship so that she could see more of *him*, nothing could have been further from the truth.

A freak accident suddenly put paid to Claire's cherished independence. Would she be able to swallow her angry pride and reluctantly share the Frasers' roof?

After 25 million sales worldwide, best-selling author Penny Jordan presents her 50th Mills & Boon romance for you to enjoy.

Available January 1987
Price £1.50.

Mills & Boon